KILLING SACRED

Also by Nancy O'Hara

KILLING SACRED

An Alex Sullivan Zen Mystery

Nancy O'Hara

Author of **ONE HAND KILLING**

Published by NOH Books, New York, New York

Cover Art by Carl Graves

Book Design by Cheryl Perez, www.yourepublished.com

ISBN: 978-0-9848938-7-4

"The occurrence of an evil thought is a malady,
Not to continue it is the remedy."
Zen Saying

Prologue

Albuquerque, Tuesday, September 11

Marco's back was on fire. It felt like he'd fallen asleep for hours under a hot sun and burned to blisters. He also wasn't helping himself by not covering his shaved skull and wearing a black shirt in the desert heat. But there was a job to finish, so he pushed away the pain-pleasure as his training clicked in. Having the horns and eyes etched into his back was a brazen flouting of the rules. He didn't care. After today they'd have no choice but to honor him and put him on the fast track to warrior.

Be prepared. It was the first vow. Still, he'd have to keep the ink his secret for now. Tattoo Jack had enough dough in his pocket to keep his trap shut, the almighty buck working better than trust or a man's word. The time was near for him to take his rightful place in the circle with all the others. He'd paid his dues, plus some.

One more stop and then dinner, a quick fuck if he was lucky, a few hours' shut-eye, then head north in the morning.

He strolled up to the front entrance of San Felipe Church, camera dangling from his neck, feigning tourist. The curved, flesh-toned adobe walls looked more like soft skin than hard clay. White wooden crosses jutted skyward from every large and small spire atop the rosy rooftop. The church was a tourist stop, so his visit would hardly be noticed. He'd just slip in and then back out with booty in hand. He'd scoped it out the day before, saving the easiest for last. Sort of like dessert, the main course tucked away in his backpack. He'd make them proud and then they could all move on to the Big Prize of Eternal Power.

"I'm sorry, sir," said the security guard with the baby face and belly spilling over his belt, blocking the doorway. "I'll have to search your bag or you can leave it with me while you're visiting."

Marco wondered where the hell rent-a-cop had come from as he tried to push past him. He hadn't been there yesterday.

"Sir, you cannot go in with that bag!"

"Since when?"

"Since now. Today is only 9/11! Duh! And I'm sure you've heard about the Spiritual Looters, quote-unquote, stealing valuable statues and such from churches. Well, steps are being taken and no one gets by me without getting searched."

This guy doesn't even have a gun. How pathetic. Don't make a scene. Don't make an impression. Don't be noticed. Vow number three: Be vigilant.

"No problem," he said, even though it was a big one, a major problem. "I'll just drop this off at home and come back. Whole life's in here you know, can't be leaving it lying around." He gave the guard his back and hugged his backpack to his chest.

"Sure thing," the guard said.

Damn, now I'll have to skip the booze and come back late. I'll need my wits. Fuck.

He walked across the street to the plaza, past the gazebo smack in the center and headed toward a bench on the far side that faced away from the church. It was the only unoccupied seat in the small park. As soon as he sat down he knew why. It was blistering hot. But he needed to sit and think about what to do without calling attention to himself, so he stayed put and endured the pain.

The final object of this self-assigned mission was in that church. He had to make a plan to get inside. Or did he? He had plenty enough already, but his heart was set on the small, golden statue of St. John. It would please the others.

Next time ... he could wait till next time. But here he was now. No waiting. No putting it off. He would get it—somehow he would.

But where to stash his bag? The other loot? No way could he leave it alone in a room with a flimsy lock. No way could he trust anyone to guard it. No way could he let rent-a-cop put his lazy bug eyes inside. So now what?

His warrior sixth sense was aroused. Told him he was being watched. He felt this same way when he was a teenager and his stepfather would creep around outside his room while he jerked off under the covers. But he did nothing wrong then or now, even if priests, cops and self-righteous assholes would say different. So why did he feel so dirty? Maybe it was just the sun beating down. He needed a shower. His back reminded him of his assignment. He drew his breath in and steeled himself against the pleasure of the pain. *Stay focused! Vow number four: Wake up.*

He would wait. It felt like a hundred eyes were boring into his back. He turned and saw no one.

Dark wasn't coming quickly enough. He needed shadow light to walk back into the church. Patience finally settled into his bones. The night was long. He would return to his room, shower, eat, meditate, maybe sleep a bit. Fortify and prepare himself. Engage his warrior training regimen. Now that he was on this thought train, his body felt grounded, his mind weightless. No regret that carnal pleasure had to be forsaken.

Walking back to the hotel, even with laser-sharp focus, he couldn't shake the feeling that he was being followed. He ducked and detoured his way back to his hotel, which was only two blocks north. The circuitous route took him to another small park, the Natural History Museum, and some shopping areas. The streets were hot, his back burned, he had no water, and he got all turned around. At one point he found himself in a residential neighborhood that made him very nervous. He was often the only one on foot and he got lost in a maze of private, earth-colored houses surrounded by high-desert flora. He wouldn't have looked more out of place if he'd been wearing his meditation robes. Finally, he found his way back to Mountain Road and got his bearings. He saw no one that seemed to be following him, but whatever had been lurking on the periphery of his energy field for the past hour was still there when his key released the lock to his hotel room and he reached inside for the light switch.

He was in. He was alone. He laughed off his paranoia. He convinced himself that he was all but invisible in this town. And he'd be gone before the morning sun woke another soul. The smell of him would remain only till his sheets were flapping clean in the wind, the desert breeze replacing any hint of him.

When he turned around to lock himself in, the door was thrust open into his face. It slammed him backward onto the musty, chenille bedspread and took with it all sense of relief and safety he had just breathed in.

Splayed on his back on top of his backpack he stared into the eyes of his enemy. How did he let this happen? He looked over at the second enemy by the door to assess the situation, all in half a heartbeat.

You?

No one, not even he, heard this last question of his life. The utterance of it was drowned in the crack of his neck breaking. Then he felt nothing. He did not have to suffer the shame of being robbed, of being off his warrior guard, of failing the cause. In fact, he suffered no more.

If he'd been able to watch from the edges when the police found him the next morning, he would have taken some satisfaction with him to his grave. There was no ID. There was no bag of sacred treasures. There was no one to mourn his death.

But he had no after-death insight.

He was just dead. John Doe dead.

1

New Jersey, Route 9W

Alex Sullivan's head was not the first body part to hit the ground. Which is why she registered the loud smack on the road. Her new titanium bicycle sprawled out in front of her, curbside, her back to traffic. She lay there stunned. On her left side. She knew she'd landed hard, was hurt. She lifted her head up off the asphalt. Found the broken spot on her forehead. Her half-gloved left hand felt the blood rushing from the open wound in her left temple. She could move. She hadn't blacked out. That was good. The blood wasn't. Her body felt okay, nothing broken. Maybe she was in shock. It didn't feel like it. She got up. There were people there now helping her. She made her way to the curb and sat down. A woman handed her a box of tissue to help absorb the blood and then called nine-one-one. Alex asked her name, it seemed important to know that. Elisa.

Except for the blood, Alex felt fine, good enough to get back on her bike and continue riding. She'd been exhausted. She probably shouldn't have gone out in the first place. It wasn't her fault. It was an accident. Are accidents without cause? She didn't think so. She thought Zen monk Muin would blame it on karma. *At least I'm thinking as usual. Wonder what karma of mine was in play here?*

Elisa asked if there was someone she could call for her. Alex dug her phone out of her bicycle jersey back pocket, held it up and said, "I'll do it. My boyfriend's on his bike a few miles north. I'll call him."

My boyfriend? Where did that come from? Maybe I do have brain damage.

A uniformed cop was kneeling in front of her, his first aid kit open next to him, peering into her face, her wound. His face was friendly, young and cute. He could've been a cousin or nephew if she had any. Officer McNulty said his nametag.

"Let's have a look," he said, peering into her face. "What's your name?"

"Detective Sullivan."

"Yeah?" He sat back on his heels.

"Yeah, from the city, upper west."

"So, what happened?"

"Haven't a clue. How bad is it?"

"It's too deep for me to bandage up. Gotta call a bus."

"Damn. Guess you can't just take me back over the bridge, eh?"

"Nah, sorry, wish I could. But even you don't wanna mess with a cut like that."

"Shit."

"I'll take care of your bicycle. Come pick it up when they've sewn you up." He handed her a card. Dermot McNulty.

"Thanks." Alex smiled.

The EMTs braced her head and neck and strapped her down on a gurney. She had no choice in this. They checked her vitals, asked the usual questions—what day is it, what's your name, who's the president? She passed with flying colors. It didn't matter, they took no chances. A head split open was not something to mess with. She saw McNulty chatting with them, knew he was telling them to take extra care, she was one of them.

On the way to the hospital, lights flashing, sirens screeching, it felt like they weren't going fast enough. Despite treating her special, they hadn't done a good job of strapping her down. She was off center, tipped uncomfortably to her left side, the injured side, and she felt like she was falling. There was no room under the restraints to adjust her body toward comfort. The loss of movement, of control, was the worst of it for her. At least her arms were free. She clutched her phone and McNulty's card in her right fist. Those were the links to her world: Officer McNulty would have her bike, and the phone would eventually put her in touch with Guy. He still wasn't answering, most definitely having a good ride. She'd already left enough messages, and wished she could erase all the missed calls from her. It would come across as panic once he finally stopped and looked. He would worry, that much she knew about his character. She could call Uncle Charlie, but he was in Boston for the week: Too far away to help, but not too far to worry.

The white fluorescent ceiling floated above her as she was rolled into the emergency room. She thought about dying. Head wounds were unpredictable. She knew she could be gone in a flash. The sound of her skull slamming down onto the asphalt resounded between her ears.

I was wearing a helmet. What the hell happened with that? Did it hit the ground first? Did it do its job and save me? What if this is my last day to live?

She'd been preparing for it all year in the one-year-to-live class at the Zen Temple downtown. Signed up for it when she couldn't decide whether or not to retire from the force. She'd put in her twenty years, and didn't want to wait till she was totally burned out or taken down by a bullet to move on to a safer way of making a living, so she'd been exploring her options.

If this were to be her last day on earth, she hoped she'd have a chance to say goodbye to the three men in her life: Uncle Charlie, Muin and Guy. Then it would be okay. If she lived she'd think more deeply about why Guy was on the list and why she had named him as her boyfriend. *Was it so Elisa and other lurking strangers would think well of me, would think I wasn't a loser out here all alone on my bike, would think I had people in my life who cared? Since when did I start caring about what other people think of me?*

They rolled her in, checked her in, and asked if she had a living will—she was happy to report yes, one benefit of the year-to-live class. They put her behind a curtain and left her, still strapped down, still in the neck and head brace. They couldn't release her from the restraints, someone said, till a doctor could check her out. *But they could leave me alone with a head injury? Fuck.*

She couldn't move. She was still lying crooked, her left leg belted at a different, more painful point, tighter than her right leg. Time passed. She tried to do zazen, to breathe into her belly, relax, wait patiently. And expect nothing, as her Zen master teacher, Setsu Roshi, would always say.

Zazen: The meditation she'd been taught by the Zen monks, who'd told her it could lead to enlightenment or, short of that, a clear knowing of her own mind. It was often hell to sit hour after hour cross-legged on a cushion, focused on her breathing, her mind a writhing mess of thinking—monkey mind they called it. But sometimes during zazen, and always after, she experienced a sense of peace and well-being, often even a deep knowing beyond all thought, that nothing else had ever given her.

When still a Catholic in name she had practiced foxhole praying: Calling on God to help her through a jam, or when she was scared, worried or just impatient to find relief from whatever pain she was in. The prayer was some version of: "If you're there God, help me the fuck out here why don't you? Please!" It never worked.

Now her reflex was to do zazen: No God, no higher power, nothing outside herself, not even herself—just concentrated, ego-dropping breathing practice. At this moment she couldn't sit cross-legged in a monastery surrounded by monks, but she could do zazen. Strapped down, unable to move, scared—the conditions were perfect.

She was successful for a few moments at a time. Ten minutes felt like fifty. She had to talk to someone who knew her and Guy hadn't called back yet. At this point it had been an hour and a half since she'd crashed. *What if I died? Without a word to anyone but medical staff?*

She felt something oozing from her forehead, down the side of her face onto her neck. Panic gripped her heart. They said they'd stopped the blood. Invisible behind the curtain, her fear escalated. No one had checked on her since they'd parked her there. She called out. A nurse came, took a quick look, said it wasn't bleeding, it was okay, the doctor would see her soon. Alex was not reassured. *What the hell was that then? Was I hallucinating? Did my brain get fucked up?*

Alex knew she should call Mother, but she didn't have it in her to deal with the certain hysteria that would greet her on the other end of the phone. Instead, she called Uncle Charlie. She didn't want to worry him, he was too far away to rush to her side, but he'd be pissed if she didn't.

Uncle Charlie picked up on the second ring. "Hi sweets, everything okay?"

Tears she'd been suppressing brimmed in her green hazel eyes. Zazen might help to soothe her mind, but Uncle Charlie never failed to soften her heart. She pictured his broad smile, deep blue eyes, pepper-turning-to-salt thick head of hair, and ruddy red cheeks, and imagined him sitting in his hotel lobby reading something, biding his time till he had to head to Fenway for his favorite pastime, watching the Red Sox play ball.

"Not exactly, but I don't want you to worry, Guy's on his way. I just needed to hear your voice."

"What happened? Where are you?"

"New Jersey. Had a little bike accident."

"Are you by yourself now?"

"Nope, I'm in the emergency room."

"Damn. Where are you hurt? What happened?"

Alex relayed the details of the accident. Saying out loud what she remembered sent a rush of feelings through her belly and lungs. Fear, relief, anger all mixed up together. A tear spilled out and rolled down her face into her mouth. She brushed at it with the back of a trembling hand. Uncle Charlie's voice, living its normal everyday life on the other end of the phone, began to calm her.

"I'm heading home right now," Uncle Charlie said. "I'll be there in a few hours."

"S'okay, really, please don't. Guy'll be here soon, I'm being taken care of. By the time you get here I'll be home, safe and sound. Just stay on the phone with me for a bit, till I hear back from Guy, okay? Can you do that?"

"I'm right here, sweetie, I'm not going anywhere, for as long as you need me."

Twenty minutes later, Guy was live on the phone, and at the foot of her bed thirty minutes after that, ready to play hero. After a

CAT scan of her head, X-rays of her ribs, arm and leg, the sewing up of her face, and a Xerox of her insurance card, Alex was released into Guy's care. They went to the station to pick up her bike, which had a few scrapes of its own but nothing serious, ate at the diner just across from the fateful corner, and eased into the Sunday-night-weekenders-on-their-way-back-to-the-city bridge traffic.

2

An hour later, after a shower, Alex was happy to lay on her couch. They said she'd feel even worse the next day. She couldn't imagine worse. *Maybe the pain's on fast forward, doesn't know what day it is. Maybe tomorrow will be better.*

At first, aside from the hole in her head, the scrapes, cuts and road rash on her left elbow, shoulder and forearm seemed to be the worst of it. The bruised ribs kicked in just as she began to relax. Each time she tried to take a deep breath the pain held it hostage. Any movement at all took immense effort and released new and deeper pains all up and down her left side.

"Here," Guy said, handing her four ice packs. "Put these on your ribs and anywhere else it hurts."

Alex groaned. "I hate those things."

"I know, but you're not in charge at the moment, I am."

"I'd rather take a hot bath."

"Nuh-uh. No heat for a few days, ice is what you need. Trust me, I've had enough wrecks to know what works."

Alex reluctantly took the cold blue packs and placed them on her ribs, thigh, elbow and knee. Slowly, the cold combined with Advil to ease some of the aching.

"My mind keeps going over and over the whole thing. I have no idea how I fell, what happened. It's so weird," Alex said.

"I know that corner well. There's a hole there, but it's pretty far out into the road. Do you remember hitting anything, some sand, a stone, a dip in the pavement?"

"All's I remember is seeing my wheel sliding to one side knowing I couldn't stop it. I can't remember the moment just before that."

"What's important is nothing's broken. You'll heal just fine so long as you obey Dr. Hawkes here."

"Nice that you make house calls."

"Only for special cases." He leaned over and kissed her gently on the lips. She felt it all the way down to her groin. Kept her eyes closed when they parted so she wouldn't have to look up into his copper-flecked eyes that always drove her crazy. If there were such a thing as bedroom eyes, he had them. Framed by his sandy brown, wavy hair and softly sculpted facial features, he was almost too handsome. His looks made her nervous. Sex helped take her mind off that. But she couldn't even consider sex right now, her body hurt too much.

"Treatment comes with three home-cooked meals a day I hear."

"You betcha, Chef Guy is on call for that part of the package."

"Seriously though, you really don't have to take care of me. I'll be fine. Don't you have to get back to work tomorrow?" Alex didn't know what answer she wanted to hear.

"Don't you worry that pretty little bruised head of yours, Ms. Stubborn Independence. I've already taken care of it. I've got a few days coming and I'm all yours till you kick me out."

"Okay then." She smiled deeper into the cushions. She didn't have the strength to argue and was happy not to be alone. It went against her nature to allow someone other than Uncle Charlie to take care of her, but in surrendering to Guy in her apartment on her cozy green couch she felt a pang in her stomach that made her nervous and excited about having him there 24/7.

***

A week later Alex was restless and bored, and Guy was still taking up space in her apartment. Playing Queen Sheba—with Guy the pampering, ready attendant—felt a bit like wearing a gorgeous pair of shoes a half size too small. She couldn't find a quiet corner anywhere in her own apartment. So here it was, the secret of cohabitation that no one ever talked about: Forget about solitude. And being out on sick leave left her with nothing to do, no monsters to chase, no puzzles to solve. There was only so much Sudoku she could play. If this was a taste of what retirement would be like, she was definitely not ready.

The bickering started on day four when she reached her limit of tolerating his teasing about the monastery and her sitting Zen practice, not that she was doing it all that much with him there, another thing that grated on her. He kidded her about the weird sect she belonged to and how it reeked of cult and what were they all hiding beneath their robes. She wasn't laughing or sure this was the hill she wanted to die on, but she defended her monks as if she were Joan of Arc, even though she harbored doubts herself.

Queen of Sheba one minute, Joan of Arc the next, didn't make for a peaceful domestic scene or inner calm. What she needed was a heart-to-heart with the two other men on her shortlist of who to call if she were dying.

Two phone calls later she'd arranged a lunch date with Uncle Charlie, back from Boston in the morning, and Muin, in town on zendo business. A weekday lunch date—how quaint. Maybe she could get used to being a lady of leisure. Now all she had to do was break the news to Guy that he wasn't invited to the party.

Next morning at breakfast, the few feet of table that stretched between them felt like a moat the size of the Hudson River that she didn't want to cross. She didn't even know why she was so mad at him.

"Did you know Muin was in town?" Guy asked.

Is this a trick question? How'd he know? What the fuck should I say?

"Muin?"

"Yeah, I just ran into him on the corner when I was out getting the paper."

"Hunh. What'd he have to say?"

"Asked if I'd be joining you guys for lunch."

Shit.

"I was just about to mention this. I'm getting my stitches out this morning and having lunch with him and Uncle Charlie after."

"Why didn't you tell me?"

"What?" *Is this another secret of cohabitation, that every detail of one's life has to be shared?*

"That you were going out today?"

"I—"

"You haven't wanted to go out that door all week, and I have to find out from your ex-boyfriend that you're going to lunch with him?"

"And Uncle Charlie ..."

"Might want to let your ex know that. He seemed to think he'd have you to himself. He was gloating and I felt like a schmuck."

"Muin doesn't gloat, he's a monk for god's sake. And he's not my ex, it was—"

"What? Just sex? That what monks do? Have sex and then pretend to be holier than the rest of us?"

He pushed his half-eaten bowl of oatmeal to the middle of the table and started to get up.

"Look ..." Alex tried to contain her anger. "You don't have to worry about Muin ... and I was planning to tell you about lunch ..."

"And invite me?"

Alex stared at him, words trapped in her throat.

"Nothing to say? Maybe I was wrong, maybe it's you who has something to hide. I feel like I don't even know you."

"Oh man." Alex twined her arms across her chest as if that could contain her racing heart and lungs. "Like I said, I 'preciate all you've done—"

"Now go?"

"What?"

"Now you want me to go? I get it. Not to worry. I'll be gone by the time you get back today." He slammed his chair into the table and turned to walk away.

Alex was numb, had no clue what to say, what she wanted, or how to say it. The anger in her belly got tighter and harder, blinding her to the right action. The table between them had become a deep, unbridgeable chasm.

"One thing about me that you might want to know ..." She said this in as soft a voice as she could muster, but it was laced with anger, which wasn't lost in the gap between them.

"I'm listening," he said, turning round to face her.

"I've been alone for so long and having you here all week has messed with my head. I don't know what's going on with me. Being cooped up all week, not able to work, barely able to move—I'm going crazy. It's not just you."

"Not just me, but some of it's me."

"No ... I don't know ... I can't even think straight. I need a little space, that's all. I need ..." She was about to say that she needed to sit on a cushion for at least a week, but didn't want his ridicule just now, not about that.

"What?" Guy asked.

"I don't know. I don't even know what I need or want. I'm sorry." Alex didn't mean it but she needed to end this, her head was spinning.

Guy's shoulders relaxed. He walked around the table and reached out his hand.

"C'mere," he almost whispered.

She took his hand and stood up. He wrapped his arms around her. She sunk her cheek into his chest.

"I'm sorry too," he said. "Guess I got a bit jealous."

They stood locked together, breathing, saying nothing.

Guy relaxed his hold, cupped her chin in his palm and kissed her forehead.

"You go have a nice lunch today with your other men, I've got a shitload to do and I'll get my stuff outta here by tomorrow, go back to my place, give you some space back. Okay?"

All she could do was nod.

"Don't say a word. I'm not going away forever ... can't get rid of me that easy. I'll see you for dinner. Maybe if you're up for it we can go out someplace and celebrate the stitches coming out, my treat."

"Okay, but I can't promise—"

He put his fingers to her lips. "I know. If you don't feel like going out I'll make you something special. We'll talk later ... now go." He slapped her ass. "Or you'll be late for your appointment. Say hi to the boys."

Alex's anger was no longer full blown, but it hadn't disappeared. She was mad at him for being so nice, and at herself for being a coward.

3

U ncle Charlie was sitting in their favorite booth with a coffee cup and the *Times* spread out in front of him.

"You are a sight for me old eyes," he said as he rose to greet her, arms spread wide.

"Careful not to squeeze too tight," Alex said as she floated into his embrace. "I'm still a bit fragile."

"Damn, sorry Petal. I nearly forgot. I'll be as gentle as a lamb."

In his arms, Alex sighed from a deep place that only Uncle Charlie could reach.

"Lemme look at you," Charlie said when they separated. He eyed her scarred forehead. She raised her sleeve to show off her purple and yellow arm.

"Swwwww," he whistled. "Those're some flashy colors. Looks like they did a good job sewing up the ol' noggin."

"Yeah, not too bad. Almost wish it was worse, give me a little character."

"Honey, you got plenty o' that without messing up your looks."

"Couldn't hurt to look scary and dangerous, my line of work. Some creeps I know might be impressed, might ..."

"'Cept you're gonna be done with all that soon, right? Less you changed your mind about working with me."

Alex plopped herself down. "I haven't a clue what the hell I'm going to do, Uncle C. I need some help here."

"Maybe I can be of assistance," Muin said as he slipped into the booth and gently slung his arm around Alex's shoulders.

"Jeez, Muin, where'd you come from? Give a girl a heart attack sneaking up like that."

He kissed her cheek. "Nice to see you, too."

"How are you, Charlie?" Muin and Charlie reached across the table and shook hands.

"Couldn't be better, but Alex has seen better days."

"I'm fine," Alex said. "And I'll be even better after I eat. Can we please order? I'm starving." She wasn't quite ready to launch into her woes.

"How's the new boyfriend treating you?" Muin asked.

Leave it to Muin to get straight to the point. "Can we please eat first?" Alex whined. "Besides, nothing I say on an empty stomach counts. Why don't you two talk while I sit here and stew?"

"Tends to get a bit cranky when she's hungry," Charlie said to Muin, his hand shading his mouth as if that would block his words from her earshot.

Alex glared at Uncle Charlie.

"Don't I know about that." Muin winked his left blue eye at Alex.

She was too angry to say a thing, knew she'd regret it. That was some progress she'd made over the years. The rage in her gut wasn't caused by the two men at the table, but it wanted her to lash out and hurt somebody. She just sat on her hands and bit her tongue.

"Heard you were up in Boston, Charlie, got to see a Red Sox-Yankees game, you lucky son of a gun." Muin gracefully changed the subject.

"Yeah, it was sweet, sitting right behind first base. Sox were in great form."

They ordered, they chatted and they ate, with Alex chiming in once in a while. With a cappuccino in front of her after all the plates were cleared away, she said, "I have to ask you guys something and I need you to tell me the truth no matter how much it might hurt. No trying to make me feel good, okay?"

"That sounds ominous," Muin said.

"I've never lied to you and I promise I won't start now," Charlie said. "Cross my heart."

"Muin?"

"Of course, you know me, I'll give you the straight dope. Monk's honor."

They stirred the white foam in their cups, sipped and waited till Alex was ready. Her men would give her all the time she needed.

"Do you think, and please think about it before you say anything, do you think I've lost my edge, my sex appeal, my mojo, my whatever I had before I turned forty-four and started thinking about not being a cop anymore?"

There, she said it. Neither Muin nor Charlie said a word.

"Well? Shit, you taking that long to answer means I'm right, doesn't it? I knew it. Shit. I am over the hill. Guy's just hanging around because of my bike accident, feeling sorry for me, you guys love me I know, and you will even when I turn grey and wrinkly. But shit ..."

"I think her head trauma knocked something loose up there, don't you, Charlie?"

"Totally. Something's just not right with her."

"Don't tease, I'm serious here."

"Darling Alex," Charlie said, "you know you don't look a day over thirty-five, tops, and being your uncle it wouldn't be kosher for me to comment on your sex appeal, but I'm damn sure you got a few more good years in you to chase bad guys, or good ones for that matter, if that's what you want to do."

"And please allow me to say something about the sex thing." Muin straightened his spine and twined his hands together atop the table as if he were praying. "Charlie, you can excuse yourself if you don't want to listen to this."

"I can handle it, but not sure she can, so be careful."

Muin twisted his upper body to face Alex. "Soooo ... if I wasn't a monk, you know I'd marry you, we've talked about this. Even though I could marry as a monk, but then there's the monastery life that I can't leave and you can't ... well ... that's not what we're talking about here. So let me get to the point.

"You are the sexiest girl I know and have known and seen walking those streets out there, with your green eyes and, what is that hair color? Auburn? And that new hairdo the way it frames your face, and that you don't even know you're a knockout makes you even sexier to most guys, and—"

"Okay, okay, I shoulda known you guys would be nice," Alex said, blushing. "Still, it feels good to hear it, but shit, I feel so old and worn out. I don't know what to do, having Guy in my place all week has made me crazy, I don't even know if I like him anymore. I think there's something seriously wrong with me, besides having fallen on my head."

"What you need is a nice long vacation," Charlie said.

"Or a few weeks up at the monastery," Muin said. "Or both. The combo would set you straight again."

"I completely agree," Charlie said.

"Where would I go? Who would I go with?"

"What about New Mexico? Go visit your friend out there ... what's her name? The cop you used to work with?" Charlie asked.

"Kate."

"Yeah, Kate. You've been talking about going out there since you got back from your last trip, when was that, about five years ago?"

Alex nodded.

"You haven't been out of this city in a while, the desert would be the perfect antidote."

"It's an idea." Alex closed her eyes and imagined being in the heat and color of the desert landscape. "Hmmm ... not a bad one," she sighed.

"I think it's perfect. In fact, I think it's more than perfect," Muin said. "I have an old friend at a monastery north of Santa Fe. You could sit with his monks, and play with your friend Kate. And you could do me a huge favor by going."

"What's that? Get me off the east coast, out of your life for a while?" Alex pouted.

"Aww Alex, you're not in my life enough when you're here. What's with all the self-pity?"

Her insides recoiled from this accusation but she knew Muin was right and the only person in the world she'd let get away with saying it. She couldn't even look over at Uncle Charlie.

"What's the favor?"

"We're making a bunch of rakusus to send to the monastery out there." Muin looked across at Charlie and said, "Pieces of fabric we Buddhists hang around our necks to let us know we're Buddhists ... long story ... case the robes and shaved heads aren't enough of a reminder."

"Very clever, you Buddhists," Uncle Charlie chuckled.

"That's one way of looking at it." Muin turned to Alex. "My friend Shoju in New Mexico would be so pleased to have you show up with his rakusus. Personal messenger is so much better than UPS. Actually, I'm not even sure UPS will deliver packages way out there in the desert, so he'd have to drive to town and, well, it'd be such a help if you could do this. And besides, since there really are no coincidences, and I had no clue about your connection to New Mexico, and I have to get some rakusus there, I think you must go. It's karma at work. What do you think?"

"I don't even know if I'm going yet, I have no idea if Kate is even around or wants me there, or if I can get a cheap enough flight, or if the doc will let me fly—I've had some vertigo this week after my fall." She saw a look of worry on Charlie's face. "It's not serious Uncle C, don't worry, it's just something I have to check out."

"Well, if you get the okay from your doctor I'll spring for the plane ticket," Uncle Charlie said.

"Really?"

"Yup, we'll call it an early Christmas present."

"Wow, that is tempting."

"Okay then, I should have the rakusus by the end of the week. You won't leave before then will you?"

"Whoa, slow down, I'm not even sure I can go, or get a flight, or ..."

"Okay then, let me know when you know and we'll make arrangements. Deal?"

"Deal." This didn't settle the issue of Guy though. She'd have to figure that one out on her own.

***

By the time Alex got home she was exhausted and the vertigo seemed worse. Perfect excuse to stay close to home, not go out to dinner. Her sore-to-the-touch left side felt like a wall between her and Guy as they lay in bed that night and she listened wide awake to his sleep-breathing and watched the night shadows dance on the walls. The one-year-to-live theme played its background music in her head. She'd started the class eight months ago, so theoretically she was down to four months to live.

Unable to sleep, Alex ruminated. *If I knew I only had a year, four months, a day to live, would I live it like this? Would Guy be next to me? Would I be in New York? What would I be doing? What would make me happy to be alive in this moment?*

She was happy to be breathing, not so happy to be restless and unable to curl up against Guy's taut, comfortable body. *Why didn't I agree to change sides so my right side faced him? If I can't make that minor adjustment how can I ever make all those others that are required in a relationship? What if I really was dying? Cold truth is each day lived is one less day I have to live. All this thought about death makes me feel ancient.*

She could feel the warmth of Guy next to her. An old, familiar Daddy's-little-girl loneliness tugged at her heart. A single tear slid down her temple into her ear. The pain of losing Daddy when she was ten had become a dull sadness over the years. Tonight its rawness surfaced as if no time at all had passed. Her father was dead but having him so alive in her heart had her wondering what dead actually was.

***

Alex knew she had to escape to softer surroundings to contemplate her future; the edges in New York were too hard and she was literally running into all of them. And even though Guy had moved back to his apartment and wasn't at her place all the time, they had dinner together most nights and he often spent the night. But she still felt like she needed more space from him. So she decided to take Uncle Charlie up on his offer to send her to New Mexico. Kate was delighted and thought she could take some time off in about a week. On Wednesday night, while savoring Guy's famous seafood paella, Alex broke the news.

"I think that's a fantastic idea," Guy said. "What about the vertigo? Have you talked to the doc about that?"

"Yeah, she's given her blessing. Thinks the dizziness is all in my head,"

"Serious?"

"Yeah, says there's nothing physical to explain it."

"That's crazy."

"Yeah, maybe I am." Alex laughed.

"Not what I meant." Guy didn't laugh along. "Besides, you're not any crazier than the rest of us. Maybe a second opinion's what you need. I don't like the idea of you flying so soon after a head trauma."

"I think I'll be all right. I appreciate your worry, but she might be right, with all that's been going on, maybe I just need a vacation. I gotta trust she knows what she's doing."

"I sure hope so," Guy said. They ate in silence for a few minutes.

"I just had a brilliant idea," he said.

"Uh oh, here you go ..."

"No, really, it is. I've got some vacation accrued, and could join you out there in about a week. If you'll have me, that is. I've never been to New Mexico, haven't had a vacation myself in I can't remember when. A change of scenery'd do us both good."

Alex finished chewing the mouthful of food she'd shoveled in while he was speaking to buy herself some time.

"Okay if I let you know about that once I'm out there?" She had no clue if she wanted his company but it would be easier to say no from a distance if it came to that.

"O'course. You get settled, have some girl fun and call on me if you get lonesome. Just need a few days warning is all."

"Sounds like a plan," Alex said.

Five days later she was 30,000 feet up and heading west.

4

Albuquerque

Kate stood with her arms crossed against her chest and looked down on the dead body. There was no blood, but there had been nothing natural in the dying. The distorted angle of the head, legs and arms akimbo, body spread on the rumpled bedclothes as if it had been dropped from on high, told part of the story. The absence of all personal effects told the rest. She was sure the ME would later confirm what she knew in her cop's bones. It didn't take a genius. Murder, pure and simple, stared up at her.

Kate's long, straight blonde hair was pulled off her face and wrapped in a twisted bun on the back of her head. A few loose strands of hair were in her face, annoying her. She swiped at them to no effect and grumbled something under her breath. Her partner, Pete, stood on the other side of the bed, his eyes bloodshot, the slump of his shoulders making his usually beefy chest look like it was caving in on itself. They were both exhausted from two weeks of twelve-hour days without a break.

"Wasn't a heart attack, that's for damn sure," Pete said. "Neck had something wrapped around it and I doubt it was a piece of jewelry."

"Yeah, this wasn't by his own hand or his higher power's," Kate said.

"Animal goes by the name human wreaked havoc on this poor slob."

"Wonder what he did to get someone this pissed. 'Cept for the shaved head he looks pretty ordinary." Kate leaned over the razored head to look closer at the neck. "Pete, take a look at this, could be blood."

Pete walked around the bed and they both bent over to get a closer look.

"Shit, I take back the regular guy bullshit." Kate stood up and rubbed her lower back. "Nothing normal about that. S'not blood, looks more like ink, maybe a tattoo. We'll have to wait for Plotzie to turn him over, get a good look."

"These ain't normal guy pants either," Pete said. "Elastic at the ankles, drawstring at the waist, and they're not sweat pants. No way this guy was hanging with locals."

"Nothing here says it, but I'll bet he was connected with those church robberies."

"Yeah, maybe why this place is cleaned out. Whoever did this took the loot."

"Shit, Alex will be pissed."

"Who's Alex?"

"Friend from back east, coming to visit. Meant to tell you I was planning to take some vacation time I got coming."

"She the cop buddy you told me about?"

"Yeah."

"She'll get it then."

"Yeah, she'll get it. Okay ... I'm the one who's pissed, she'll understand. She's from the streets of New York, so she's seen more than her fair share of dead assholes—not to mention having plans fucked with all the time.

"It's just, well, damn, I was looking forward to some time off, spending it with her. Now there's no way the captain will allow it. Not that anyone's gonna mourn this character"—Kate indicated the stiff on the mattress with a tilt of her head—"but killing's killing and even this guy, dead or not, criminal or not, deserves some sort of justice. And the motherfucker who did this is still out there to kill again."

Kate jammed her fists into her pockets, scowled at the corpse as if it were all his fault and muttered to herself for a while. After a few beats, the task of dealing with the crime scene took over and settled her into a working groove. She had three hours till Alex touched down.

***

"It's been what, four or five years since you were here last?" Kate fastened her seatbelt and handed Alex a bottle of water. "Here, keep the liquids flowing ... dehydration can be a bitch."

"Thanks ... four years is just about right, plus a few months." Alex took a long pull on the water and luxuriated in the dry desert heat.

"Too long, my friend."

"Exactly. I can hardly believe how fast time shoots by. I was coming up on my fortieth, remember?"

"Mmmm. We had some fun." Kate pulled out of the No Parking space and hit the horn twice at the SUV that was slowly cruising the curb. She looked over at Alex. "Once you got over your freak out about being thirty-nine going on forty, that is."

"Oh god, don't remind me. The Chrissie Hynde and Neil Young concert almost made me proud to be so old, they still looked and sounded so amazing."

"Yeah, those rockers, even with all the fast living, if they're still playing and singing they are almost ageless. I bet you'll look as good as she looks when you get to be that old."

"Thanks for that, but she's got something I'll never have. The cool factor. That's what makes her look so great."

"Aw c'mon, Alex. You may not have a guitar strapped to your body and maybe you can't belt out a tune, but even she'd call you cool for carrying a gun and chasing bad guys."

"Maybe back then. But now I'm forty-four and old enough to retire for God's sake! Can you believe it?" Alex moaned.

"What is it with you and age? You don't look a day over thirty-four. Although that old lady attitude will put you in a home playing checkers faster than you can say granny. What the hell happened to you?"

"It's been a rough year."

"Wanna talk about it?"

"Let's get to your place first. I need a shower before I do anything. We can talk more over a beer and burrito a little later. D'you mind?"

"No problem," Kate said. "Okay if I talk?"

"I'd love it." Alex slouched down in her seat and closed her eyes, soothed by the sound of Kate's voice, the desert clime, and the freedom to do nothing.

"... and the sex, ooh man, the sex," Kate purred.

"Whoa, Kate, slow down. I must've missed something. Sex, what sex?" Alex sat up and turned her full attention to her friend. Neither of them were very good at keeping in touch between visits so there was always a lot of catching up to do. They'd reconnect as though no time at all had passed, but it took a while to get current on the details.

"You didn't hear anything else I said, did you?"

"Sorry, guess I'm more exhausted than I thought."

"We can do this later."

"Are you kidding? Tease me with sex and then stop? I'm wide awake now, you've got my attention. Do tell."

Kate had been even unluckier in love than Alex. Transplanted three thousand miles from the city she was born and raised in was a geographic solution to the problem of her abusive ex-husband, Jerry, who wouldn't stop hounding her even after they got divorced and she moved away.

Since moving to New Mexico Kate had dated some cowboys and Indians, had even tried a few cowgirls, thinking that that was her problem, but she never let anyone get too close. Alex was thrilled to hear her friend so excited about someone.

"Well, he's in the department ..."

"He's a cop?"

Kate nodded.

"Ooohhh boy ..." Alex said.

"It's not like that out here. Cops here are different than back east. And this one, he's half Indian, half Irish, very sexy. People sometimes mistake him for Johnny Depp."

"Ooh-la-la."

"Young though."

"How young?"

"Not sure I want to tell you ... you with your ageist slant on things."

"Aw, c'mon, Kate. Gimme a break. As long as he's tickling your you-know-what I don't care how old or young he is, long as it's legal."

"Oh, he's legal all right, but what he does to me must be illegal somewhere."

"I'm not sure I want to know about this," Alex teased.

"Truth is, sex is just a part of it, a fabulous part of it, no question. But I don't know ... there's something else. I really like this guy. He's only thirty! I must be crazy, tell me I'm crazy, I can't fall for him. I'm too old for him. I could almost be his mother. In fact I met his mother and she's only a few years older than me. That was weird. He likes older women. Maybe 'cause his mother raised him— she definitely has that cool factor we were talking about—after his father left before he was even born. They were never married, of course, and Sam doesn't seem to want to get married, says he doesn't want kids. But I don't believe him, he loves kids, works with Native kids every chance he gets." Kate stopped abruptly.

"What is it Kate? Why'd you stop?"

"You think I'm crazy."

"Au contraire. I've never seen you so happy and excited about anyone. I'm happy for you. When do I get to meet him?"

"Maybe tonight."

"Maybe?"

"Well, he's planning on it. But you know how police work goes ... there's this case—"

"Say no more, I get it." Alex stretched and yawned. "I've got two luscious weeks with nothing to do. Surely he'll sneak some time to see you while I'm here and I won't be far away.

"And," Alex added, with a threat of mischief, "he'll want to meet someone who knows all about you."

"Don't you dare tell him what a nerd I used to be. He thinks I'm a hip, sexy, city girl."

"And whatever I tell him won't change his mind about that. Hope he doesn't get jealous about us spending so much time together while I'm here."

"He's not the jealous type."

"Far cry from Jerry then, eh?"

"Couldn't be more different." Kate didn't have the heart yet to break the news that she'd be harder to pin down than a shadow during Alex's vacation and wouldn't have the time to spend as they'd planned. But Alex was a big girl, she'd understand. Still, she felt guilty.

"It's so good to see you, Alex. We just don't see enough of each other. I wish I had the nerve to visit New York, not leave it all up to you coming here."

"You think Jerry would know or even care at this point?"

Kate looked at Alex as if she'd lost her mind.

"Oh, right," Alex said. "I forgot. He's a bastard."

"Got that right. And till he finds a replacement to torment, I'm still it."

"That sucks."

"Yup. He ..." Kate fell silent and concentrated on driving.

"What? He, what?"

"I don't want to ruin your vacation, let's talk about you. Tell me about this guy you're seeing. His name is Guy, right? Is that weird?"

"Let's save that for later. I want to know about Jerry. You look pissed or scared. What the hell did he do now?"

"He showed up out of the blue at the station about three, four weeks ago. I wasn't there, I'm sure he knew that. Introduced himself to everyone as my husband. My husband!"

"Shit, what happened? Did you see him? Did he come to your house?"

"Never saw the creep, but he was snooping around I'm sure of it. He's a slippery bastard though, so even if he was there I wouldn't have been able to get my mitts on him. He's gone now, so let's change the subject. Pleeeezzz ..."

"Damn. Why can't I get it after all this time that he's not one of the good guys?"

"Always been hard for you to think bad of anyone once they get into your circle," Kate said.

"S'pose you're right. It's like I got this wall up and once you're inside my instincts short circuit."

"Something like that."

"So, what? I'm not perfect? That what you're saying?"

"Something like that."

"Ooohhh, that hurts." They both laughed and then lapsed into a comfortable silence for the last few miles.

***

As they drove into Kate's driveway, Alex said, "Your house looks amazing Kate, the oasis I've been dreaming about. Thanks for having me. I'm so glad to be here."

"No need to thank me—you're welcome anytime, you know that." Kate eased slowly to the top of the drive and turned off the ignition. The noise of the engine cut off, dropping them into quietness. The contrast struck Alex as profound.

"But I have some bad news." Kate had to get it over with.

Alex tensed up. "What happened?"

"Nothing happened ... well, a lot's happened, but that's not the news. But because of all that's happened—I won't go into it now, or ever if you don't want—I may not be able to take any time off while you're here. It sucks ... you know how it goes."

"Boy, do I ever."

"The bad guys just won't honor our vacation schedules. There's a big case right now and the department can't afford to have me gone. Besides, I want to catch the bastards."

"What'd they do?"

"Let's save that for another time. You're on vacation for Christ sakes..."

"Guess I'm not so good at that."

Kate took Alex's suitcase out of the trunk. "I can take a few minutes, help get you settled, then I've got to get back."

Kate unlocked and opened the front door and they were met with a cool, shaded living room. The hidden swamp cooler, the ceiling fan, and the shades drawn against the heat of the sun did their jobs making the space an inviting respite from the dry, sunny outdoors. It felt like a cool drink in the shade on a scorching hot day. And not nearly as startling as walking into a cold, air conditioned room on a hot August day in New York. There was harmony here between the inside and outside. Walking into Kate's home made Alex feel welcome and the thought that she could live in this climate made its usual appearance.

"I'm sorry you can't take some time while I'm here, but I'm not surprised."

"I feel awful about it."

"Don't worry, I'll be fine." Alex wouldn't say it out loud, but she was a little relieved. As much as she loved Kate, she wanted some time alone in the desert.

"It's not you I'm worried about, it's me. I haven't had a break in months," Kate moaned.

"I know the feeling."

"But I'll try like hell to sneak at least a day while you're here."

"I hope so. We'll go up to Ojo Caliente, get a massage, soak in some mud and hot springs."

"God, wouldn't that be yummy? But right now I gotta run. There's a ton of food in the fridge, plenty of beer and other liquid refreshments. Help yourself, take a nap, the hammock in the backyard is a great place for that."

A car horn tooted softly out front.

"There's Sam now. Here's a set of my house keys, and my car keys, in case you want to go out. The car's yours while you're here. Sam's offered to chauffeur me around. We're on the same schedule ... sort of."

"That's very generous of you."

"Selfish really. I love being treated like a queen. Never knew that about myself, but hey, it fits."

"Looks good on you, too. You deserve it."

There was another toot of the horn, not insistent, just a gentle reminder.

"Now go, get out of here."

"There's—"

"I know where everything is, I'll be fine, really. Go to your Prince Charming."

"Okay, bye." Kate hugged Alex. "I'm so glad you're here. And I promise not to spend every night with him. I've so looked forward to a late night gab session with you."

"Yeah, me too. We've got lots to catch up on. See you later."

The door clicked shut, the car backed out of the driveway and wheeled away out of hearing. Alex was alone. It was quiet except for the soft whirr of the fan overhead and the purring of Ed, Kate's nineteen-pound orange tabby that had been around since Kate's first day in New Mexico, in the corner rocking chair right where Alex had last seen him almost five years ago.

Will I be happy five years from now if I leave the force and start living the life of Ed? What the hell would retirement mean anyway? And what the hell would I do next?

She had no energy to face these questions. Instead, she took a quick shower, changed into shorts and a T-shirt, grabbed a tumbler of iced tea and her Tony Hillerman book, and flip-flopped her way to the shaded backyard. She stretched out in the hammock and fell asleep in the first paragraph.

Something shocked her awake an hour later and she couldn't tell if it was in her internal or external environment. She bolted upright and nearly spilled over onto the ground. *Fuck, I hate hammocks.* She finally got her feet to the ground and stood up, becoming mildly dizzy. There was nothing to hold on to. She stood still until the vertigo passed. Her patience for the healing process was stretched to its limit and a small worry nagged at her deep inside a brain she couldn't trust anymore. She wished she could remember how she fell off her bike in the first place. *Maybe my brain was on the fritz even before the accident? Damn it. I will not make a good old person.*

5

"That was delicious, Sam, thank you." Alex, Kate and Sam were relaxing after feasting on Sam's special quesadilla dinner. "You and Guy will have a lot to talk about if he makes it out here."

"Hope he does." Sam leaned back in his chair, his long legs stretched out under the table in front of him, crossed at the ankles of his cowboy boots, a toothpick between his lips.

"Ain't it great having a man that cooks?" Kate looked back over her shoulder at Alex as she stood at the sink finishing up the dishes.

"Sure, except it sorta makes me feel like I'm missing a certain gene," Alex said. "Not complaining though, I love a man in an apron. I guess some people love to cook and they need people like me who love to eat."

"Speaking of eating." Kate walked back to the table drying her hands and stood behind Sam. "I've been invited to a lunch in Santa Fe tomorrow that I just can't go to. Alex, would you be a dear and go in my place?"

"Thanks, but no thanks, I'm bad enough in social settings when I know everyone. Being surrounded by strangers and no way out would be torture for me, you know that," Alex said.

"Course I do, but I gotta call Skip and cancel and he won't be happy. Thought you could help ease the pain, give you something to do," Kate said.

"Don't you worry about me, I'll have no trouble finding something to do. Sam, you know about this guy Skip?"

"Yup, ex-cop from New Yawk, got in touch with our Ms. Kate here when he moved west. Seems like a nice enough guy, though I was not invited to this lunch." Sam winked at Alex.

"Kidding, right?" Kate stroked the top of Sam's head and then sat down. "Damn, I was trying to do a good thing here by not inviting you."

"I know honey, it's okay, just joking." Sam reached out and took her hand. Kate's body sighed and relaxed.

"Skip worked Brooklyn," Kate looked at Alex. "He and I met on a case right before I moved out here. Guess I told him my plans so he looked me up when he got here a few years ago. I really don't know him so well but he's a nice guy ...

"We'd have a drink, bite to eat here and there. Talked about New York mostly. Then he met Cissie, his now wife, and I hardly ever saw him again. He'd call once in a while when he needed a favor from a cop. Never even met the wife. Though I did visit her gallery once just to get a look—didn't strike me as someone I wanted to know. Once he got married, I hardly heard from him."

"And he invited you to lunch at his house tomorrow?"

"He called outta the blue last week probing for information on this case I'm working. Anyways, I mentioned you were coming, trying to change the subject, get him off my case. So he invited us both to lunch. Said it was the real reason he called. Said he was having a little get together to introduce his newish bride to some people."

"Well, now I really know I don't want to go, especially without you."

"The whole thing seemed a little odd. I think he was just on a fishing expedition about this case I'm on. And, he's been married a year, so his wife isn't exactly his new bride anymore, is she?"

"I've got an idea," Sam said. "How about you call him and say something's come up, you can't be there tomorrow, and then we invite them here in a couple of weeks for dinner? Things should settle down a bit by then. Even if they don't, let's do it while Alex is here, have a little get together of our own, show how entertaining we New Mexicans can be."

"Really?" Kate asked.

"Really and truly and madly, yes ma'am."

"Ugh, please don't call me ma'am," Kate laughed and rose from the table. "I gotta call him, get it over with. Why don't you guys go relax in the living room and I'll be with you in a jiff."

Less than five minutes later Kate walked in and held a phone out to Alex. "Skip wants to talk to you."

"Damn it, Kate."

"Sorry, he knows you're a cop from New York, I think he's homesick. He's okay, really, it'll take a minute."

"Shit." Alex struggled off the lounge chair, took the phone and walked toward the front door. "This work out on the porch?" she asked, raising the phone up above her head.

Kate nodded.

By the time she walked back into the house she'd been roped into a lunch fifty miles away with a stranger. She'd been too whipped to put up much of a fight.

***

By 9:00 the next morning Alex was behind the wheel of an old Jeep, on loan from Sam, taking the long, scenic route to Santa Fe. Randomly selecting a CD from Sam's collection, she slipped it into the dashboard player. The sound that filled the cavity of the Jeep was reminiscent of the live flute music played on New York City street corners by groups of native South Americans, but this was softer, more airy and meditative—seductive even. She glanced at the CD cover—R. Carlos Nakai, indigenous and native. It wouldn't be her choice back home, but it suited her just fine here. It helped to send her swirling thoughts to the deep interior of her mind as the arid landscape seeped into her bones.

At ten minutes after the designated hour of noon, Alex stood at Skip and Cissie Hunter's cobalt-blue front door and rang the bell. At least she'd get to eat, one of her favorite pastimes. The sprawling adobe house just outside of town sat on top of a winding hill with a panoramic view. It was shut up tight, no cars in the driveway, no sign of life anywhere. Except for the gentle desert breeze wafting over her cheeks, the whole neighborhood was sitting still as if holding its breath waiting for the residents to return: A well-manicured ghost town ripe for a gang of burglars. *Damn, will I always view the world from a jaded cop's perspective? Where the hell are all the friends who are supposed to be at this lunch?*

Alex pushed the bell a second time and thought she heard a faint ringing inside but couldn't be sure.

If a bell rings in a house with no ears, does it have a sound? A quote from some Zen text floated into her mind: *Listen for it and you can't hear it.* Her brain registered anger at the paradox and inscrutability of Zen. Reflexively, her left fingertips felt the nearly invisible scar and small bump on her left temple. She raised her face skyward and felt a twinge of vertigo. Her left ribs ached slightly, so she dug through her bag for more Advil.

Whatever patience she had for this outing had been spent during the two hours she'd wasted strolling around town buying silver jewelry from natives who resented her long legs and money. She couldn't blame them. She let them gouge her. It was the least she could do. And now she was spent and had no energy for socializing.

She leaned on the bell a third time. Her Irish was in a lather and she was starving. *Why had I said no to Guy when I meant yes and yes to Skip when I meant no? Fuck.*

She needed to eat. Her inner grouch was yelling at her. Along with her hungry ghost creating havoc in her brain, she was pissed at someone she'd never met for being stood up at a lunch she didn't want to go to.

What I ought to do is walk away, accept the gift of the cancelled lunch without question. I'll call it: The universe doing for me what I can't do for myself.

Except now I'm starting to worry. Maybe something's wrong. I can't just walk away without finding out what the hell happened.

She punched Skip's cell number into her phone and banged on the door. The house was sealed up like a fortress, no openings to peek into any of the windows, and the six-foot adobe wall that wrapped around the property, attached to both sides of the house, stood as a barrier to seeing much of anything beyond the front yard.

As Skip's phone was ringing, she buzzed and knocked again. If he were in there she'd wake his ass up.

"Hello?"

"Skip, it's Alex. I'm at your front door."

"Oh shit, right. Hang on, I'll be right there." He hung up.

She stared at her phone. How had he not heard her at the door if he was inside all the time?

There was movement on the other side of the door, the turn of a dead bolt, then another and another. The sun bore down, the breeze rustled the branches of the lemon tree overhanging the side fence, and the loud punctuation of the unlocking locks disturbed the stillness of the suburban cul-de-sac behind her.

Skip was bigger than Alex had imagined, redder in the face, and greyer on top than the photo Kate had shown her had revealed. He stood in the doorway, blocking her view.

"Hey Alex, look, I'm sorry. Meant to call you, forgot all about you coming. Something came up. Had no choice. You know how it is, work takes over and, well, hey, I'll make it up. Call when you're heading back this way. We'll do the lunch. But look, I gotta go. Say hi to Kate."

He started to close the door. She hadn't said a word. He didn't seem to notice or care.

Reflex had Alex thrust out her arm to hold the door ajar as her other arm automatically went for her gun—only to find it wasn't there, she'd left it at Kate's. The sudden movement sent a spasm of pain through her left ribcage. She held a grunt deep in her throat and blinked away the pain.

"Whoa, whoa ... it's not a problem, I get it. But would it be okay if I use your bathroom first? I'll just be a minute."

"Uh, sure, okay." With reluctance, he let her in. "It's down the hall on the right. Be quick, would ya? I've got a client coming any minute."

"Sure thing." Alex didn't have to pee, she just wanted to get inside to see what was behind that door. *Why all the heavy duty locks? What's he hiding? Who the hell is this guy anyway?*

I have to start using a different word to refer to men and reserve the guy word for Guy. How can I be with a guy named Guy anyway?

Ten steps down the hall she was stopped in her tracks at the sound of the three dead bolts turning and locking into place behind her.

***

Back in Albuquerque at the morgue, Kate and Pete stood over John Doe's stone cold body as Abe Plotzer, medical examiner, was explaining cause of death.

"COD was compressive asphyxia—a heavy weight was applied to his chest, probably someone's knee—the force was enough to compress his lungs, reduce oxygen flow and kill him. They broke three ribs in the process. Simultaneous with the knee, a heavy object was applied to his neck, or a not-so-heavy object with some muscle behind it. Left some weird indentations and bruising, looky here." He pointed out the pattern of small, circular bruises on the neck.

"Yeah," Pete said, "we saw that, looks worse now. What the fuck'd cause that? Ever see something like it?"

"Seen the effect, not sure of the cause in this case. Not yet anyways. Whatever it was, it produced cerebral ischemia and a fractured hyoid bone. Either the chest compression or this would have killed him. One or the other was overkill. Hard to say which came first. Someone wanted him dead in a hurry. Died instantly is my guess."

Kate smiled at this tic of Plotzie's. He never made guesses, always knew what was up, wouldn't say a thing otherwise.

"What else you got?" Kate was dying to see what the hell was on the back of the stiff's neck and shoulders, maybe down his whole back. She'd play Plotzie's game, let him bring it up, or else he'd tease her with it, shoo her away, make her come back after sitting with the not knowing a bit longer. She wasn't in the mood, then again she never was. But this was his sanctum and she respected that.

"What you talking about?"

"Dunno, saw that look in your eye like you had a surprise for us."

Abe squinted at her as he raised the glasses that were dangling around his neck up to the bridge of his nose.

"Oh, all right. Help me roll the body over."

Pete backed away as Kate and Abe turned John Doe onto his belly. Pete hated touching dead bodies even through gloves and Kate never seemed to mind. They were good together like that, her yin to his yang, him willing to do the things she hated and vice versa.

"Get a look at this," Abe said.

All three stared down at an unfinished, freshly inked tattoo. A wild looking creature with half a face stared back at them. The face was an angry red, or maybe the expression in the eyes made the color feel angry. Gold horns jutted from the top of its head and black hair framed the partial head. Eyes were wide, round and possessed with a crazed demonic glare.

Plotzie put the words to it. "My guess, that tattoo is fresh, probably the same day as he met his misfortune. Thought he had more time left. Probably planned to go back, get the bottom half next week or next month."

"Damn," Kate said. "That must've hurt."

"Yeah, well, someone put him out of his misery for good." Pete stepped nearer and leaned over to take a closer look. "What the hell is it?"

"Wouldn't want to guess on that one," Plotzie said.

"But you've done some looking into it?" Kate knew he had but she had to frame it as a question or she'd get nothing.

"Some, not enough yet."

"C'mon, Plotz, give a clue," Kate pleaded.

"It's gotta be connected to his current condition." Pete threw a warning glance at Kate to keep the emotion in control. Plotzie would clam up if it got to be too much.

"I'd bet my wife on it," Plotzie murmured. Abe Plotzer wasn't married, far as anyone knew. Or he was, and loved his wife more than his own life. Only thing the two detectives knew was that every time he used this expression his hunch was right on target.

"Here." He handed Kate a photo of the red-faced, horned creature etched on John Doe's back. "Go talk to Jack. He'll know something. Only one in town could do a tat like this with such elegance and detail. Quite impressive, really. Don't you think?"

"I don't know about that, but it's damn ugly," Kate said. "Who the hell would want something that hideous on their body, unless it had some sort of cultish significance?"

"Sure wouldn't be attracting no girls with it," Pete said. "Except the weirdos, those who go for the criminal element, guys behind bars etcetera."

"Exactly my point. Now go, so I can work in peace. You're both breathing too much for my taste." Plotzie gently swept them out of his sanctuary and got back to work.

***

Alex spun around and asked with as much innocence as she could muster, "What's with all the locks, Skip? I'll only be a sec."

"Oh, right. Not about you. Sorry. Old habit from the city. Just can't seem to break it."

Alex left the lie hanging, went into the bathroom, took a minute, flushed and was back out faster than possible if anyone had been paying attention.

Skip was pacing back and forth all nervous in the middle of his living room waiting for her. Alex had already overstayed her welcome.

A quick scan of the room revealed nothing special. There was framed art leaning against walls and stacked in corners. Kate had mentioned that Cissie had an art gallery out on Canyon Road so that set off no alarm. The dining room table was laden with small statues, pottery, and sculpture. Everything appeared indigenous Native American.

Except for the painting hanging over the enormous stone fireplace. It had to be five feet tall and three wide and practically leapt off the wall. It was a portrait of an ugly red-skinned demon wielding a large metal-studded club. Its mouth was open as if shouting, large yellow teeth, with two long pointed fangs jutted out at crooked angles from the top and bottom gums. Horns protruded from his head.

The shrill ringing of the doorbell interrupted her viewing and sent a jolt through her body. Skip panicked.

"Shit, I knew it. Listen, you gotta do me a favor and go out the back." He took her by her still-bruised left elbow and led her to the backyard deck. The door chime continued as if stuck. His fingers were wrapped tight enough to leave another bruise.

"Okay, okay, lighten up on your grip, would you?" Alex said as she tried to pry his fingers off.

Skip loosened his hold but did not let go. Outside, he pointed to a gate in the side yard.

"Slip out there," he whispered, as if anyone could hear him over the now relentless and annoying doorbell, someone's finger and impatience bearing down hard. "Then give us a minute before you walk around to the front ... oh damn, did you park your car in the driveway?"

"Where else? ... Look, Skip, are you okay? Can I help here?"

"No, no. It's just a fussy client, thinks he's the only one I have. Hates to see other people here when he comes. So long as you don't see him it'll be okay. I'll handle it."

The bell stopped its noise. They stood immobile in the loud silence and stared at each other for a flash of a thought. The ringing resumed, rudely piercing the stillness. As if that were their cue, they sprang into motion, Alex out the back and Skip toward the front door.

Damn, that's more than enough reason not to become a PI. No way could I deal with a client like that.

In her brain, on the spreadsheet entitled *What To Do Next With My Life*, she penciled *crazy clients* into the cons column next to PI.

After unlocking the gate, she let herself out onto a narrow lane between the tall fence on one side and four-foot-high desert shrubs on the other.

What the hell just happened? I've gotta call Kate. But first things first, I gotta eat. I'm starving. She adjusted her newly purchased, expensive, silver-buckled belt, took a deep breath and quickly made her way to the car.

Skip's client had arrived in a black Hummer whose windows were almost as dark as its body. It dwarfed the Jeep it had parked too close to. The Mutt and Jeff-ness of it made her laugh. *Passive aggressive bastard. Or maybe just plain aggressive. Bastard for sure.*

She got into the passenger side of the Jeep, climbed over into the driver's seat and got her ass out of there. Whatever was going on, it wasn't any of her business.

6

Alex was unable to reach Kate all afternoon to report to her friend how bizarre Skip's behavior had been and find out if it was in keeping with his personality. Her cop's gut kept nagging at her. Maybe it wasn't her business, but when did that ever stop her? Something wasn't kosher with him and his supposed client, and she couldn't let it go. So, when he called her an hour later, despite wanting to be left alone, she took his call, curiosity once again winning out.

"Alex, listen, I really want to make it up to you, it's important to me, my behavior this afternoon wasn't very friendly and well, I can't imagine what you think, but our aborted lunch is now going to be dinner, tonight, we want you to come, you have to come meet Cissie, she's counting on it, and in the meantime I want you to be my guest at Ten Thousand Waves, this truly amazing spa up the mountain, a good friend of ours is the owner there and they're waiting for you to give you the red carpet treatment, you can't say no, I insist—"

"Whoa, Skip, take a breath, slow down."

"Sorry, sorry, I guess I get excited sometimes, especially when I've done something wrong and want to make it up, and anytime I can treat someone to a luxurious spa treatment, especially a female as I know they appreciate such things, I get excited for them. So will you?"

"Will I what?"

"Go up to the spa for the afternoon and then come join us and a few friends for a celebration dinner at seven?"

What could it hurt?

"Sure, why not. Just tell me where to go."

"Perfect! I'll text you the info, spa's number, manager's name etcetera. Any questions you just call there and be at our house around seven tonight. Okay?"

Guess I can't accept the spa gift and refuse dinner...

"Sure, okay, thanks."

"Have a blast!" Skip hung up with no goodbye on either end.

***

"You went to a spa and now you're spending the night at Skip's?" Kate whispered into the phone in her darkened kitchen. It was late, Sam was gently snoring in her bed, and she didn't want to wake him. "What the hell's got into you?"

"Yeah, it's pretty weird. I think it must be the desert air. I almost hate to admit it, but I loved it up on that mountain, getting pampered, soaking in an outdoor hot tub butt naked. Girl could get used to that." Alex kept her voice down even though she was at the far opposite end of the house and was sure Skip and Cissie were passed out from all the wine they'd drunk. Still, she felt a need not to disturb the peaceful night air.

Kate padded her bare feet back to the red vinyl dinette chair as Alex chatted on about the spa experience, with a spoon and a pint of Ben & Jerry's Cherry Garcia in hand, phone cradled between shoulder and ear. She was up and talking to her best friend, her man tucked comfortably in her bed, so she figured she might as well pretend she was on vacation. Listening to Alex talk about her day soothed her and began to open up a clear space in her mind between obsession and worry, both to do with police work.

"Damn," Kate cooed, once she settled back down. "Can you believe I've never been to that mountaintop spa? Maybe by the time you head back this way, this frigging case I'm on will be done and we can go together as planned."

"How's it going?"

"That can wait. More important right now is how the hell did you wind up back at Skip's house for the night, especially after his odd behavior when his client appeared? Jeez Looeeze." Kate filled her mouth with creamy sweetness and listened.

"He called me after his client left—he is definitely weird when it comes to his clients—takes the private in PI way too seriously.

"Anyway, he wanted to make it up to me—his rudeness, cancelling lunch without notice, his bad behavior all around. He's friends with the owner of the spa so he offered me a free afternoon of massage, mud baths, the works —*if* I'd come back for dinner, he was having that party he cancelled at lunch.

"I figured what the hell. Besides, I'm on vacation with no real plan and I was curious. He is most definitely a character, but his wife, Cissie, now she ..."

"Do tell, what's she like?"

"Like a hummingbird—all night, up and down, up and down—flitting from one person to the next to the next—setting down nowhere. She would perch every once in a while on Skip's knee, peck at his face and then move on. She was a blonde blur most of the evening, nattering on about this artist and that craftsman and antique relics and her food—which was fabulous, by the way, she does know how to cook. But the whole evening was excruciating!"

"Oh gawd, I'm so sorry I sent you up there in the first place. I'll make it up to you, I promise," Kate said.

"Don't worry about it. I'll go home with a quirky vacation story."

"Speaking of that, dinner with Skip and his wife is one thing, but how the hell did you wind up spending the night?"

"Long story short, there were no decent rooms left in town—I procrastinated as usual in making a rez, it was late, and they insisted I stay in their guest room. By that time I had no energy to argue or traipse around in the dark looking for a bed. It was a little weird, but safe enough. Fact is, it's rather cozy. I'll buy a piece of Cissie's art as payment and she'll be thrilled.

"How're things on your end?"

"Talk about weird. We got church break-ins and robberies all over the state. We got one dead body that we think is linked—he was IDed by a church security guard, guy had given him a hard time about checking his backpack, which is missing—but there's no prints, no clues, no nothing. We can't even figure out why anyone would steal this shit. There are a couple of pieces worth some bucks, but they'll never be able to sell them on the open market. Rest of the stuff's only of sentimental and religious value to church people."

"What? There's something else," Alex said. "I can feel it. What is it?"

"It's nothing, really, I'd rather not talk about it."

"C'mon Kate, it's me, your old friend."

"Old is right!"

"Very funny!"

"And you know me too well."

"Okay, out with it."

"Okay, okay. I think Jerry's in town again. I can't be sure but I've been getting calls at home at the weirdest times and there's always someone on the other end of the line but he won't say a word. I can hear breathing, or at least I think I can. And I swear it's Jerry."

"Damn it, what is his problem?"

"He's sick, that's what, and obsessed with me. It's beginning to freak me out again."

"Oh man, anything I can do?"

"Yeah, find him another girlfriend, take his attention off me."

"Now there's an idea. I could put an ad on Craigslist, set up some interviews ..."

The two old friends chatted on into the late night, girl talking, catching up, laughing and sharing, as old friends are wont to do.

***

Alex crept out of the house the next morning before the sun crested over the mountain and Skip and Cissie had their last dream. A half hour later she hated herself for wishing a mall with a Starbucks or Dunkin' Donuts would appear on the horizon, but a strong cup of coffee was becoming an urgent need. Jonesing for a shot of caffeine, she almost felt sorry for the street drug addicts she had to tangle with on the job.

Finally, just before 7:00, she found a town awake and serving breakfast. Sitting in a restaurant with plastic tablecloths, sipping coffee and waiting for her huevos rancheros, vacation mode grabbed her and shifted her brain into park. Coffee never felt so good.

By noon she was on Chama Canyon Road to Abiquiu Desert Monastery. She had checked into the Abiquiu Inn, decided to get her favor to Muin over with sooner rather than later, and then become Jane Q Public on vacation. No formal Zen, no police work, no city grime. Georgia O'Keeffe country was the perfect place to start and she was in the heart of it. She would visit the monastery, meet Muin's monk friend Shoju, drop off the package of rakusus, and go on her merry way. An afternoon for Muin wasn't all that big a sacrifice.

The landscape seduced her and at moments it took her breath away. High canyon walls on her right, pink and layered like a frosted birthday cake; the river below her on the left, snaking through the rocky, shrub-laden canyon floor; and the narrow, winding dirt road. She never imagined the desert could be bursting with so much color.

Even with the Jeep it was slow going and would take a good hour or more to get to the monastery, a mere twenty miles in. What a perfect place for peaceful contemplation, the southwest version of the monastery landscape back home in the Catskills. She started chanting the heart sutra. The cadence of Buddhist chanting had always reminded her of a Native American ceremony. The tempo now felt in harmony with the setting, a natural container for her incantations. She was "in beauty" as the famous Navajo tribal policeman Jim Chee would say.

Halfway through the chant she became aware that she kept repeating the same twelve Japanese syllables over and over and had no idea how to get past them and on to the ending. It was the place she always hummed her way through when chanting with the monks.

What better time and place to rest and finally learn the damn thing?

She stopped the Jeep, turned off the ignition, dug her sutra book out of her bag and walked down to the water's edge. There she spent a half hour memorizing the tricky section. By the time she got back to the Jeep the foreign sounds were in her head. Now she just had to chant it enough to get it into her bones and the memory cells that resided there.

The Jeep wouldn't start. She was miles from nowhere. The noon sun was bearing down. She closed her eyes and took a deep breath. Sam's warning came back to her. "She's a little finicky, tends to stall out once in a while on rough terrain, but patience and a gentle talking to'll get her moving again." Alex had kidded him about being a Jeep whisperer. They had had a good laugh.

Not funny now, nope, not funny, and patience was not her strong suit. Maybe she could learn something about that out here in Indian country the way she'd just learned the chant so easily. There was no phone service in the valley, but there were still eight hours of daylight left, which gave her plenty of time to walk back to Abiquiu or forward to the monastery if she had to. A passage from the Tao flew into her consciousness.

Do you have the patience to wait
till your mud settles and the water is clear?
Can you remain unmoving
till the right action arises by itself?

She had no clue about any of that. But panic was not an option and she had some time, so she decided to do a little zazen in the great outdoors, see what happened.

Sure enough, a half hour later, just as Sam had promised, the Jeep started up and purred as if nothing was wrong. Alex rolled down her window and began chanting again, from her deep belly, as she'd been taught. She chanted into the valley wind. No one but the local wildlife heard the echo of her voice off the canyon walls.

***

While Alex was en route from Santa Fe to Abiquiu, Muin's friend, Shoju, sat in meditation at the monastery, anxious and afraid. Knowing that it was delusion, illusion or hallucination didn't help ease his mental torment. The fear that gripped his imagination felt real. And when the han—a wooden board hanging outside the door of the zendo—was hit with the mallet, calling an end to the morning services, it pierced the silence like a rifle shot and sent a charge through his heart. The continuing rat-a-tat-tat, slow and then fast, seven times, then five, then three, slowly began to ease his racing pulse. It was just the usual beating of the han, not gunfire.

When the ceremony of the han was finished he struck the inkin bell, got up from his seat, bowed and led the other monks to breakfast. The silent meal would give him time to think what to do about his imminent guest.

His old friend, Muin, was sending some ex-lover cop friend of his to drop off a package of rakusus Muin had made for him. When she'd called and spoken to Andy in the front office, she asked if she could visit for a bit, maybe sit with them in the evening. Andy had told her it was fine before checking with anyone. It was not fine, not today. Shoju would make some excuse, ask her to come back in a couple of weeks. Or never. He couldn't have a stranger lurking just now. Especially a cop—even if she was thousands of miles from her regular beat. He'd have to use his Zen charm to get rid of her.

7

Alex almost missed the turn into the monastery road, it blended in so well with the surrounding terrain. She wondered what other structures she had missed along the route and realized she'd been expecting something bigger and grander than what greeted her. After parking the Jeep in the parking lot, she actually gave it an encouraging pat on its hood and left it there with the wish that it would start when she was ready to leave. As she walked toward the main building she decided she would not spend much time there, just drop off her package, take a look around and leave. It wasn't as inviting as her home monastery and didn't look like much of anything till she got up close.

There were a series of about five or six unattached buildings surrounding a courtyard and a certain comforting flow about the whole arrangement the closer she got. Magnificent manicured gardens and meandering stone walkways wended around the buildings and off into the desert landscape. A sculpted rock garden sat outside what appeared to be the meditation hall. Wild desert sagebrush, cactus and juniper trees were plentiful all the way up to the canyon walls.

Shoju met Alex at the door of the monastery, but that was as far as she got.

"Muin told me you were coming. Thank you for the package of rakusus. I'm very sorry, but we're incredibly busy right now preparing for our silent retreat next week and really don't have time to spend with you. You can come back in a couple of weeks and I'll give you the grand tour." Shoju practically slammed the door in her face.

"Okay if I spend a little time here walking around outside? When I spoke to Andy this morning he never said anything about any of that and—"

"Andy is a new student here and shouldn't have given you permission to come today."

"But I'm here now—"

"Okay, fine ... but only till four, three would be even better. Don't stray too far, it can be dangerous out there." At that he closed the door and disappeared.

Must be some bizarre virus going around New Mexico that causes temporary insolence. First, Skip's lack of social grace, and now Shoju booting me away without ceremony. Jeezus.

When her phone started ringing it took awhile to realize it. At first she thought the Chi-gong chime signaling a call from Muin was a bell coming from the monastery. She had assumed there was no phone service way out there in the deep valley so it took five rings to register with her.

"Muin?" she whispered into the phone.

"The one and only," he said, as clear as the valley stream.

"I can't believe there's cell service here, I'm at the monastery. Your so called dharma brother just turned me away."

"What're you talking about?"

"Shoju. I gave him the rakusus, he hardly said thank you and then told me I couldn't stay, he had no time, they were preparing for sesshin, or as he said, 'our silent retreat' as if I didn't know what a sesshin was, and could I come back after next week. Got the clear message that coming back never was what he really meant." Alex walked away from the monastery buildings. The wireless signal was still clear and strong. She looked around for a cell tower.

"That's strange. ... Hold on a sec, would you?" Muin put her on hold. Alex walked farther away and saw not a soul. The scenery kept her attention. Familiar with the star-studded sky in other parts of the state, she wondered how many more stars would reside in the darkness here. She wanted to stay the night if only for the light show. The only sound was the distant river. No noise at all coming from any life inside or in the vicinity of the buildings.

"Just as I thought," Muin said when he came back on the line. "I just checked online. There's no sesshin on their schedule for next week."

"Maybe they didn't update the website?"

"No way, something fishy's going on."

"Sure feels that way to me."

"Let me call Shoju, I'll call you right back." He hung up without a goodbye. She looked agape at her phone. *Damn rudeness virus is spreading east.*

***

Back in Albuquerque, when it became clear that Kate and Sam would both be working late that night, Sam suggested they take "a quickie lunch break" at Kate's house. "I'll fix you up something special." Fifteen minutes later clothes were off, shades were drawn and the breathing was heavy.

"This feels illicit," Kate said.

"It does, yes ma'am, it does. So arrest me." Sam sweetly kissed Kate's neck, and comfortably entwined his legs with hers. The breeze from the overhead fan wafted over their naked skin.

As they lazed in the after effects, Kate's phone blared intrusively into the moment.

"Don't answer it," Sam said.

"What if it's the department?"

"They don't know you're here. Wouldn't they call your cell?"

"You're right. Who the hell could it be at this hour?" She looked at the phone. "Caller ID says OUT OF AREA. I've been getting a lot of these weird calls lately." She sat up on the edge of the bed, picked up her blouse from the floor and punched her arms into the sleeves.

"I'm gonna answer this, find out who the hell keeps calling me. Spell's been broken anyway, and goddamn it we gotta get back to work."

"Want me to answer it?"

"Hmmm, that's an idea." Kate took a moment. "Thanks, but I think I gotta do this.

"Hello? Who is this?"

She sensed someone on the other end. "Jerry, is that you? How'd you get this number?"

No answer.

Kate hung up the phone. "Fuck," she said, under her breath.

Sam let her be, said nothing. They got dressed in silence.

"I'm starving," Kate said. "You?"

"Sure am. How 'bout I make that quickie lunch I promised?"

"Oh, you meant food?"

"Yes, I did, but someone distracted me from that mission," Sam said.

"Think we have time?"

"Yup. Be done in a jiff. I'll make it to go, we can eat in the car if we have to."

"I'll help."

"Okey dokey. And for dessert I'll hook your phone up later tonight so you can trace those calls, find out who's been calling. Probably just a wrong number and now that they've heard your voice and realized it, they'll stop calling. But just to be sure, I'll take care of it. Okay with you?"

Kate nodded and hugged him tight. "It sure is nice to have a techie around the house."

"You betcha. Now let's see about some grub."

"Shit," Kate said.

"What is it?"

"I just remembered I'm supposed to meet Pete downtown right about now at Jack's tattoo parlor, talk to the owner about the ink on that John Doe who got himself dead."

"Alrighty then. I know that place, know Jack, too. There's a great taco place just next door where we can get a bite. I'll drive, get you there in no time. Let's go."

"Okay, perfect, thanks sweetie. I'll call Pete, let him know we're on our way."

***

Alex headed toward a small butte—or was it a mesa, she wondered, and made a mental note to look up the difference—about four or five hundred yards northwest of the buildings, hoping she'd be able to climb up and view the area from on high. Peering back at the monastery it emanated peacefulness and appeared to be in harmony with the natural landscape, as if it had grown roots there and flowered as any other desert plant or creature would.

Just as she got to the bottom of the hill and was scoping out the climb, Muin called.

"Okay, here's what I found out. Shoju really didn't want to tell me, but I dragged it out of him so long as I told no one."

"Except me, though, right Muin?"

"I didn't tell him that, but I'll let you in on some of it." Muin paused. "But you can't say that I did."

"Right."

"Just as I suspected, there's no sesshin on the schedule, but there's been an event. Something happened that they want to keep in the family so to speak, deal with it themselves without outside help."

"That sounds ominous and un-Zen like," Alex said.

"Now don't go making it into a big deal. Shoju's sorry he was so rude, promised he'd make it up to you when you come back."

"Okay, so what happened?"

"Well, as you saw when you were inside the monastery—"

"I never got in, not even one foot, he came to the door and shooed me away," Alex said.

"Okay, okay. Anyway, they have a lot of antique and valuable bells and gongs and statues from the East, mostly Japan, and someone stole a very famous, very precious, very old gong and everyone there, especially the Roshi, is quite upset about it."

"Do they have any idea who took it?"

"They think it was one of their old monks who had a theological parting of the ways with Renku Roshi and left to form his own zendo many years ago. One of his students was visiting recently, and putting two and two together they've decided that that student stole the gong and brought it back to the monk, his teacher. It was quite large and heavy and they haven't figured out how he accomplished this feat, but they're convinced it was him. Apparently there's a plan in place for Roshi to visit this monk in some neutral space sometime soon, within the next week I think, and negotiate the return of the gong."

"Has the monk admitted to stealing it?"

"Not sure about that. That was all Shoju was ready to tell me."

***

Kate, Sam and Pete were eating tacos after their visit with Tattoo Jack.

"Damn." Pete was staring at an eight-by-ten photo on the table that Jack had given them. "That creature is uuug ...ly!"

"I dunno," Sam said, "it has a certain dreadful beauty to it."

"Maybe in the photo," Kate said, "but to etch this monster into your skin? Covering your whole back?"

They ate and stared at the demon, lost in their separate thoughts as they fed their hungry ghosts.

"Think Jack was being straight with us about our John Doe being his only customer for this demon ink?" Kate asked.

Sam and Pete shrugged in answer, their mouths full of beans, taco and spicy rice.

"He didn't even know the guy's name? Paid cash? Spent hours being stuck with needles and never said his name? Jack never asked? A little hard to believe," Kate said.

"Yup," Pete said. "Puts us back to knowing just about nothing."

***

After Muin's story of the stolen gong and all the precious statues under the monastery roof, Alex was reminded of Kate's sacred objects larceny case and felt a need to see some of the treasures resting on the altars of Abiquiu Desert Monastery. *What the hell is it with religious groups and all their paraphernalia? Aren't they supposed to be focused on a higher power and purpose in life rather than object worship?* Even her precious monastery back home wasn't exempt from this phenomenon, and it rankled.

She had an urge to investigate. She wouldn't be able to live with herself if she left this hanging. It would be like having an itch and not scratching it, something she was trained to do while sitting on a meditation cushion, but trained not to do as a cop. She was standing up and moving and not even close to a meditation cushion, so she gave herself permission to scratch away.

There were five outlying buildings that looked to be the residences, with the main, center building reserved for Zen ceremony, sitting, chanting and eating rituals. That was the structure her curiosity settled on and wanted to explore.

Other than Shoju, Alex hadn't set eyes on another breathing soul since she turned off the Jeep's ignition an hour ago. There was no sign of life anywhere. It felt unnatural, just as it had at Skip's place, but at least there were no locks on these doors. It was a piece of cake to slip inside unseen. If caught, she'd use the needed-the-bathroom-it's-a-long-drive-back excuse.

Alex removed her shoes at the main entrance and snuck into the cool, darkened interior of the main monastery building.

8

Kate, Pete and Sam were finishing up their latish taco lunch when Pete's and Sam's phones buzzed with urgency.

"Damn, it's another church theft over on Lead," Pete said.

"Yup, and there's been a casualty this time," Sam said. "So it's escalating."

"Wonder why I didn't get the call?" Kate stared at her phone. "Damn, my battery needs recharging."

"I got a charger in the car, let's go." Pete grabbed his jacket off the back of his chair and sped toward the parking lot.

"Looks like it'll be a late night." Sam planted a quick kiss on Kate's cheek as they headed in opposite directions.

"No doubt. See you when I see you." Kate waved and smiled as she followed behind Pete.

***

Alex stood stock still for a few breaths once inside the monastery, and then spun around in a full circle engaging all her senses. Upon completion, she knew she'd be able to move around with ease. The only person inhabiting those walls with her right now was Andy, the new student who'd given her permission to visit, manning the phones in the main office. She could avoid him. And even if he caught her trespassing, she knew he wouldn't give her any trouble.

The four large rooms that she explored—zendo, dharma hall, kitchen and dining room—gave away nothing other than the feeling that they'd once been used by Christian monks. A few stained glass windows and an antique wooden pulpit sitting in the corner of the dining room hinted at that secret.

Some of the icons on the altars in the zendo and dharma hall looked ancient and of museum quality, which led her to wonder. *Who is Renku Roshi, the Zen Master in this place? And, being a Zen monk, where'd he get all that money?*

The only thing she knew about him was that he was Japanese. So she chalked up the opulence to the many rich people in Japan who liked to bankroll men in robes.

There were three other things that piqued her curiosity more. One was a room with a locked fire door, unheard of in all the monasteries she'd ever visited or knew about. *What the hell is in there?*

And then, on the wall in a smallish room that was probably used for sangha business meetings, greeting guests and sharing a cup of tea, hung two suspicious photos.

One was a photo of Skip's wife, Cissie, standing with a regally robed monk, probably Renku Roshi. The other was of a huge statue in a garden that looked remarkably like the ugly demon in the painting hanging above Skip's fireplace.

Alex thought back to dinner the night before. She was sure she'd told Skip and Cissie about her plan to visit the monastery. And she was just as sure that neither one had said a thing about it. Their silence on the subject had her assuming that they had no interest in and certainly no intimacy with the place. The photos she was now staring at told a different story, at least for Cissie.

***

An hour later, just as she got to the Jeep, her hand out ready to open the door, she swung around to stare back at the monastery. She'd felt, more than heard, something behind her. Whatever it was had vanished, leaving her holding her breath. Her ribs hurt from the sudden movement and a soft wave of vertigo rolled through her head, not enough to throw her off balance, but enough to set off a worry that all was still not right with her brain.

Aside from the monk-less monastery, and the locked door inside, something else had spooked her. From habit, once again she began to execute her crime scene ritual as her left-brain scoffed at the gesture. Closing her eyes, she began to turn slowly in place, breathing, sensing, and trusting her muscles and bones to tell her a story. Once she settled into her body, she half-opened her eyes, taking in the terrain, not really seeing anything in particular, but not not-seeing either. Her focus was on the space, the air, the nothingness out in front of her. She turned ever so slowly so as not to shock her brain and incite vertigo.

This was her usual crime scene ritual but there was no dead body here, no assignment, no crime. Just her instinct, arched like the back of a frightened tomcat telling her that something was not quite right, not quite safe, not quite serene as it first appeared.

By the time she completed the circle, someplace deep inside she knew something was not quite kosher with the monks who resided there, and that Skip and Cissie were somehow involved. Leaning back against the car door, Alex stood as still as the rock walls. Breathing from her gut, she set her gaze out into space, focused on nothing, and let the scene in front of her just be there until she became part of the scenery. Ten minutes later she felt better, more at home in her body, and keenly aware of how much she missed everyday police work.

She'd have to find a way to channel her proclivity to solve puzzles, especially those involving bad guys, and not conjure up trouble where there was none. She might be thinking about retiring from the NYPD, but she sure as hell wasn't ready to do nothing. That much she knew.

***

The eerie beauty of the monastery interior and what she'd seen and hadn't seen remained with Alex as she drove the slow, rocky road back to Abiquiu. Guy was along for the ride in her head. It was getting pretty damn crowded up there.

Less than a mile away the phone signal disappeared, so talking to someone else would have to wait. She sorted through the facts as though they were clues in a case, making a list on the chalkboard in her brain:

1. A soulless monastery—empty of moving monks, no one home. Where were they all?
2. One locked, fireproof door, whose corresponding outer walls had barred windows with drawn shades. What was inside that room?
3. The two pictures in the meeting room.
4. The missing gong.
5. The riches on the monastery altars.
6. Skip's and then Shoju's hostile and obnoxious behavior.

This wasn't her case. In fact, there was no case. She just had to let go and stop manufacturing mystery where there was none. There was no crime here and no more inscrutability than normal everyday life. *Will I ever stop thinking like a cop? Stop seeing the world and every event as a possible clue to some wrongdoing somewhere?*

Chanting always helped to quiet her chattering brain. By the fifth mile, a mere half hour later, just like magic, her obsessing mind had calmed down. Guy was all that was left and she didn't want to push him away anymore.

Warm desert air, soft pink cake-layered canyon walls, the slow shushing sound of the river, and the hard bumping of the canyon road underneath her, assaulted her senses. Soft and hard. Pleasure and pain. Her nerve endings came alive. She felt warm desire between her legs. Maybe they were right. Maybe, being in her forties, she was at her sexual peak. That was some consolation she supposed.

She slowed down and looked for a spot to pull over, face the river and get off the road. No one was likely to come by, but she wanted some privacy. She pulled between two juniper bushes and turned off the ignition. She leaned her head back and closed her eyes. Never had she done anything like what she was thinking of doing, except when she was drunk back in the day and couldn't recall the event the next morning. Doing it in the open air felt risky. *But what the hell.*

She got out of the car, walked down to the river, took off her jeans, and sat cross-legged on her jacket in her underwear. The dry breeze on her thighs and between her legs felt scrumptious. Her panties were wet. It was as if the visual and aural sensations of the canyon, with Guy in her brain, had been the foreplay. She closed her eyes and imagined Guy right there with her as her fingers began to play. She lay back and let herself go. She hoped no one was looking.

The possibility added an edge to the experience. Not unpleasant. Her own sounds surprised her. A hint of embarrassment appeared but was drowned out by the pleasure of release.

She opened her eyes. The ground underneath was rough but her whole body relaxed into it. She laughed softly out loud. Wait till I tell Kate about this. She knew she wouldn't tell Guy, not just yet. But she might bring him to this same spot, have her way with him and then tell him. She laughed louder. She sat up and hugged herself.

The late afternoon sun was sitting on the top edge of the western canyon wall. Soon it would dip behind and cast the monastery in shadow. Alex heard a thunderclap in the distance as a chill coursed through her body. There wasn't a cloud in sight. She got dressed and walked back to the car.

***

By the time Sam got to the church, his team had strung yellow tape across the front door to keep all but his crew and a few cops on the outside of it—curious citizens and passersby who had congregated like bees to pollen hoping to take something away to sprinkle into their next conversation and bring forth the oohs and aahs that naturally flow from a good story told.

There was a dead pastor near the altar up front, probably some missing objects, though that hadn't been confirmed yet, and a number of staff people in the office area in shock.

Once the scene had been contained and the coroner was on his way, Sam and his team began to work methodically from the back of the church to the front, shining their flashlights between and under the rows of pews, searching for anything that might connect to the murder-robbery that was in wait for them up front. It was as if they were sweeping a roomful of sand and collecting it all into one big pile to sift through and dispose of.

The heap that they'd end up with hours later would hold a dead pastor, shattered religious icons and with any luck some clues about the what, when and who of it. The why was not their business. The why Sam and his crew were happy to leave to the detectives and God. The why never had a clear-cut answer and to Sam's scientific mind only confused the truth.

It wasn't as if Sam had never been in the same room as death, but today the closed-in space was a high-ceilinged sacred one meant for rituals other than murder and it rankled. His Irish half was angry at the violation, his law enforcement and crime scene training had him assessing the scene—an almost empty altar pointed to the church bandits once again, a few broken shards of ceramic icons scattered at the altar's base indicated that things hadn't gone so smoothly this time, and the dead pastor suggested that he'd been the interruption, the surprise visitor, an unplanned consequence of the break-in. And the small part of Sam's blood that was Navajo had him wondering if the spirit of the priest would forever be trapped inside the church. This idea shuddered up his spine as he snapped on his latex gloves. After this was all over he'd look into having a traditional Navajo cleansing ceremony performed, to prevent ghost sickness. He didn't know if he believed all that but some of his genetic material was on fire at the moment and it wouldn't hurt to explore his heritage.

The dim lighting in the church was meant to create a contemplative, spiritual atmosphere for the faithful who would enter there and pray for themselves or their loved ones, but tonight the high shadows and dark corners cast a chilling spell. It might be perfect for calling forth the deities, but it was not conducive to police

work and seeing clearly. Klieg lights were on their way from the
station, and till then Sam and his team would do their best.

***

After dinner and back in her room at the inn, Alex paced and
thought and thought and paced. It was only 9:00 and she had
already exhausted all her local entertainment options. Something
was bugging her, something connected to something she'd seen and
heard since her plane had touched down in this corner of the world.

She wanted a cigarette. Ten years and her brain-body still
wanted to inhale nicotine as the thing to do when alone and stuck in
indecision, or with company and having fun, or just for the activity
of it. She wanted to call Guy but needed some ballast first, so she
dialed Kate. She'd been trying for an hour and there was still no
answer. Uncle Charlie was no doubt asleep with a book open on his
lap and this wasn't serious enough to wake him. An empty pocket
opened up in her stomach and ached to be filled. She couldn't call
Muin, his evening meditation wasn't over and the monastery phone
was off for the night. *If retirement looked anything like this, it sure
would suck. Have I ever known how to vacation? How do other
people manage?*

She had to talk to someone. She called Uncle Charlie. Even if
she woke him he'd be happy to hear from her. It took him four rings
to answer.

"Sorry to wake you, Uncle C, I can call back in the morning if
that's better for you."

"Don't be silly. Talking to you is a much better tonic than sleep.
I can sleep anytime. How's the wild west?"

"Weird. I'm bored and a bit antsy. And I'm suspicious of
practically everyone. You know me, always on the lookout for bad

guys. I see them everywhere. Can't tell the difference anymore between good and bad. Don't even trust myself since I frigging fell on my head."

"Yeah, not always easy to tell, but you'll be back to your old intuitive self before too long. You trust me, don't you?"

"About the only one I do trust these days."

"Okay then, here's what you do. Are you ready? I'm not sure you're going to like it."

"Will it help?"

"Absolutement! Guaranteed."

"Okay, shoot."

"Relax and have some fun."

"Oh, that. The F word."

"Speaking of which, how's Guy?"

"Uncle C!"

"Fun, I'm thinking fun. Not sure where your mind went." Charlie laughed.

"Yeah, well, I was about to call him, but needed to hear your voice first, to settle me down."

"Try not to be so serious, Petal. Call him up, take a risk, let go a little."

"I'll try. Thanks Uncle C, I feel better. What the hell would I do without you?"

"You'd manage, of course you would, but I for one am glad you don't have to."

"Me too."

"Now you go call that guy of yours and be as sweet as I know you can be."

"Yessir."

"Okay then and good night."

"Night. I'll call you soon."

"Just have fun. Uncle's orders."

"Got it."

Alex hung up and speed dialed Guy before she lost the mood, her gut flopping around like a beached fish.

***

By 2 A.M., Sam was the last remaining tech on the crime scene. His team had gone home to get a little sleep, the pastor's body was in the morgue, and there were two uniforms stationed outside in the parking lot to keep an eye on things. He turned off the bright lights and prepared to leave. The place was bathed only in the streetlight coming through the windows. All was quiet.

When he heard the side door that led to the pastor's office creak open, he turned to admonish whoever it was for being back there.

Sam didn't see, hear or feel the bullet as it pierced his heart. But somewhere deep in his bones as he fell to the floor he panicked at the thought of his spirit never being free, always being there under that particular ceiling. "Kate" was the last word he uttered. His assailant shot a second bullet right between his eyes.

9

Alex was awakened at 5:00 by an hysterical Kate who made little sense. She threw on yesterday's clothes, woke someone up to check out, and sped back to Albuquerque. Cruising along Route 50 she slipped the mala bead bracelet off her left wrist and worried the wooden orbs between thumb and fingers—an attempt to calm the murderous rage in her brain. She squeezed each bead as if to crush it, twirling the string of beads round and round, thinking, hating, missing, worrying, Daddy, Kido, people killing people, disease, murder, a year-to-live, it all ends in death, no escape, no reason, just death. *Why Sam? Why now?* She rolled the smooth beads between palm and thigh. Cruiser lights flashed and zoomed up behind her. She eased her foot off the gas and dropped the speedometer to a lawful sixty. The state cop wasn't after her, but there was no need to tempt him. The silent strobe of speeding light streaked past her.

Her grip on the beads turned softer, slower. The rage subsided but cracked open the Daddy-Kido scar deep in her heart that for years had sealed off the searing pain of love-wrenched-away-too-soon. Daddy killed by a drunken driver when she was ten, Kido taken by AIDS just after she'd asked him to be her teacher. Her heart now ached for Kate. Nothing she could say would ease that pain, her own now raw and inconsolable.

An hour later she found Kate curled up with Ed on the couch, mutely frozen—female and feline locked together, deep in a cavern of grief. She kissed Kate's head, stroked Ed's fur and slipped her mala bead bracelet onto Kate's left wrist. Kate stared blankly up at Alex.

***

Cissie locked eyes with herself in the mirror long enough to see through the decorative touches of makeup and silver jewelry straight down to the ugly girl. Her stomach went cold and her eyes turned into hard self-hating orbs. The light tinkle of the bell on the door announced a visitor. She dabbed more red on her lips and pasted on a smile before turning to greet her customer. They were few and far between these days—at least those willing to spend a few bucks on pretty wall hangings and clay sculptures—and she couldn't afford to be sullen.

Perk up missy, this ain't a funeral. Stop looking as if someone died. Her long-dead mother still nagged at her from the grave.

Smiling at the tourist couple, she silently invited them to browse, take their time, while she pretended to be busy. Five minutes was her rule of thumb. If they left within five, nothing she could say would convince them to buy. More than five, she could almost always close a sale. She'd never calculated it precisely, but figured her closing rate was up above eighty percent. Made her feel better about herself. Not bad for a poor trailer-park girl. She refused to say trash even if the word sat in her brain ready for use.

The married-looking couple lingered over the two thousand dollar desert watercolor. No one spent that much time in front of a painting if it had a price tag unless they know the artist or couldn't imagine their life without it. Cissie had a good feeling about these two. Her own art was in the timing, pouncing sweetly at just the right moment. Her instinct today told her to give them a little more personal time.

Something she wished she could give to herself—alone time— but being without company was torturous for her. She dug her nails into the palm of her hand, the pain a momentary distraction from her racing mind that fluttered from one to another to another man. She had to sort through the clutter of testosterone she'd piled up around her to fill the voids. Jerry would be the most difficult to get rid of. The other two she could manage—it would take a few tricks but she had more than enough up her sleeve and elsewhere. She forced herself to think good thoughts of her husband. Poor, dear Skip, she had to do right by him.

Ah, they were ready. In her strapless high-heeled sandals she clicked her way across the wooden floor over to the couple that was back in front of the pastel—one of Cissie's favorites. Everything would turn out okay. Life would be good.

***

Alex sat for hours with Kate until she couldn't any longer. She left on the pretense of getting some food neither of them wanted to eat. Alex's own lack of hunger was a surprise, stress and anger usually triggered insatiability, a call to her hungry ghost to wake up and start screaming for something.

Kate's gun sat on a table behind her head. Alex buried it in a kitchen drawer and stuck the clip in her rear pocket. Maybe she couldn't assuage Kate's pain, but she could make it harder for her to hurt herself. Kate barely registered Alex's movements and departure.

Closing the front door behind her, Alex stepped softly into the heat of the day. *What next?* She had no clue. But she couldn't sit idly by while Sam's killer was still roaming the earth.

She longed for someone to leap out of the sky or just hover over her and whisper in her ear what to do next, who to be, how to act, where to go. Some higher being that she didn't believe in to tell her what to do—not that she'd trust it or do it, but she hoped for it. She didn't know her own mind yet. Maybe something or someone else did. Was that too much? Give up all hope is what Kido would have said. Rely on yourself were Buddha's last words. Easy for them to say: A Zen monk and an enlightened being. Just sit and expect nothing Setsu Roshi would say. *Yeah, right! Even when a friend is suffering so? Even when a friend's lover has been brutally murdered and taken from life? Even when the bastard who'd wreaked this wrong is still free to do it all again? Don't think so. Not this day, not this time, not this life.*

Her phone buzzed. It was Guy. She sat down on the front step.

"Hi."

"I was able to get a flight out later today. I'll be there by ten tonight. Can you pick me up or should I rent a car?"

"I don't know if—"

"This is not negotiable. I'm coming."

Alex was relieved. Words stuck in her throat.

"So, what do you know? Any clues who did it? Have you spoken to Sam's chief? Who's on the case over there?"

"I don't know a thing yet."

Alex's cop brain woke up and slapped her lost brain into gear.

"I just walked out of Kate's—she's a basket case of course, hasn't uttered one syllable since I arrived. Hate to leave her alone, but I thought I'd head down to the station, see what's up, ask some of those questions."

So now I know.

"You need anything from me you call. Okay?"

"Yup."

"I'll be available till seven my time. Emailing my flight info to you now as we speak."

"I'll call soon as I know something."

"Good ... and Alex?"

"Yeah?"

"Despite the circumstances I look forward to seeing you."

"Mmm. Me too."

That wasn't so hard.

When Alex opened the Jeep door, the earthy smell she'd come to associate with Sam whooshed out, heat crashing into heat. She tried to imagine what she'd be feeling if Guy had been the one gunned down: Her stomach lurched and then flipped about and fluttered like a schoolgirl's as her thoughts moved to seeing and touching him later that same day. She knew that meant something, but she was damned if she knew what, other than lust. And then the guilt slammed into her gut for letting lust even have a say under these circumstances.

***

Whether they all knew Sam personally or not, it didn't matter, he was one of theirs and the grief and anger were palpable as Alex pushed open the door of the Albuquerque police station. Alex was ushered by the front desk sergeant back to a chair outside the captain's office and offered a cup of coffee while she waited, which was a tad tastier than the burnt, muddy water back home.

An hour passed. Cops walked by, checked her out, ignored her. She became part of the furniture. She caught snatches of conversation:

"... brain matter ..."

"... not a thing to go on, fuck me ..."

"... ballistics ..."

"... my wife ..."

"... know where Kate ..."

She itched to be part of it. Raised voices behind the captain's door and then dead quiet. In waves. *How long do I have to sit here? Where else would I go?*

Scooting herself off the chair and onto the floor, Alex crossed and tucked her legs under her, rolled up her denim jacket and fashioned it into a pillow, stuck it under her sitz bones and relaxed into position. *Might as well do zazen, make use of the time.* Just as her mind began to settle into her belly, the captain's door flew open and eight legs walked out and past her. Always happened like that. When she was a daily smoker, as soon as she lit up the bus or whatever she'd been waiting for would come. Had to crush a perfectly good cigarette. *Damn.* She unfolded her body and rose to greet the captain who stood at his door unfazed by her floor sitting. Try that in New York and no one would call you sane let alone a cop worth talking to.

The captain held out his hand.

"I hear you're a friend of Kate's, knew Sam."

She nodded her head and shook his hand.

"Sorry for your loss," she said.

She'd uttered these four words so many times under myriad circumstances they'd been zapped of all feeling. The emotion behind her face as she said them now took her by surprise.

"Likewise," the captain said. "Have you seen Kate?"

"About an hour ago. She's rather shellshocked as you can imagine."

"Come in, come in."

He marshaled her into his office, leaving the door open. Sure sign she wasn't going to get anything useful out of him. Niceties, pleasantries, but no real dope.

"You're not gonna tell me much are you?"

"You're a New York City detective, that right?"

"Yeah."

"Then you know—"

"Right."

"All I can tell you is we don't know a thing yet. But my guys are on it and they won't stop till they find the fucker."

"Yeah, well, you need an extra gun, you call me." She laid a card with her phone number on his desk and rose to leave. *Waste of time, this.*

"Why don't you go to Kate? See her through this. Tell her she's got the week off of course, more if she needs. We can't get through to her, she won't pick up her phone."

He held out his card for Alex to take.

"Keep in touch."

"Sure thing."

Alex snatched the card from his fingers, u-turned and left without another word.

10

Alex squinted through her Ray Bans against the sun's hard beat as she leaned against Sam's Jeep in the station parking lot. She could feel the freckles popping up brown one by one. If she didn't layer on some lotion soon or don a hat, she'd be burnt to a crisp in no time.

The huddle of officers by the front entrance hurled a suspicious eyeball over to her every few minutes. Whether she was the topic of their conversation or not didn't matter—it was clear they wanted her gone. They could smell cop on her—cop from not around here—and they didn't want her messing in their business—their nerves were all on edge, their fingers itching to pull on something.

She ought to go over and make nice, but the game of that was old and anathema to her. They had plenty of reason to be pissed. But why direct it at her? One of them split from the group and was walking over to her, nonchalant as all get out. Her phone buzzed against her ass, she pulled it out of her jeans pocket, looked at the number and chose Skip over the cowboy cop.

"Hey, Skip," she said as she unlocked the Jeep and slipped behind the wheel. She eased out of the parking lot, hateful darts being cast her way now, no more pretenses. *Shit. They don't know me and I'm in Sam's car. What a jerk I am. I should go explain.*

Skip was blathering away at her. She hadn't heard a thing.

"Hold on, Skip, give me a minute. I gotta go find a place to park so I can talk. Call you right back."

Against Skip's protests, she hit the red button and tossed her phone onto the passenger seat.

***

"In New York maybe you got people crushed up against you breathing their stink into your face twenty-four-seven." Skip turned to face Alex. "But here the town's so small everybody knows everybody—you don't look out they've got one hand down your pants and the other one down your wife's bra.

"You gotta help me," he pleaded. "I can't ask anyone here. You I don't know. Them I don't trust. Instinct tells me to bet on you."

Skip and Alex were sitting in Skip's car sipping coffee out of paper cups. He'd insisted on keeping their conversation private. "One never knows who's lurking and listening."

"What about you?" Alex said.

"What do you mean? What about me?"

"Why don't you go look for your wife? You know her best, know who she knows, where she's likely to be."

When Alex had finally called Skip back, he was in a panic, in Albuquerque. Had told her briefly what he wanted her for: "I can't leave here right now, I got urgent business to deal with, I need your help." She decided to meet him, thinking that the distraction might help her decide her next move. His wife, Cissie, was "gone, missing, someone took her." The drama queen act fit the behavior she'd witnessed at his house.

"She's likely to be at her gallery, but she isn't there, is she? And I may not know all there is to know about my wife but I know one thing: She would never, ever, not in a million years leave her precious art, just walk out, leave the door unlocked, no one there, leave her purse and her money. She would not do that. No one would do that. Unless they had a gun to their head, or worse."

"Did you check the hospitals? Maybe she had an accident, had to be carted off?" Alex flashed to her bike crash, almost catching a glimpse of what had caused the fall, but it was still just out of reach in her brain, like a dream after waking. What she did know was that personal belongings meant nothing after the hard landing, in fact, she never did recover her favorite bike cap. *But how could Cissie have had anything so jarring happen inside her shop? Even if she'd fainted and cracked her head open the EMTs would not have left her store unattended—a cop would have been called.*

As if he'd read her mind, Skip said, "Even if she'd blacked out for some weird reason—she's been known to faint now and then—if they'd taken her to hospital the cops wouldn't leave the place unlocked without a uniform standing guard. Besides, I called around. She's not in any hospital or morgue."

***

Kate felt Ed's head nudging her hand hanging off the edge of the couch. Ed was gently persistent. She moved her hand out of his reach. He sprung up onto her chest and began to rub his face into hers. He was hungry. She'd have to get up. Ed kept at her, insisting that life goes on. She didn't care. For her it felt over. She stroked Ed's soft orange fur and wrapped her arms tightly around him. She felt him breathing, heard his loud throaty purring. He allowed her to hold him down for a few minutes before he started meowing in protest. He was definitely hungry. *How long has it been since I fed him? How long have I been lying here?* The sun was shining, looked to be about midday. *What day is it? Where is Alex? Where is Sam now? Oh god,* she didn't want to imagine it, but she wasn't in control of her mind. She saw his body laid out naked on one of Plotzie's tables. His face was not in focus. Ed wriggled free, leapt off the couch and walked into the kitchen. Kate struggled to sit up. Ed meowed from the kitchen. Kate felt light-headed. Maybe she needed something to eat, too. *What about Nona, Sam's mother? Has anyone told her? Of course, of course. Oh my god, she must be devastated. I should call her.* She could hear Ed pushing his bowl around the kitchen floor.

"Okay, okay, you wild beast. I'm coming, I'm coming."

Kate stood up and made her way to the kitchen.

***

"Who's minding the store?" Alex asked. "If you're here, and she's, well, not there, how'd you learn about it?"

"Guy in the café next door called me," Skip said. "A customer asked him 'bout her—if he knew where she'd gone—he checked it out, called me right away."

"He didn't call the cops?"

"Nah, phoned me first. I made some excuse to him about her erratic behavior of late—said a close relative had died and she was all broke up about it, no predicting what she'd do, no surprise to me. Asked if he'd lock up—her keys were sitting right there on the counter—said I'd be by later, not to worry. Told him I was sure she was okay. But I'm not, of course, as I said. And—"

"Okay, okay, let me think a minute." His chattering was annoying and her brain couldn't or didn't want to take it all in. But he was offering her a puzzle to solve, her calling in life. A flash of worry erupted in her brain.

They sat in loud silence for half a minute. Way too long for that small a space.

"I don't think I can leave Kate just now—"

"But—"

"You have heard about Sam?"

Skip nodded. "Why I'm so beside myself about Cissie. It feels connected somehow."

"You're kidding, right?"

"I don't know. All I know is something's wrong. First, the pastor was killed in that church, probably connected to the robbery, so whoever's doing that shit is killing strangers. Then a cop was killed, Sam, someone we know! Way after the robbery, so that was probably personal. And I'm getting all kinds of undue pressure from my client since then, which is maybe unrelated, maybe not. And now Cissie's missing. I can't help thinking there's a link somewhere between all of these things."

"Seriously? Between Sam's murder and Cissie's unexplained disappearance? And the robberies and dead pastor?"

"Yeah, I know, sounds crazy face value. But I've been at this long enough I got instinct, intuition, you know, a cop's sixth sense. I know you know what I'm talking about."

"But what the fuck's the connection?"

"That's what I don't know yet, and much as I hate to admit it, I need help. For the first time since leaving the force I need help. Maybe cuz it's Cissie, maybe I'm getting too old for this shit, maybe ... fuck, I don't know. I got no one else to ask here, you gotta help. How 'bout I pay you for your time, that make a difference?"

"Look, Skip, I'd really like to help, I would, but I have some company flying in tonight." She couldn't strand Guy at the airport. "And Kate needs my help."

"What time?"

"What do you mean?"

"What time is your friend landing?"

"Ten."

"Okay, if you go to the gallery you'll be back with time to spare and I'll check in on Kate. Quid pro quo sorta thing. All you gotta do is check things out, ask some questions, see what you can see."

"If I do this"—Alex took a long breath for effect—"*if* I do this, you gotta do something else for me. As it stands, it's more like quid pro nada."

"What?"

"Tell me who your client is and what you're working on."

"I told you I can't—"

"Look, fair's fair. If you think there's a connection and I'm gonna be traipsing all over the desert looking for your wife while I neglect my friend, you gotta be straight with me. I gotta know all the facts and all your theories."

"Okay, okay. But what I tell you stays here between us and these four doors."

"Course."

Skip let out a loud sigh that smelled of coffee. "I don't know where to begin. It's a long story. How 'bout you get on over to Santa Fe, see what you see and we'll talk later, here or there. I may be done by about eight tonight."

"Give me the Cliff's Notes version."

"Jeezus, you're persistent."

"No more than you. And I'm going nowhere till you tell me something. With what I don't know now I won't find out any more than the café guy did."

Skip turned and stared out over the steering wheel. His jaw pulsed as if he were thinking with his teeth. He turned back to face Alex.

"Look, I take the private in private investigator very seriously—"

"No shit. I got that first time we met, loud and clear."

"It's sorta like a doctor or lawyer, investigator-client privilege and all—so I won't give you names, not yet, unless I think it'll matter, I'll just give you the broad strokes. Deal?"

"Fine." Alex's phone hummed. It was Kate.

"Hold that thought. I gotta get this … Kate? Where are you? You okay? Is something wrong?" Alex grimaced and swore under her breath. *Shit. Of course something was wrong. What an idiot.*

"Did you see my gun when you were here?" Kate ignored Alex's questions.

"Why?"

"Well, I can't find it. I'm worried. I feel like I lost a day. I don't remember where I put it. I just need to know it's not lost."

"It's safe, don't worry. I tucked it away before I left."

"Good, are you close by? I gotta go see Sam's mother. I don't think I can face her alone. Will you come with?"

"Of course. I'll be there in about twenty minutes. That okay?"

"Sure, I'll see you then."

Alex hung up and was about to apologize to Skip, but he got in the first word.

"Maybe you could take Kate with you? The distraction might do her some good. I know when I'm upset, like now, keeping busy is the only solution to not going crazy. And that isn't really working right now for me 'cause I don't have enough to do and I can't stand just sitting around. There's a lot of that in this business so if you ever think of going private talk to me first—there's a huge downside to it, but then again the upside is sometimes worth it except for times like this—"

"I got it." Alex put her hand on the door handle. "And I gotta go, so I can't go find your wife. Sorry, but I gotta take Kate to see Sam's mother. That's what I gotta do now." She opened the door and was about to step out of the car.

"Let me drive you to Kate's. Seeing Sam's car won't do her any good in the condition she's in—we can work out getting it back to you later—and I can fill you in on our way. Then you'll see what there is to do. If you decide to invite Kate you can use her car—it's faster and more comfortable than the Jeep, so it'll take you less time to get there and back. And if she doesn't go with you I'll pick you up later and bring you back here for the Jeep. C'mon, close the door, let's move, time's a wasting."

He has a point. A couple of points, come to think of it. I have to admit I'm curious. She shut the door and snapped on her seatbelt.

"You're sure it'll be safe leaving the Jeep here?"

"Sure as I can be about anything."

"Good enough for me. Let's go. And start talking."

11

It was early evening by the time Alex and Kate got to the locked door of Cissie's gallery. They'd spent an hour with Sam's mother. Kate didn't want to be alone, so she accompanied Alex to Santa Fe. Every little and big thing, every three dimensional object in her house and the empty spaces between them reminded her of Sam. She needed to get her mind off the absence, the not-being that once was Sam.

They talked of other things on the way and sat through interludes of silence, neither one uncomfortable with the lapses. But when the silence entered their brain and demanded to be filled they struggled against their respective internal chatter. Kate fought with grief and anger. Alex worried and obsessed about her mental faculties and Guy's arrival. It was so not sexy to worry so much.

To take her mind off herself, her diminishing sex appeal, and her guilt about even thinking such thoughts while her friend sat next to her, emotionally shattered and wracked with grief, she turned her thoughts to what Skip had told her. None of it made much sense but something nagged at her.

Part of an old Zen koan rose up out of her long-term memory file. *Smoke over the hill indicates fire. When you see horns on the other side of the fence, you know there is an ox there. Given one corner, you grasp the other three.* Skip had given her three corners and claimed there was a fourth that would complete the puzzle. Alex wasn't convinced. All she saw were three separate corners looking for their three missing pieces with none of the finished squares at all related.

One of his clients had lost something: It had sentimental value and could have been stolen by an old rival. Client Two, who knew Client One, engaged Skip to investigate something else. Skip said this something else had nothing to do with Client Two's relationship with Client One, far as he could tell. Which was why he'd taken on both cases. Neither client wanted the other client to know what they were asking Skip to do, neither client knew that the other client was even working with Skip. The water was getting muddy, the secrets were getting harder to hide, and Skip was ready to walk away from both jobs. But he needed the money. Not that Client Two had much to give him, but One had plenty, which made up for Two's lack, plus he liked Two better and wanted to help him, so he stuck with both cases.

So, two clients, two corners that might be related, might not. The third corner was Cissie's disappearance, which Skip insisted was connected to Sam's murder—maybe that was the fourth corner, which would square it all together? He didn't say why he thought there was a connection except that his instinct told him it was true. For all the talking Skip had done, he hadn't told her much at all. Alex's grey matter was a knotted web of confusion. She was glad to be driving. It gave her something else to focus on.

***

It took a half hour to get inside Cissie's gallery. The café guy had gone home, left a note with his number, and they had to drive fifteen minutes back the way they'd come to pick up the keys. This was just the sort of thing that pissed Alex off—people who didn't think. Period. Café dude *should've* called Skip, who *would've* called her, who *could've* picked up the keys on her way into town and saved a half hour's time and a few cents in gas, not to mention she was doing a favor. Coulda woulda shoulda. Used to set her Irish blood to boil. But not today. She was on vacation. She was with her best friend who needed her.

Kate seemed unfazed by the delay so Alex decided to be unfazed as well, at least on the surface. Nothing she could do about how it festered deep inside, but that particular rattle was always with her, the outer circumstances too often determining the degree of internal cacophony. *This is exactly why I sit on a meditation cushion whenever possible. And I need it bad right now!*

The longing to be sitting still in a serene, visually calming place battled internally with her temper in need of a flame. She and Kate prattled about nothing and lapsed into long silences as they drove to pick up the keys. Alex listened, interjected an mm-hmm or uh-huh or a chuckle once in a while, leaving her mind free to wander. It floated to her belly. She envisioned two avatars of herself slugging it out down there. One stood on a black zafu cushion decked out in black robes, black headband and red boxing gloves. The other balanced on a bed of hot coals in a leopard skin bodysuit, black gloves and long flowing hair. She wasn't sure which one she rooted for to win. That was a sure signal that she needed a mind adjustment. A trip to the monastery for a few days would do it. Maybe after the funeral on Friday. Maybe Guy would want to come with. Her mind went to him, her stomach tensed, the two avatars disappeared. Guy took their place.

Alex turned off the ignition. They were finally back at the gallery, keys in hand. It was twilight. Guy would be landing in a few short hours.

"Care to come in? Or do you want to wait here?" Alex asked.

"I think I'll stroll around out here, see what I can see. My legs need a stretch," Kate said.

"Okay. See you in a few. This won't take long."

***

At the desert monastery, Shoju sat in the meeting room waiting for his teacher, Zen Master Renku Roshi. He was being a good monk, abiding by the second vow of the Sōhei Warrior: *Be obedient!* Roshi had asked him to be there, to wait for him, and so he would. He gazed out the window and watched two young monks at their work. They were garbed in blue work clothes, samu-gi, each with a small towel wrapped and knotted onto their bald heads. One was raking the rock garden, the other loading a truck with bins of compost.

If only life were as idyllic and simple as all that, thought Shoju. Once upon a time it was. When he had first arrived in New Mexico, eight years ago, he was lost and miserable, not knowing if he still wanted to be a monk. He'd been ordained by Endo Roshi on the east coast in 1993, but had left after the sangha had erupted in a sexual scandal that by some accounts involved the Roshi. The evidence seemed clear, but Endo Roshi had denied all accusations. When the dust had settled, Roshi was left with only two loyal acolytes, a monk and a nun. The rest were scattered to the wind, including Shoju.

Sexual acting out between consenting adults was one thing, and with no vow of celibacy in their lineage it happened all the time, but preying on young, vulnerable girls in Dokusan—a sacred, private time between teacher and student meant solely for discussion of one's meditation practice—that was another thing entirely. Abusing the power of the robes in that way was unconscionable and, in Shoju's mind, unforgiveable, especially without any admission of guilt or willingness to make amends.

Disillusioned, Shoju traveled around the country looking for another teacher and found nothing. He went to Japan for a year and almost settled there permanently, but when Gempo Roshi, the Japanese Zen Master he'd become devoted to, died at ninety-two, Shoju became homesick and returned to the States. Making one last effort to hook up with a teacher, he visited Renku Roshi, one of Gempo Roshi's dharma heirs, in New Mexico and decided that if it didn't work out he'd move to San Francisco, work in a soup kitchen, and give up the business of being a monk altogether.

Renku Roshi's charisma and unique style of teaching, reminiscent of his first beloved Japanese teacher, convinced him to give monkhood one last try. And for eight years he had no doubt whatsoever that he'd made the right decision. He loved Renku Roshi. His own practice deepened as a result of their relationship. He was as captivated with Roshi as those young girls had been with his previous Zen boss. Until recently, when Renku Roshi's character flaws, which Shoju had accepted as merely human limitations and mostly turned a blind eye to, were becoming harder to ignore: The hair-trigger mean temper, the elitist attitude and tastes, the egocentric lust for power. This thought made him cringe at his own biggest shortcoming and for acting out on the lust he had kept under control for so many years. It seemed that everything around him was out of control right now, even if much of it he couldn't label. He knew regret and hoping for a different life was useless, but at this moment he wished he were ladling soup for the homeless rather than wasting time waiting.

The monks in the courtyard finished their assigned tasks. Shoju peered out at the serene landscape, empty now of monk activity. He turned to look out the western window at the mesa in the distance. Stillness prevailed. It was early afternoon. He knew the scene on the other side of the mesa was a beehive, all the monks gathered for their daily warrior regimen, a session he rarely missed. He listened. The pulse of the building and the surrounding nature was all he heard.

Where was Roshi? Why did he have him sitting here alone, waiting? What was all that warrior business anyway? Gempo Roshi had never talked of it, never practiced it. Shoju felt uneasy sitting alone in the empty monastery. He had a bad feeling. And something that felt like fear clutched at his diaphragm. He didn't want to disrespect Renku Roshi but how long must he sit here? Roshi had never demanded this level of obedience from him. From others, yes, especially when he was angry. What had Shoju done to rile him up so? Had he discovered his one secret? They'd been so discreet he couldn't imagine how. Had she given them up?

He hated himself for having succumbed. He'd been weak. He had to end it. He would. Where the hell was Roshi? Now he was getting pissed. Maybe he'd move to San Francisco, start his own zendo. It was time, he was ready. He was tired of being under the thumb of another man. He was no longer enamored of Roshi. He could leave. He had to honor the memory of Gempo Roshi and do it according to the rules. He was tired of rules, tired of vows. He let his thoughts go. He settled into his belly, into patience, into his role as a good monk. He would wait.

***

None of the six keys on Cissie's key ring fit smoothly into the gallery door lock. The rabbit's foot and the two-inch gold C hanging on the orb told Alex they were the right keys. The door was locked so the key had to be one of the six. She tried each one again, finally getting to one that with some jiggling fit all the way in and turned the bolt on the other side. But this didn't release the door. A smaller lock at the base of the door was engaged. Alex remembered all the locks on Skip's front door and wondered which one in the mismatched couple had a security phobia. She easily found the bottom key and it worked as it should. Someone had tampered with the upper lock, but probably hadn't gained entry. She became mindful of not leaving her fingerprints.

Tossed behind the white Formica counter, stuck square in the middle of the floor, was Cissie's gold purse. Alex recognized it from the evening she'd spent at the house. Spilling out of the purse was a neon pink wallet. Peeking out of it was the corner of a twenty-dollar bill. It didn't take brilliant deductive powers to know for certain that there were three more corners of the twenty in there, making it real money, and that if something nefarious had happened to Cissie, robbery hadn't been the motive.

Alex checked every square foot of the place—a quick calculation told her there were about five hundred of them, including a small bathroom in back. There was no blood, no sign of struggle, and except for the discarded purse and no sign of her cell phone, there was no corner of anything else to ascertain a clue—it was as if Cissie had evaporated into the thin mountain air with just her phone. There was one big empty space on the wall and a receipt for two thousand dollars, less 10 percent, on the counter. *Good for her, she sold a piece of art this morning.*

She took a few snapshots with her phone to prove to Skip that nothing else was amiss and was about to execute her crime scene ritual of turning in place when she looked out to check on Kate and saw her sitting in the passenger seat staring straight ahead. Alex couldn't recall if Kate had even stepped out of the car. She had to go, tend to her friend. She was about to flick off the lights when she heard a faint sound of music. She held her breath and listened. It stopped. Then immediately started again. Sounded like a ringtone—coming from a drawer in the counter, which was locked. The key to it wasn't one of the six she held in her hand. *Damn.* The sound continued. She knew the song but couldn't quite grasp the name of the artist. Out of reach, like the moment before her bike crash. She saw it, she knew it, she wasn't quick enough to name it. The music stopped.

Alex looked carefully through Cissie's bag for the drawer key. She searched the other drawers in the unit that had no locks and came up with nothing. The ringtone pierced the silence once again. *I have to find that key. This is definitely a corner worth investigating. Whoever's on the other end of that phone is damn persistent.* Finally, taped to the underside of a drawer, Alex found the key. *Looks like Cissie's the paranoid one. What and who was she hiding? And from whom?*

By the time she got the drawer open the ringing had stopped. It was a cell phone, as she suspected. *Why would she keep her phone hidden like this?* There were voice messages. She'd need a password. That would take time. There was one text message:

*Ou the f *** r u? I came by. u shut down. what goes on?*

Using the French 'ou' for 'where' nudged at Alex's memory. She once knew someone who did that, but couldn't remember who.

She hit the green send button twice to find out. The caller picked up on the first half ring.

"What's up, baby? Are you okay?"

Alex said nothing. She wanted to keep him talking. She thought she recognized the voice but needed more of it.

"Cissie?"

Breathing on both ends. Alex finally gave in. "Who is this?" she said.

Nothing. Alex longed for the old days when you could hear someone click off in your ear, when you knew they'd hung up.

Deadness on the other end, she couldn't tell. "Are you there?"

Nope. He'd hung up.

Something about the text language, the voice, bumped up against something else in her brain. It was as if all the little and big pieces of her life had been dislodged from their resting place in her grey matter and were scattered to the wind, some of them shattered into tiny fragments, lost and looking for their missing bits. Maybe when her head had cracked open against the road it had created a brainquake. The voice, the text, the weird secrecy all added up to something, to someone she thought she knew, but maybe it was just familiar because of the many cases she'd worked and the asshole on the other end of the phone was just that—another jerk involved in something outside the margins of normal. Cissie was probably having an affair, simple as that. *But where is she? Not with her lover if that was him on the phone.*

She feared this was going to end badly, that Skip had been right, that Cissie was in trouble. A woman who carried a purse like Cissie's wouldn't leave without it, wouldn't leave her art unlocked, wouldn't leave her lover's phone behind for curious fingers to find.

Alex locked up and drove back to Albuquerque in relative silence. She told Kate none of it, didn't want to burden her with unnecessary badness. She'd talk to Skip, and in less than four hours, to Guy.

In the Buddhist way of looking at the world, everything was interconnected—so there was that. But for solving crimes and catching criminals, that always seemed like too wide a net to cast. Trusting her instinct, she was certain now that a link existed between Cissie and Sam, that Skip had been right. What she wasn't sure about was if this connection was in the broader Buddhist sense or in the smaller criminal sense. Cissie took up one corner, Sam another. Skip's clients lived in the third corner of what was quickly becoming a square in search of its fourth corner.

12

Guy's schoolboy nerves couldn't sit still. He wished they would jump out of his skin to relieve the tension in his cramped body. The hum of jet engines was his only comfort. He kept fingering the small package in his jacket pocket, taking it out, flipping it open and staring at the green jewel nested in velvet. Was he mad? Thinking she'd say yes just because she was worried about her advancing age and not on her home turf? He *was* mad. He never met a more independent stubborn woman. And he was never so deeply madly truly head over heels for anyone.

He snapped it closed, jammed it back into his pocket. Left his hand curled around it. He liked the sound the small box made when it closed. There was something definitive about it. He kept opening and closing it. *Snap. Snap. Snap.* Would she be just as definitive? He took it out again and stared at the gemstone set in gold. He'd chosen emerald to match her eyes. He'd been told it was associated with fertility: Not so important. And rebirth: With her uncertainty about the future, this could come in handy. Plus it supposedly brought wisdom, growth, and patience—a feature he wouldn't share with her as she'd likely take it as suggesting that she lacked these qualities. But the green gem was also symbolic of love and fidelity, which he'd take care of.

He'd chosen the emerald over the classic diamond. It reflected her better. He couldn't imagine her wearing a diamond—she so much as told him she thought the whole idea was an old-fashioned sexist waste of money. So he chose green. He was old-fashioned but willing to bend. Green. She hated green. It was the color everyone bought her to match her eyes. She rarely wore it. The green her eyes became when she was near green was almost too hard to look at. He loved it. She wore her heart in those eyes. She tried not to, but couldn't keep the truth from staring out. Yet deep inside sat an impenetrable mystery. He loved that too. *Snap. Snap. Snap.*

He could wait. He would wait if he had to. With all that was happening in New Mexico to disturb Alex's vacation, the timing might be off for matrimonial matters. He believed that no matter how tough skinned, every woman wanted to be adored, Alex included. His mind wouldn't move off his big question. He'd only asked it once before. They were young, just starting out in their careers, both newly recruited agents. She'd said yes. Was then ripped away from him in a drug bust that had gone tragically wrong. The crack in his heart was now scarred over and he could hardly remember her laugh anymore. Since then, he'd never let himself get that close to another woman. Till now. Just his luck: He had to choose someone with commitment phobia. A shrink might say that showed his unavailability. He didn't agree. He opened his computer and pressed the power button.

***

It was close to midnight. Alex had made a huge pot of green tea. Neither Skip, Kate nor Alex could sleep, and Guy was a night owl, so even though it was two hours later for him, he was happy to be up.

They sat in Kate's living room with not much to say and nowhere to go. They figured on a long night.

Kate had insisted that Alex and Guy stay with her and sleep in her bed. She didn't know when she'd be able to get back there, the empty half of it too hollow a reminder. And now that she had company she didn't want to be alone.

If Guy was disappointed Alex couldn't see it. He was okay with abstaining from showering affection on Alex in Kate's presence. Alex knew it would be the salt in Kate's wounded heart. A small part of her was relieved—she still didn't know how she wanted to be with Guy around friends or how she felt about being with him at all, she was aware of some residual anger from their last argument. Another part of her, she supposed it was her selfish, narcissistic side, was pissed that her vacation was turning into business as usual—dead bodies popping up, people gone missing, everyone wanting something from her. She just wanted to be alone and she hated herself for it.

She sat on the edge of the tub feeling slightly dizzy. She'd come into the bathroom to grab a few solo moments to gather herself. Sam's murder, Kate's heartbreak, Cissie's disappearance, Skip's barging in and making a ruckus, and now Guy's physical presence. She had a squeezed in feeling, like when she sat between two big men on the subway in seats made for much slimmer asses. *Did I cross some imaginary line into old age when I turned forty-four? One day being able to handle anything and everything that came at me, and the next day dropping into overwhelm at the fall of a body?*

She got up and braced herself for the rush of vertigo. At least that was getting better. Felt now like a slight hangover. She flushed the toilet and ran the water in case anyone was listening. The cell phone she'd found hadn't rung since she'd answered it back at the gallery and she was sure it wouldn't again, but it was a clue regarding Cissie and she had to give it up to Skip. She'd talk with Guy first, if she could get him alone.

Alex walked back into the pin-drop quiet living room. "Okay, Kate, we'll stay in your room, though I hate taking your bed away from you."

Kate smiled up at Alex, relief moving across her face like a cloud, followed by sadness.

"That okay with you?" Alex said to Guy. She knew it would be.

"That works for me," he said as he got up from the rocker, gently picking Ed up from his lap and placing him on the floor. "I'll get our bags."

Alex followed him out to the car.

***

"Sure you're okay with this?" Alex whispered over Guy's shoulder as he held her close.

"It's fine," he said, kissing her neck. "Course, I'd rather get you alone."

His kisses moved from side to front to ear to cheek. Alex closed her eyes and soaked it in, his strong body wrapped around hers, his lips, his whispery deep voice. She felt it in her groin.

"But any way I can have you is fine with me. Kate seems to need you."

"Maybe after—"

Guy stopped her words with his lips. They melted into each other.

"As I was saying," Alex said, "before being so smoothly interrupted..."

They unlocked their embrace and walked toward the car.

"... maybe after the funeral we can steal away together. Kate's sister is coming so she won't be alone."

"When's the funeral?"

"Friday."

"Okay then, two days more. I can do that."

"Thanks for being here and understanding."

"I've really missed you, sweetie."

"Yeah?"

"Yeah."

"I think I've sorta missed you too." Alex kissed him on the cheek to soften the sting of her ambivalence.

"Well, that's saying something."

"Oh jeez. What I mean is so much has gone on I've hardly had time to be here, let alone miss you or home or the job or anything." Alex wasn't sure if she meant any of it. "You know how it is. The one who stays behind in normal surroundings is always the first to start missing."

Guy put on an exaggerated hang dog look to poke fun, but she knew she'd hurt his feelings.

"This is not coming out right. What I mean is—"

Guy pulled her close, picked her up and twirled her around.

"Don't be so serious. Relax, you're on vacation. We're on vacation. We'll get to all that, okay?"

Alex nodded. Held onto his arm for the last twenty feet to the car. She was still spinning.

I guess I have missed him. I will tell him. After all the Kate and Skip business is over and I'm back to normal in my head. I will. I'll tell him.

***

The phone Alex had found hidden in Cissie's gallery was ringing when Alex and Guy walked back into the house. Kate looked scared and Skip looked guilty, his hand in Alex's bag. Kate was curled into herself on the couch, knees in her face. Her eyes darted to Alex and fixed on her, helpless and afraid. Skip put the bag down. The phone continued to ring deep inside.

"Sorry, Alex, didn't mean to pry but that ringtone scared Kate half to death. I was just trying to find it to turn it off," Skip said.

The ringing stopped.

Alex wrapped her arms around Kate.

"What is it, Kate? What's going on?"

"Are you in touch with him?" Kate moved away from Alex's hug.

"With who?"

"Jerry. Was that him calling you?"

Something clicked inside Alex's brain. A second or third corner came into view.

"Jerry, calling me?"

"But that's his special ringtone. And I've been getting hang-up phone calls here—Sam was going to try to trace them. It had to be him. Do you think it was him?"

The phone played again. Then stopped after three chords.

Frozen tableau. Two guys standing. Two women sitting, one giving comfort, the other inconsolable. The men not knowing what to do or say. The enemy invisible and unknown.

"Maybe he did it." Kate whispered to her knees.

"Did what? Who?"

"Jerry."

"Did what?"

"Killed Sam."

Alex swallowed her first reaction—*don't be ridiculous*—and let Kate talk. Guy sat down in hearing range. Skip walked into the kitchen, his mind too full of Cissie to participate in the unfolding drama. He'd give them some time before pushing them back to his main worry.

Kate rambled. "It makes perfect sense ... thought it was connected to church bandits but that never felt right, it didn't fit, and the hang-ups and breathing ... he was taunting me, probably spying ... knew Sam and I were happy, had to destroy it, destroy me ... I should've killed him when I had the chance, he's a slippery bastard ... there's no evidence, he'll beat this one, too ... he should've killed me, why hasn't he ... prefers the long slow torture, goddamn him." She took a breath and sat up straight, brought her feet down to the floor.

"We have to find him Alex."

"Who?"

"Jerry, that's who. Don't you see? He did this. He killed Sam. Just to punish me. And he won't stop unless we stop him."

"Okay. I'm going to make some coffee. We'll talk about it. Looks like we're not gonna get much sleep anyway." Alex got up and moved toward the kitchen. She needed to clear her head. *Is Kate's grief and hatred in control or could there be some truth to what she said? Last thing I want is coffee, I need to sleep! Fuck. I'm so tired of bad guys and death.*

13

Three hours later they were all tucked in. Skip in the guest room, Kate on the couch, Alex and Guy in Kate's bed. They'd succeeded in quelling Kate's suspicions about Jerry a bit, especially once Skip agreed to check out his whereabouts. The phone was found locked in his wife's drawer and he had no other leads, so it would give him something to do. Worry ran high among the foursome. No one expected to sleep much.

"I know you just got here and I feel guilty as hell just thinking about it," Alex whispered under the sheets in the dark. "But I'm exhausted and there's nothing more I can do right now for Kate ... I could really use a couple of days on a meditation cushion ... I know what you think about that whole business, so please be kind and keep—"

"Not a word, I promise," Guy said.

"Good. Then how would you feel if I took a two-day trip by myself up to the monastery?"

"Much as I'll miss you I think it'd be a good time for you to go. Why you came here in the first place, right?"

"Yeah, but everything's changed and now you're here ... Course you could come if you want." Alex didn't really mean this and knew he'd hate just the thought of it, but it was out of her mouth before she could stop it. She was relieved when he said, "Nah, but thanks, not my thing yet. Maybe one of these days I'll check it out, but not this week. But, hey, didn't you say the monks weren't very welcoming? Are you sure you want to go there? Maybe—"

"It's fine. I spoke to Muin this morning. He talked to Shoju, the monk I met, straightened everything out. According to him, they'd be glad to have me. Seems whatever the problem was has been solved... so..."

"Long as you're okay with it, so am I. And I can stay here with Kate, help her out if she needs."

"Mmmmm ... I knew you were the sexiest guy I ever wrapped my arms around." Alex snuggled closer. "And that just clinched it, you are now officially the most generous. Thank you." She kissed him, he kissed her back. They got lost in each other's heavy breathing and were careful not to make too much noise, which heightened their sweet surrender when it came.

Skip was already gone by the time they got up the next morning. By 9:00 the rest of them were in Kate's car heading north. Kate had nothing to do before Sam's funeral on Friday and didn't want to hang around home. She and Guy would spend time in Abiquiu while Alex sat with the monks. They were all glad just to be moving.

***

When Alex arrived at Desert Monastery, Shoju couldn't have been nicer. Back home a guest like her would have been greeted and handled by a lesser monk or one of the students, but Shoju himself met her at the entrance, carried her bag to her room, oriented her to the schedule, the layout of the zendo and the details she needed to know about the monastery rituals and rules.

"You just missed lunch, but if you're hungry I'm sure there's something we can scrounge up for you," Shoju said.

"Thanks, I ate before I left Abiquiu," Alex said. "Wish I'd known ... if the food is half as good here as back home at Muin's zendo I would've been here sooner."

"If you get hungry before the evening sit, there'll be some food in the dining room about five. Very informal, but it'll give you a taste of our southwestern Zen cuisine."

"Perfect."

"Roshi would like you to join him for a cup of tea now."

"Roshi knows I'm here?"

"He likes to keep track of who comes and goes, and when I happened to mention that you were a detective from New York, sorry about that, but he went a little monk-crazy and just simply had to meet you. He's a huge fan of Sherlock Holmes you see ..."

"Well, shit, I'm no Sherlock Holmes."

"Let's not tell him that. He's never met a real live detective before—he's like a kid on Christmas Eve waiting for you right now—so I hope you won't disappoint him. Just tell him a juicy story about catching a criminal and he'll be elated. That be okay?"

"Sure, why not." Alex shrugged. Though it was about the last thing she wanted to do.

"Good, then let's not keep him waiting any longer. I'm sure he's wondering where the hell we are." Shoju lowered his voice. "I shouldn't be telling you this, but for a Zen Master he can sometimes get a tad impatient."

They walked in silence to the tearoom. Roshi was sitting with eyes closed, a look of discomfort on his face as if he were straining to rid his body of an irritation lodged either in his brain or his rectum. An elegant Japanese teapot and tea bowls were set out on the table in front of him.

Alex took Shoju's lead, bowed at the door and quickly sat on the floor at the table.

"Ah, Miss Alex the detective." Renku Roshi opened his eyes and looked at her. It seemed the storm had passed and the sun was now shining, his face lit up and softened into a beatific Buddha-smile. "Welcome to our humble monastery."

Humble is definitely not the word I'd use to describe this place. Alex smiled and took in his golden robes, the ancient Buddha statue that sat behind him on an altar that must have cost a fortune, and the elaborate tea service in front of her. *Nope, humble this monastery is not, if just the material opulence was being considered. Will reserve judgment on the interior lives residing here.*

"Thank you for having me. You're very kind. It's lovely here."

She was in the room in which she'd seen Cissie's photo, during her first secret visit. But she'd sat down so fast she hadn't noticed if it was still hanging on the wall directly behind her. *It would be rude to twist around and look right now, but I am damn curious.*

"Lovely, yes, it is lovely," Roshi said. "But that's not the point is it?"

"Sorry?" Alex said.

"Never mind, it's not so important. I want to hear about this detecting business of yours. I'm a big fan of Mr. Holmes."

"Yes, Shoju mentioned that."

"Ah so, then tell me, did Mr. Conan Doyle get it right? Is real life detective work so elementary? Are you more like Holmes or Watson?"

"I hate to admit this, but I haven't a clue. I've never read Sherlock Holmes."

"No? Well, that's too bad." Alex noticed a slight tightening of his jaw. "Too many villains on the job you'd rather not read made up stories of bad men?"

"Something like that, yes."

"So, tell me then, Miss Alex, who was the worst, the most evil, character you ever nabbed?"

"Nabbed? Hmmm, let me think. ... That'd be hard to say right now. One thing I do know is there's lots of evil men out there who haven't been nabbed, getting away with murder."

"Ah so ... you say evil men. Do men have the corner on this evil you talk about?"

"Yup, pretty much. Ninety-nine percent I'd say. Maybe more."

"Mmmmmm ..." Roshi closed his eyes and tilted his head back as if he were swallowing this hard nugget of truth.

He then focused his attention on the tea things and in silence began an elaborate preparation of tea, pouring tea into each cup and then back again into the pot, three times, with care, grace and patience. When Roshi finished, Shoju took over. He stood up, placed one cup in front of Roshi, one in front of Alex and one at his place. Roshi then placed his palms together and bowed to the tea, picked up his cup and sipped. Shoju nodded at Alex that she could do the same. They drank in silence until their cups were empty.

"Shoju, you may leave us now." Roshi's voice cut through the stillness like a sharp knife slicing through flesh.

And then in a soft, velvet tone: "Miss Alex must stay and tell me her stories of evil. You have work to do."

Shoju rose without a word, winked at Alex as he collected the tea paraphernalia, as if to reassure her that all was normal there, quietly closed the door and left them alone.

Roshi pushed himself up off the floor and walked behind Alex. His robes brushed up against her back as he passed, and what felt like fingers, or maybe the sleeve of his robe, waved across the hair on top of her head. The breeze of his movements raised the hair on her neck. *What the fuck* was all she could think.

He swished his way to the burgundy leather couch set between two windows that faced Alex where she sat. He could have gotten there faster without passing behind her. Benefit of the doubt: Maybe it was Zen custom to avoid walking in front of the Buddha statue. Whatever, she felt a bit creeped out.

Roshi plopped himself down and patted the seat next to him. "Come, Miss Alex. Come sit with me, tell me a story.

"Is okay. I won't bite. Ha ha!" Roshi threw his head back and laughed, his beatific smile once again appearing. "That is a funny expression, don't you think?"

"What the fuck," Alex whispered to herself as she got up off the floor. She'd play along.

"For all I know you could be a vampire," she said as she made her way to the sofa.

"Ha ha, a detective with sense of humor. You would make good Zen nun."

"Now look who's being funny. Fraid that's not in my future."

"Ah so, but you are Setsu Roshi's student, yes?"

"Yes, but student to nun is a pretty big leap."

"Not so much."

Alex wanted to change the subject. "Do you know Setsu Roshi?"

"Indeed, indeed." Roshi nodded his head. "We became monks together, same teacher, same year, same monastery in the Haku Mountains of Japan.

"We were dharma brothers like this." He raised his hand and crossed two fingers. "Sad how time changes even the closest of brothers."

He paused to consider this loss. "Now we are more like this," he said. He lifted both arms, put his palms together and then separated them as if he were demonstrating the size of a fish he'd reeled in.

Hands still raised, he twisted sideways to face Alex. When he lowered his arms, his right hand landed on her thigh. He squeezed just above her knee and left it sitting there.

"But that is history," he said, "and now that I have you here, tell me about the so-called evil men you chase." He patted her leg and lightly squeezed it again.

Alex crossed her legs to get rid of his hand and turned to face him. If he hadn't been a Roshi she might've slapped him, and surely flung his hand back to his side of the couch.

"Well—"

"First, let me ask you something." Roshi picked up her left hand and held it between both of his, as if he were making a hand sandwich; she the meat, he the bread. *This guy doesn't take a hint.*

"Do you think evil exists?" Roshi asked.

Alex's insides were a riot of squirm, her outsides as still as the wall she stared at. *What the fuck? If he weren't a Zen Master, dharma brother to her teacher, I'd be up and out of here in a flash.* She tried to think of him as a too-friendly uncle and casually withdrew her hand to scratch her head, then set her clasped hands on her lap out of easy reach.

"Yes, evil exists." Alex did not want to talk about this. She did not want to talk about this with the shaved man in robes sitting next to her. She did not want to be in the same room with this man, alone and behind a closed door.

It suddenly dawned on her as she looked at the picture gallery wall facing them, that the photo she'd seen of Cissie and Roshi together during her first "illegal" visit was no longer there.

"What do you think Sherlock Holmes would say about evil?" Roshi asked.

"Haven't a clue," Alex said.

"Are you okay, Miss Sullivan? What is problem?" He reached over and wrapped his fingers around her hands. "You can talk to me. Think of me as your teacher, twin of Setsu Roshi. What is it?"

Alex flung his hand away, stood up and looked down on him. Now that she was towering over him, he looked like an innocent, gentle monk.

"I'm sorry, Roshi, for being so rude. I'm not myself, a good friend's boyfriend was killed this week, another person is missing, it's too hard right now to talk about evil men. I came here to sit and be quiet, try to forget about all that. Please forgive me."

When Roshi looked up, Alex saw his jaw unclench and a black flash of anger recede back into his skull. By the time he stood up he was back to being the kind-hearted, non-threatening, gentle man she'd been introduced to just minutes earlier.

He placed his palms together and bowed to her.

"I am the one to be forgiven. So sorry to disturb your already disturbed state of mind. Sorry to hear of the loss of your friends. If we can start again, no talk of evil, or Sherlock Holmes—we'll save all that for another time—maybe I can help."

"Thank you, Roshi, but what I need right now is to be still and quiet."

"Yes, yes, just so. That is in abundance here as you will see."

He walked to the door and opened it. "Please," he said, "go find some comfort now."

"Thank you." Alex put her palms together and bowed to him.

When she raised her head, his two black orbs pierced like darts on a corkboard straight into her eyes.

"And don't be afraid to face the darkness inside," he said, staring into her face. "It is safe here to do that."

Alex had no retort. She just walked out and down the hall to her room. On the way her body and breathing relaxed. It felt as if she'd been gripping and holding it the whole while she'd spent with Roshi. Being alone with him was something she'd try to avoid for the duration of her stay.

After collecting herself and heading out for a walk, she called Muin.

14

"What is it about you monks?" Alex asked.

"You mean how special we are?" Muin replied.

"You could put it like that, though I would use another word ... more like weird."

"Yeah, that too."

"All that talk about non-dualism, the Middle Way? Is that s'posed to apply to the absolute world or the everyday world?"

"What do you mean?"

"Well, Shoju couldn't have been nicer when I showed up here at his precious monastery today—there was no trace of the rude guy I met last week. Either that was his evil twin or he's got a seriously split personality."

"You forget something very essential to this point."

"Yeah, what's that?"

"We monks are just human like the rest of you. In fact, we may be a little more flawed than the rest of you—probably why we choose this life, to work through all that shit."

"That's an interesting theory."

"Yeah, well, I asked Shoju to give you the royal-red-carpet-Zen-Master treatment. Glad to hear he's complying."

"Have you ever been here?" Alex asked.

"Once, a long time ago—about the time Shoju arrived. And just after Renku Roshi got there."

"Not sure what it was like then, but compared to our monastery this place is a castle. There are expensive statues—some that look centuries old, in every room, on every flat surface. Then there's a room that's all locked up with barred windows and tightly drawn shades."

"Not the place I remember. But it was a long time ago, like I said, and Shoju and Roshi had just landed there. I guess a lot has changed."

"Someone here's got money. It's rather understated, but there's opulence dripping off every altar. So much for the vow of poverty."

"Have you seen the ancient gong that was stolen? Shoju told me it was back."

"Nope, but I overheard someone talking about it. If it's here it must be living in Roshi's quarters or in the locked room. I wouldn't be surprised if it was under armed guard."

"Now don't go getting all cop suspicious on me, Alex. ... Have you met Roshi yet?"

"We just had a cup of tea together. Which was weird in itself since I was told they don't have too many lay people visit here and they rarely spend the night. I got the impression that they discourage guests except during sesshin, but even then it's just a few old-timers as Shoju described it. Maybe it was the strings you pulled to get me in here. ... And I got a practically engraved invitation for a private tea session with the Roshi."

"You're welcome. And yeah, it's a more serious place than this one as a monk-training monastery. Their practice is Rinzai squared—too intense even for me."

"Oh shit, thanks a lot. Wish you'd warned me. Will I even be able to make it through their evening sit?"

"You'll be fine. So, c'mon, tell me, how was Renku Roshi?"

"He's a trip."

"Do tell."

"Well, he was all charm and gracious host. Definitely one of those Zen Masters I've read about, the ones with a fat cat lifestyle. The outfit he was wearing must've cost a fortune."

"Hmmm. I guess some of us monks exist more deeply in the human realm than others."

"Subject to the three poisons? Greed, anger and delusion?"

"Something like that."

"Ego driven, maybe?"

"Yup."

"And he was clearly practiced at the art of entertaining women."

"Damn. I'm getting so tired of that shit. What'd he do?"

Muin sounded so crestfallen Alex didn't have the heart to get into it with him.

"It was nothing. Just surprised me how casually friendly he was, s'all, especially given how strict this place is in terms of practice."

"You'd tell your old friend Muin here if he were a lech, right?"

"O'course. Don't you worry your bald little head about me, you know I can handle any man who gets out of hand."

"True enough." Muin laughed.

"What scares me is the three hours of zazen tonight."

"Want a little advice from your now even more favorite Zen monk?"

"But of course. Please do tell me what to do."

"As if that would ever work!"

"No, really, I actually mean it this time. I'm out of my realm here."

"Why don't you just chill? Sit with the monks, recharge, don't worry about any of the monastery business. You've got enough to think about."

"Got that right."

"Is Guy with you?"

"Nah. I left him and Kate in Abiquiu—this just wasn't the moment to convert either of them. Plus, I wanted a night to myself surrounded by men in robes."

"Ha! Great. Then just *be* a Zen student. Take a day off from being a cop."

"I'm trying, really I am. It's just that there was a picture on the wall in the tearoom that I saw last time I was here, and now it's gone."

"Really? A picture is missing and you're alarmed? How did you even remember one picture on a wall when, as I recall, you were sneaking around uninvited?"

"Because it was a picture of this woman Cissie, married to Skip, an ex-cop friend of Kate's, whose house I stayed at, but that's another story. What matters is, she's gone missing, and she had some connection to Roshi, the picture being the evidence, and now that's gone, too."

"Did you ask Roshi about it?"

"No. First of all, how would I explain my knowledge of it? Second, I just wanted to get out of that room. I didn't feel completely safe alone with him behind a closed door."

"Now you're worrying me."

"It's okay, really, I just have to steer clear of him. He's just a very strange dude. And it was a really weird experience. I'm not often uncomfortable in any room with anybody, but he put me way off my game. I don't know if he's a true Zen Master but he's certainly a master at something, if only taking charge of a room and manipulating the people in it."

"Zen Masters sure do have their eccentricities."

"I was charmed, entertained, fascinated, delighted, suspect and finally pissed off. All in a matter of about fifteen minutes. One of the oddest experiences I've ever had. At one point I thought he was even coming on to me. If I'd played along I'm sure I could've been between his sheets tonight. But I was beyond shocked and pretended not to hear the come on. And now I don't even trust myself that I'm remembering it right. Anyway, he gave me the creeps."

"Alex?"

"Yeah?"

"I want you to answer the next question without thinking too much about it before you do. Okay?"

"Okay, sure."

"What does your gut tell you? No hesitation now, the first thing that pops into your head. Are you safe there?"

"Yes."

"Okay, good ... now do yourself a favor. Just sit there tonight with him and his monks. Get some sleep and none of it will matter in the morning."

"I s'pose you're right."

"Not me, the practice, the zazen. That's what's right. And it will straighten you out like nothing else."

"Yeah, maybe even better than sex—"

"Well, now, let's not get carried away."

They laughed.

"By the way, did you know that sex and meditation have the same effect on our brain?" Alex asked.

"Oh, really?"

"Yeah, really. A scientific study, no less."

"Hmmm, scientists, eh? Has no one told them that stimulating the brain is not the point of sex?"

"Very funny," Alex said. "By the way, and not so beside the point, I sure am glad Kido was my very first monk and that there was no hint of sexual danger with him. And then you were my first monk in the biblical sense, shall we say."

"You mean there have been others since?"

"I didn't mean it that way. I just meant if I had met these guys before meeting you two and then Setsu Roshi, I'm not sure I'd be sitting in a Zen temple at all."

"Well, I'm glad I was and still am your favorite living monk."

"That'll never change," Alex said.

"Till we're both dead," Muin said.

"Ha! Let's just hope that's not in the near future."

***

Alex had a few hours to do nothing before the evening meditation began. Much as she craved do-nothing time, whenever it opened up she was at a loss and fell out of sorts, missing the links to her normal if hectic everyday world, a place where she was comfortable in her discomfort. Here, with all that stripped away, no markers to tell her who she was, how she belonged, with time in front of her like a gaping chasm that she feared leaping into, she felt a beautiful terror.

She was familiar with this state, from doing seven-day sesshins back home at Nekoji Monastery with Muin and Setsu Roshi and the other monks and students she knew and trusted. Here, the flavor of the fear had a new twist to it: Strangers acting strange, deep in a desert valley far from anyone she knew.

Conjuring up bogeymen was a desperate cry from her ego to keep her off the cushion, a creative mind game she employed to avoid facing the real bogeyman inside of her: The empty void, the nothingness, the egoless mind. Or the "darkness inside," as Renku Roshi put it. Maybe that was what had scared her. But she also knew from the few times she actually quieted down enough to exist in that place for a bit, it wasn't so terrifying. In fact, it was liberating.

She actually disappeared for moments at a time and it was sublime. But getting there was a warrior's path. And some days she just wasn't up for it. Like today.

Now that she was an invited guest, Alex freely walked through the halls of the monastery toward the zendo where they'd be sitting tonight. She wanted to check out the seat they'd assigned to her, make sure proper cushions were in place. She saw, felt and heard no one. Siesta time, perhaps; the post-lunch, pre-afternoon work period, with everyone getting a little rest and a few private moments alone in their room.

The walls smelled of incense and, just as in the monastery back home, there seemed to be a faint echo of chanting filling the silent spaces. There was no one chanting live—she was perfectly alone— but each time she stopped moving to listen harder, she heard some incantation. It was different from the sounds in Setsu Roshi's temple. This sound wasn't an aural memory, this sound wasn't a memory of any kind. It was real. And it was coming from outside the walls of the monastery.

She quickly set up her place in the zendo with everything she would need later to help ease the inevitable pain of sitting and then walked outside. There was really no place to go, but enough desert to explore without straying too far. And she wanted to locate the chanting monks.

***

The desert sun bore down on Alex's unprotected whiteness, her Boston Red Sox cap mitigating the worst on her already freckled face. The cool September air was a pleasant contrast to the ubiquitous sunshine.

Alex walked slowly around the monastery perimeter trying to get a fix on the muted, constant humming. It wasn't quite chanting, but gutturally human. She saw no sign of life, animal or otherwise.

The drone was nearly absent on the south and east sides of the buildings. Directly west and slightly north sat the butte/mesa—she still wasn't sure what it was: *Mental note: Google it later*—that she'd wanted to climb during her last visit. She headed in that direction.

It was an easy hike up, the hum getting louder as she reached the top. It was not a friendly sound. Her brain clicked into cop mode. She didn't want to be seen or heard.

Stealthily, she made her way across the top of the hill. She lay down on the rock and until she saw the scene below her she had the thought that she was being silly and paranoid. *I'm at a Buddhist monastery for God's sake.* But that idea burned away instantly when she saw the tableau in front of her.

Down below, there were thirty or so bald, shirtless, barefoot men wearing only yellow, loose fitting pants. *Must be the monks. 'Cept, other than having shaved heads they don't look anything like the men in robes I saw within the monastery.*

Then she recalled Shoju's hostile attitude during her first visit and knew he was down there among them.

Half of the men were sitting on the edges of a cleared, circular arena, chanting and watching the other half who were engaged in what looked like a dance or sword fight. But they weren't wielding swords. Whatever they were swinging at each other was too thick to be a sword. And they weren't making body contact, just club to club. The soft thud, thud, thud, echoed off the canyon wall, a drum beat for the chanting. The movements of the warriors were aggressive and fierce—that much she could discern.

Too far away to perceive some of the smaller details, the longer she stared, the blurrier things got. *Another mental note: Have eyes checked.* A wave of vertigo rushed through her brain. She closed her eyes, saw the bike wheel falling in slow motion, but not the moment before. Slow motion speeding past her eyelids. *How is that even possible? Why can't I see what caused the fall? Damn it.*

Her vision sharpened when she opened her eyes. All of the men below were bare-chested, yet some seemed to be wearing something on their backs. The way the colors and what looked like an image moved—the exact same design on all who had it—appeared to be inked right on their flesh. What sort of monk would tattoo his whole back? There were no nuns in the group.

She knew many monks and nuns who had piercings and small tattoos here and there on their bodies—all done before they took their vows—but what she was witnessing was something else. *These tats were most definitely etched into their skin post monk-dom. Unless they'd all been in a cult together before the monk thing, and the monastery was just a front for something weirder. Maybe they're not monks at all!*

Her brain was fried, she couldn't make sense of what she was seeing. The color and shape of the tattoo seemed familiar but she couldn't quite place it. Her brain was not itself. *If my brain changed, would I still be myself?*

Slowly, she crawled back from the edge and made her way back to where she started. Whatever the hell she'd just witnessed had nothing to do with a monk's life as far as she knew it, and everything to do with why she should get the hell out of there. Something was awry not only in her brain but also in this desert paradise.

As Alex approached the main building, angry shouts pierced the air. She saw no one and couldn't detect exactly where the noise was coming from.

She slinked up to the side of the building and peeked around the corner. There was Roshi, frothing at the mouth, unleashing vitriol into a monk's face. She could only see the back of the monk's bald head, but Roshi's face was clear as day and red with fury. The monk was still and quiet as a stone.

"NEVER EVER defy me again. I will be finished with you and you know what that means." Roshi was winding down. She'd missed most of it.

"Are we clear?"

The monk nodded.

Then Roshi wrapped his arms around the monk, a radiant smile transforming his features into the "nice" Zen Master she'd met just a short while before.

In the next instant, Roshi cast off the monk as if disposing of a piece of litter and walked inside. The monk turned and headed toward the parking lot.

Alex waited for the monk to collect his bags, curious to see his face, and she wanted to give Roshi enough time to disappear into the bowels of the monastery before going inside. She was determined more than ever to get her butt out of there and did not want to run into him. She'd seen behavior like that before in some criminals she'd dealt with, but never in a monk. It was unadulterated evil.

As the monk neared the entrance, bags slung over his shoulders, Alex corrected her sexist assumption. It wasn't a wayward monk returning to the fold after all. It was a nun.

15

Shoju's heart pounded against his ribs and blocked his breath. His head felt as if it would split open. Enjou was back. Roshi had promised he was done with her. The others were bound to snap back too, metal to his magnet, or maybe hers. The scenario playing out in his mind's eye was a nightmare turned to something worse.

For all of Roshi's posturing being the tough guy, stern master in charge of his flock, he let his bevy of dragon ladies push him around, do whatever their sadistic little brains conjured up.

He shuddered, knowing that Akiko was right behind *her*. God, would he love to get both of them in the arena. But women weren't allowed there—one of Roshi's rules that he hadn't broken yet. They had their own training regimen, which only Roshi was privy to.

Calling them women was too generous. They had breasts and vaginas, which made them biological females. Even cunt was too kind of a word. He'd have to make up a word to describe them. No matter, as the Diamond Sutra would declare: Cunt is merely a name, there is no such condition as being a cunt. They needed not a label. Everyone who came in contact with them knew what they were.

If he had any sense he'd pack up his bags this day and get far away from the imminent madness. As soon as he was confident

Cissie was safe and out of their clutches, he would hightail it. But he owed her that much for making the introductions in the first place.

Where the hell was Muin's friend, Alex? He should never have agreed to her staying the night. On his way to the first sit of the evening he walked out to the parking lot to get some air, see if her car was there. She hadn't responded to his knock on her door.

His phone quivered in the sleeve of his robe. It was a text from Cissie.

I'm fine. Will b in touch later ;)

He breathed easier, the worry clouding his mind dissipated. Now he could meditate, and perchance find some clarity.

***

"Muin, it's me, Alex. Call me soon as you get this message. It's rather urgent. Something weird's going on here and I need you to talk me down, or help make sense of it ... I left the monastery. I'll explain when you call. It didn't feel safe ... I'll probably be out of range for thirty or forty minutes so keep trying. Please. I'll call you back when I reach town."

Alex threw her phone into the passenger seat. No need to end the call. There was no service. *Did the call even go through?*

***

Alex called Guy as soon as she got a signal and asked him to make some excuse to Kate and meet her in the hotel parking lot in about a half hour. She'd text him when she got there.

Guy was walking toward the lot as soon as she drove in, and got to the Jeep before she'd put it in park.

"It's nice to see you, Alex, and don't take this the wrong way, but what are you doing here? And why the secrecy?

"Not that I don't love having you all to myself, but I can think of sexier places than a parking lot."

Guy leaned into the open window and kissed her full on the lips, his left hand caressing her cheek.

"Mmmm ... that helps ..." Alex leaned her head back a few inches from guy's face. "How's Kate?"

"About the same as this morning." Guy moved away and rested his forearms on the roof, his face still at her level. "She's trying 'cause she doesn't know me, but she's in such a fog ... there are moments she can't figure out how she got into a hotel with a strange man far from home. She'll be glad you're back. Why are you back, by the way?"

"Can you come in here for a minute?" She patted the passenger seat. "I don't want to talk in front of Kate just yet. She's been through too much already."

"Sure you're not planning to spirit me off to some desert hideaway?" He stretched his neck out to kiss her again. Her fingertips halted his lips from reaching hers.

"I need a reality check. Can we do that first?"

"Course." Guy sprinted around the front of the car and hopped in. "At your service."

"I just saw a couple of things at the monastery that freaked me out and I don't know if I'm being paranoid or what."

"I'm all ears, hope I can help. I'm not sure what normal at a monastery looks like, so with that in mind, give it to me."

Alex described the morning introduction to Roshi, his come on, the combat scene and the Roshi-nun exchange, in her cop-reporting-just-the-facts mode.

"Sounds pretty weird. Have you called Muin for his perspective?"

"I told him about Roshi's behavior and he said not to worry. All the other stuff happened after he and I spoke. I tried calling him again, but he's not answering."

"I say we wait for his input before I give you my two cents."

"But you think my instinct to leave wasn't off the deep end?"

"What's going on with you, Alex, not trusting yourself?"

"I don't know." She slouched in her seat. "Ever since I cracked open my skull, I feel like something's missing, just out of reach in my brain. I'm tentative, I don't fully trust what's coming up, and I hate it."

"Yeah, that sucks." Guy knew that coddling her would be exactly the wrong thing right now. "How's this? I think you made the right decision to get out of there."

"Thanks, that helps." Alex let out a long breath. "Let's go see how Kate's doing ... how can I explain it to her, me being here? I made such a fuss about needing quiet time, blah, blah, blah."

"Tell her you just couldn't stand being away from me for another minute."

"That'll make her feel awful."

"Oh shit, you're right." They both thought of Sam. "How about you missed both of us and preferred spending time with us rather than in silence with a bunch of monks you don't even know?"

"That's good. That'll work. I can pull that off. In fact, it is how I feel. I'm glad to be here."

She cozied up to him as they walked into the Inn. He kissed the top of her head.

"I'm glad you're here, too."

***

Shoju sat in the monastery car outside the dark gallery for an hour, continuing his zazen. Cissie had texted and he'd come running. He hated himself for that. He still wanted to end it with her. And still didn't. He was pretty sure Buddha would say that sitting on a fence was not the Middle Way.

He looked once again at his phone to make sure he'd got it right.

2night 9:30 can u pick me up @gallery? Ready 2 hear all what u have 2 say. Hope it's good. Miss u.

Blinds closed. No light seeping through. Her car was nowhere in sight. Where the hell is she? He tried phoning, texting, got nothing back. He'd give her till 11 p.m. Maybe her husband was delaying her. That thought alone should be enough to send him away. Cuckold. That's what he was. Disgust shivered through his bones.

He'd been trying to save her and then fell under her spell. At first he blamed her for seducing him, but he was wrong. She was just being herself and he let his dick lead him right smack into the first hindrance: Sensuous lust. For about a week he had deluded himself into thinking it was a different organ that spoke to him, the one in the center of his chest. And then he got honest with himself. It was pure lust masquerading as love.

He was as bad as Roshi. In trying to save her from Roshi he became the devil. She trusted him, she felt safe, much like a child with a parent. And then he betrayed her.

It started as an innocent kiss, a turn of the cheek, lips getting in the way. They both recoiled, felt the electrical charge between their legs. They confessed weeks later while lying naked after skin-to-skin sex. A chance touching of lips between a celibate-by-choice monk and a sexy-décolletage-blonde escapes the realm of innocence in that split second of touching.

Red, oft-kissed lips upon long-chaste ones: Who wouldn't succumb?

It had been up to him to nip it in the bud. It had awakened his nerve endings and they refused to go back to sleep. He didn't kiss her again for weeks, but when they were together, conniving what to do about the Roshi matter, he would lean into her, whisper conspiratorially, just so he could smell her.

Subtle, flowery shampoo, soft, musky perfume, the lipstick— always the lipstick—mixed together to create the *Cissie scent*. It never lingered long enough once she left a room. He wished for such an aroma in a stick of incense.

He would hold her hand to console and reassure her. He would accidentally brush against her breasts to console and reassure himself. He would hug her goodbye a few breaths past Zen monk decorum.

He hated Roshi for what he was doing to her. He was grateful for bringing her to him. He was despicable, no better than Roshi himself, no matter how much he rationalized.

Lust had him taking too many risks lately and he knew he had to stop. Leaving the zendo and not returning before the end of the evening was dangerous for both Cissie and him. He envisaged how Roshi would react and it wasn't pretty, not even close, maybe even deadly. That hadn't occurred to him till this moment. And he knew it was true.

Regret thrust him deeper into the leather seat. What had he done? He didn't care about his life anymore, only hers. Maybe he was too late.

***

Two hours later, the street was as quiet as the monastery and almost as dark. No moon tonight. No traffic, pedestrians or otherwise. Shoju felt conspicuous, the only car in view. But no one was there to see it. It wasn't a forest, but the same thing: *If a tree falls and no one is there to hear it, does it make a sound?* If Cissie was in trouble would he be there to catch her?

He felt the movement before he saw the thin figure at the gallery door, his nonchalance a parody of the real thing.

Shoju wanted to hit the horn, scare the shit out of him. His head spun around in Shoju's direction as if there'd been a sound jolt. But stillness reigned and Shoju relaxed, as he was all but invisible behind the tinted glass. He held his breath. The thin guy's back was to him so he couldn't see what he was doing, but it looked like he was trying to get inside. There was clearly no one answering the door and he didn't have a key. He gave up and strolled away. Shoju exhaled.

Near 11:00 and Cissie was nowhere in sight. He had a bad feeling. He convinced himself she was caught at home and couldn't text him without creating suspicion or a fight. Thin guy was probably the cousin she'd told him about, prowling for her, too. He hoped she was safe at home. He'd been taught to give up all hope. This situation beyond all others called it back to him. Poor Cissie, chased by men her whole life. He turned the ignition and slinked through the sleepy streets back to his cushion.

***

Renku Roshi spewed strict instructions to the three acolytes he'd chosen for this job and swore them to secrecy. No real need for that, they wouldn't be saying anything after the fact, but he humored them. He promised to take care of them when it was done. They figured one thing, he another. The paradox and perfect chaos of life as backdrop. They'd have their moment of enlightenment when he was ready, not before. And it'll be more and less than they ever dreamed. Always is.

Everything was in place as he sat alone in the back seat in the new moon blackness of his motored chariot, a glass shield between him and the driver—a new face, nameless, none the wiser, finished after this ride.

The only thing moving in or outside of the car was his mouth sucking on the Cuban wad of tobacco sticking out of it, and the curling smoke. The orange ember at its tip was the only color. His mind too, was moving.

His phone vibrated on the seat next to him. His timing was perfect, as usual. The cigar was done just as they were ready for him.

He signaled to the driver. Perfectly capable of opening his own door, he waited for his rented chauffeur to do it. He deserved to be waited on. Especially tonight.

He had to marshal all of his energy for the task at hand. He had to make it look easy, like it was the natural order of things, nothing special. He had to appear special, the one in charge, he who knew the rules.

He threw the stub of his cigar into the gutter as he stepped into the street.

"Anything or anyone suspicious comes around you call me at once on that phone I gave you."

"Yessir."

"And don't go calling your girlfriend or anyone else. You got that?"

"Yessir, I got it."

The gallery door swung open just as Roshi got to it. He didn't need to break stride. His goons were well trained.

16

Skip stood looking down on his wife, Cissie, and was almost as still. The difference was that his insides were churning like a motherfucker and hers would never move again. Except when burned to ash during cremation or turned to dust six feet under. He wasn't sure which way to go. He wasn't even sure this wasn't a dream. They'd never talked about what they wanted after death—hard enough for them to say what they wanted while breathing.

He didn't know if he was angry or sad, there were so many emotions swirling around inside him, some he had no label for.

One thing he knew for sure: Cissie did not do this to herself, someone else did. It was murder, plain and simple.

She looked more at peace than he'd ever seen her—he couldn't bear to imagine how she might have suffered. Nights when he couldn't sleep, worried about her or them or money or some client's woes, he would watch her as she slept—no makeup, hair mussed, a picture of innocence and loveliness, the girl showing just under the surface of the woman. It always felt voyeuristic and wrong, like he was stealing something from her, meant only for her, not to be shared. Even so, it became his ritual, sustaining and nurturing him whenever he felt her slipping into her darkness, that place inside where she hid from her past, her demons, herself and anyone who was breathing in her presence, including him. In sleep, her edges would soften and he could spend time pretending that they were of one mind, of one heart, close and intimate as he imagined all picture perfect relationships to be. He knew that was a delusion, but in the wee hours the fairy tale would come alive and get him through to the morning.

He preferred her scrubbed clean like that, but she had no interest in showing her face or body to the world unadorned. And that was fine with him because he alone could see through the eyeliner and lipstick down to the real darling he'd fallen in love with. He had that part of her to himself.

He hoped she hadn't suffered and wondered what her last thought might have been and if she'd been aware she was being murdered.

She had to have known her killer. Too much care had been taken with how she looked: Laid out on the gallery counter, dressed to the hilt, lipstick applied, hands crossed over her taut belly. A small, black, satin-wrapped pillow—one he'd never seen before— propped up her head. He took care not to touch anything.

There were no signs of struggle. He'd leave the forensics to the cops, who were milling around impatiently waiting for him to be done with his goodbyes.

He'd left their bed three hours earlier. When he couldn't sleep and Cissie wasn't there for him to stare at and be soothed by, he'd driven to the gallery, to be in her sacred space. Finding her like this didn't sync with any imagined scenario. Another guy, yes. But not this. The shock kept him there with her unable to take an action. It took him two hours to make the 911 call. So he had had his time with her, disturbing nothing but his gut and his dreams.

Suspect #1: The husband.

Suspect #2: Fill in the blank.

He had no clue. And if they didn't lock him up he'd find the bastard who did this to her and ruined his life ... if it killed him. Because, without her, at this moment, he didn't care if he lived or died. Without her, there was no him.

***

As soon as the cops let him go, Skip placed a call to the only person he could think of to trust right now.

"How'd you like to help me find a bad-guy-killer-motherfucker?" Skip asked.

"Wha—" Alex said.

"Cissie's dead. Found her early this morning in her gallery. Looks like suicide, first glance, but for sure it ain't that."

"I—"

"Cops here ain't gonna do shit fast enough for my liking and for this one I'm gonna need help. Never wanted a partner, but now that she's gone all I care about is finding the motherfucker or fuckers who did this and yesterday won't be soon enough."

"Wow, I don't know—"

"Are you in or not? Cuz if you ain't I gotta get moving. No time to lose."

Alex didn't even try to say anything again, till she heard at least a half-breath of silence.

"Are you done? Can I say something?"

"Speak."

"First, I'm very sorry about Cissie. You two seemed good together."

"She was the best decision I ever made."

"You're sure it's murder?" Alex cupped her hand over her mouth to muffle her words, keep them away from Kate's ears.

"Look, do you want to help or not?" Skip was hardly breathing.

Much as she was tired of death and murder and bad guys, the puzzle of it called to her. Her brain was afire. *First, the disappearance, then the hidden cell phone with Jerry's ring—Jerry, how the hell did he fit into this?*

She looked over at Kate and Guy and knew she had to bow out, turn Skip down, be with her people. If she jumped in to help everyone she met who was dealing with some shit storm she'd never have a moment's peace, let alone time enough to help them all. She thought of the photo of Cissie at the monastery, and next day the blank space where the photo had hung. *Could there be any connection here with Sam's murder? Seems far-fetched but maybe it's a way to make it okay with Kate and Guy for me to help Skip.*

"Okay," she said.

"Okay?"

"Yeah. But we're up in Abiquiu now, won't be back down till tonight. What say we meet up for breakfast in the morning?"

"You can't get here sooner for fuck's sake? Time's of the essence here, you know that," Skip said.

"I do, but ..." Alex looked over at Kate sitting lifeless, a weight of sorrow hunching her shoulders, folding into herself, as if her backbone were made of soft putty. She owed her friend a day. "... It has to be tomorrow. I'm with Kate now and I won't rush her."

"Okay, okay."

"And I might bring Guy along."

Guy looked at her, raising a questioning eyebrow. What was she promising? Who was she talking to? Alex smiled and shrugged.

"Fine. I'll meet you at the café next to the gallery at seven sharp."

"Okay."

He hung up before the word left her mouth. She didn't take it personally. She wondered if her reaction to such a loss would be more like Kate's or Skip's. *How could I know?* She didn't have a clue how to be so close to anyone, in partnership and in love as they both were. She knew it involved some kind of deep letting go, but that kind of risk-taking eluded her.

Uncle Charlie was the closest person in the world to her—if only she could call him right now. *That's what's missing! Nothing is wrong with me except that.* But he was off on his own retreat, clam-happy somewhere knee deep in a trout stream, with no cell service. If she ever really lost him, and she knew that day would come, it would be like losing her father all over again. Of course she'd handle it but she didn't want to think about it now. Then there was Muin. She didn't want to entertain losing anyone she loved. *Hmmmm, maybe I do love more than I admit. If so, is it lack of love or fear of it that keeps me from getting closer to Guy?*

She was a great one with the questions. Zen practice taught her to be in the question, not to worry about the answer. That might be okay when sitting on a cushion contemplating koans, but it didn't really work in the flesh-and-bones world, especially in the domain of the heart.

I've got killers to catch and plenty of life left to get to the other stuff.

"Who was that? What happened?" Guy walked over to her and whispered into her neck. "What are you getting me into?"

"Skip wants to have breakfast tomorrow, that okay with you?"

She didn't want to talk about another dead body in front of Kate. Cop or not, she was fragile right now and Alex would respect that.

"Did they find Cissie?" Guy asked.

"I don't know. Said he'd fill us in tomorrow."

Guy knew she was lying. Alex knew he knew. She peered straight into his hazel brown eyes and cocked her head at Kate who wasn't looking at anything but the floor. Guy got the message.

"Okay then." Guy softly clapped his hands and rubbed his palms together. "What you all want to do for the rest of the day?"

Kate spoke up. "We have to find Jerry." The fire was back in her blue eyes. "Did Skip ever track him down, confirm that he is in New Mexico?"

Alex and Guy just stared at her, both at a loss.

"He was going to do some investigating, what he does, the other night when we were all at my house, remember? He promised cuz the phone you found in Cissie's drawer had Jerry's ringtone. Have you talked to Skip? Did he come up with anything? Doesn't matter, I just know it in my bones that he's here, and that he killed Sam. We have to find him."

***

Two hours later they were back in Albuquerque, back at Kate's house, back to corner number one. A phone call to Skip brought news that Jerry was indeed someplace in the southwest, exact location still a mystery.

"You think Kate's ready to go chasing down her ex, who may or may not have killed Sam? Who may or may not be in this state?" Alex said in a whisper to Guy.

"Doesn't matter what I think. Seems clear she's about to do what she wants to do. No changing a—"

Alex shot him a look. He wanted to say woman, he wouldn't dare.

"—mind made up when it's made up, especially a cop's," Guy said.

He is quick, I'll give him that.

"I'm worried," Alex said. "She seems to be in some altered state. I empathize, I do. I'd have murder in my blood too, I were her. But what if she's wrong? Finds Jerry? Does something stupid she can't take back?"

Guy listened.

"Gun on her hip is a ticking bomb, she's driven to hurt someone, get some retribution. She'll squeeze that trigger sooner or later—hurt someone best case, kill someone, worst. Shit."

"We'll have four eyes on her, minimum two, at all times. Maybe I can get her piece and jam it up so's it can't kill."

"And then what if she really needs it? That'll be on us."

"You're right."

"Those words are usually music to my ears ..."

"Look, we're both trained for this. We'll keep her safe."

"I hope you're right. Let's go do it."

They walked into the living room. Kate sat on the edge of the couch waiting, tapping her foot, staring at nothing, all internal edges pouring out of her toes.

"Let's not forget these." Alex dangled a set of handcuffs from her fingertips. "Case we actually find him."

"I'll let you be the good cop," Kate said. "Me, I'm gonna beat the shit out of him, immobilize the bastard so you won't need them. Maybe even plant one of these 'tween his fucking eyes." She slapped the Glock on her hip.

A couple of pounds slid from Alex's shoulders hearing Kate finally expressing her rage. A slice of hope sat up there in its place that she wouldn't go all Dirty Harry on them now.

After a few phone calls, some Google searches and a quick meal of tortillas, veggies, rice and beans—Alex insisted on feeding them— they were out the door headed to town, with a list of hotels on Alex's iPhone that might be harboring Jerry. Alex wasn't buying the scheme, but it would keep Kate busy.

The annual Hot Air Balloon fiesta was in town. The throngs tended to eat, drink and bed down in the southwestern part of town, close to the launch fields. They weren't known to wander beyond a three-mile square radius till the last balloon was a pile of deflated fabric. It was as if the hot air corralled them all in place. Most went straight to the airport afterwards, no interest in seeing the real Southwest, which was always fine with Kate. Except for the revenue they brought in, Kate would be happy to never see another tourist. Reminded her too much of Times Square, visitors walking four, five abreast, blocking the sidewalks, looking up, slowing down pedestrian traffic, testing the patience of the real city folk who had to get someplace. Reminded her too much of why she left New York. Reminded her too much of Jerry.

Kate hated Balloon police duty, and hadn't been assigned to it in years, since getting her detective's badge. A perp could get lost in the mess of flesh. It was ironic that she was now off to hunt Jerry in the crowds that always brought him to her mind. A few years back, when Jerry first found her in New Mexico and communicated with her just to let her know he had her back in his sights, he mentioned balloons a few times. Threatened to come visit, see the balloons. Now she was sure he'd be somewhere near the balloon fields.

Her nose would lead her to him—she'd be able to smell his putrid self across the state border. She wished she'd gotten wind of him before now. If she had, Sam might still be alive.

***

"Kate, it's midnight. Let's go home, get some rest. He'll still be here tomorrow." Alex was being as gentle as she could be, which wasn't much this time of night, on this sorry a mission.

"I can't sleep knowing he's in one of these beds on our list," Kate said.

"You can't be sure of that, he—"

"Look, you don't wanna help, fine with me. I'll bring you home or get you a cab. I'll find him. I gotta find him. And now's the time, while he's curled up snoring. Catch him unawares, same way he did—" Sam's name caught in her throat, behind her eyes, and squeezed her brain.

"Jerry's a late sleeper, right? Always has been, right?"

"Yeah, always stayed up way past my bedtime, slept till noon when he could."

"So, there you go."

"What, there I go, where?"

"He's probably not even in bed yet. Don't you think we'll have better luck finding his sorry ass in bed in the morning, when the sun's up?"

Kate froze and then went limp all over, as if her bones had turned into Jell-O.

"Fuck, you're right. Why didn't I think of that?"

"S'okay." Alex reached out and wrapped a consoling hand round Kate's toned bicep. *I have to ask Kate about her workout regimen when all this is done.* She had begun to notice small signs of aging skin and didn't want to become an old lady with droopy, flapping skin on her upper arms that a light breeze could move.

"Change of plan." Kate sprung back into form. "We'll hit the bars."

"Not a good idea." Alex used her firm cop voice, tried to lace it with a little I'm-talking-to-a-friend-who-just-lost-her-man compassion. Kate's slapped-in-the-face reaction told her she'd failed. Guy stepped in.

"How about we take a minute here and reassess, make a new strategy for getting this creep?"

Kate said nothing but her ears were engaged. Alex was pissed, then quickly grateful for the interference.

"Tonight we might find him, we might not. It really is late, we're tired, there are lots of dark bars and drunks to wade through.

"Tomorrow we could have two goes at finding him. First, early morning, sleeping off his hangover. Easy.

"Second, if we don't nab him in the buff, we canvas the Balloon field. We could get some of your uniforms to help," Guy said.

"No," Kate said. "I want him for myself—the unies will scare him off."

"Then have them dress to blend in," Guy said.

"We don't need help," Kate said.

Alex saw this could see-saw all night, but she kept her mouth shut.

"There's a lot of territory to cover, a big crowd." Guy was still trying reason.

Kate took a moment.

"Okay, let's make a deal. I'll skip the bar scene tonight, we'll get up early, do a bed check first and get to the balloons by ten. If we come up empty at the end of the day, I'll call my captain, get some help for Sunday. That work for you?"

"Yup, works for me."

They both looked at Alex.

She wasn't quite sure how he just got Kate to his side, but he did. A skill she'd have to watch out for.

"Fine with me, too. Let's go try to get some sleep. I'm exhausted."

Alex walked alongside Kate back to the car, Guy trailing behind. No one spoke. Her gesture was given and received as an "I'm sorry." It was the best Alex could do at the moment.

17

Three text messages greeted Alex first thing in the morning. Uncle Charlie, Muin and Skip.

"Shit." She rolled over and wrapped her arms around Guy. It was 5:30.

"And good morning to you, too."

"Sorry, I just remembered I promised we'd meet Skip this morning in Santa Fe at seven."

"Call him, tell him what's going on."

"He won't care. His wife's been murdered."

"Have him come help us, then we'll all help him."

"You wanna call him?"

"Sure. Gimme your phone."

"Nah, 's'okay. I'll do it."

"Wait a sec. Maybe Jerry's his guy, as well as ours."

"He won't buy that."

"Didn't you find a phone at Cissie's gallery that might be connected to him? Same ringtone he likes his women to hear when he calls?"

"Oh shit, you're right. What's wrong with me, I forgot that."

"Ease up on yourself there, sweetie." He gently brushed a few strands of hair off her face and kissed her cheek. "Does Skip have any other leads?"

"Don't know. He didn't say much, just wanted our help."

"Call him, convince him that Jerry is his number one suspect."

"Kate's not gonna like one more in her gang."

"I'll go talk to her while you call him. She'll be fine."

"You know her that well from just one morning together?"

"Jealous, are we?" He playfully nuzzled her neck.

"No, I just ..."

"It's okay, Alex. Make your call, I'll go get Kate on board. Okay?"

"Okay."

Am I? Jealous? When he said "she'll be fine," a green-eyed bullet shot through her heart. *Damn. How could he be so sure about Kate? What happened between them when I left them alone? Was that a mistake? Am I losing him?*

Kate is so vulnerable and grief-sick right now that she could be falling for him. Alex had seen the syndrome too often to just shake it off like sleep dust: Grief-stricken widow climbing into bed with the first warm body that appeared willing. *Is Guy that guy for her? Would Kate do that? Would Guy?*

Guy kissed her seductively before his feet touched the floor as if he knew what she was thinking.

"More of that later," he said.

***

Alex checked all three texts before she phoned Skip.

Uncle Charlie: *Just arrived @ camp w/ good cell service. U ok? Need to talk I'm here 4 a bit.*

The @ and numbers for words were a surprise. Charlie hated using shortcuts and not spelling everything out properly. He thought it lazy. Something had changed, made her smile.

Alex sat up, put her feet on the floor and felt her old self returning, as if it had been off with Uncle Charlie, stuck in a corner of his suitcase for a month. Guy loved her, Uncle Charlie was reachable, she was fine. She couldn't wait to have a long chat with him. She'd try him later, and be good as new after that.

Muin: *Got half message from u 2 late 2 call. Was off on Roshi mission. U ok?*

She shot them both a quick text that she'd be in touch later.

Skip: *Reminder: 7AM café near gallery.*

No surprise there. She found his number, tapped her phone to connect. Guy was right, he had no leads. He'd head out immediately and meet up with them wherever they were at. He sounded relieved to have some kind of plan.

***

Three hours of checking beds turned up nada. They hooked up with Skip, grabbed a couple of tacos to eat on their way to Balloon Fiesta Park, and piled into Kate's car.

Alex and Kate knew what Jerry looked like, but the boys would need a photo. Alex sent them an old one she still had in her phone address book. She dialed the number for the heck of it, and Jerry's voicemail answered.

"Shit, I can't believe he has the same old number. Listen to this guys." Alex hit speakerphone. "He's so Brooklyn you'll know him as soon as he opens his mouth, case his looks have changed and you have any doubts it's him. Kate, you can cover your ears."

They listened. No comments.

"I sent a picture of him to your phones. Kate, you want one?"

"I know what the bastard looks like."

"'Course, but what about to show around?"

"Fuck, I s'pose you're right. Better send it to me."

***

Fiesta Park, host to the annual Hot Air Balloon festival that attracted tourists from all over the world, was a riot of color. The foursome split up to cover the wide expanse, and agreed to text in every half hour. There was no separate staging area for the balloons—spectators, pilots and balloons mingled, the crowds helping when asked to hold down the balloons or open them for air to be blown in. The weather was dry and chilly, the sun not yet warming the ground, the atmosphere festive.

Kate's and Skip's sorrow was blown open and exacerbated by the cheery ballooners, poignantly reminding them of how Sam and Cissie both loved the yearly festival. Sam had been training to be a balloon pilot; Cissie, childlike in her excitement, attended every year since her arrival in New Mexico, and every day of the nine-day event.

Purples, reds, oranges, yellows: Primary, happy colors were strewn on the green field in various stages of inflation. Whooshing sounds as fires ignited. Many already up and away, a blaze of color splashed against the blue canvas above, willy-nilly.

Alex marveled at the good-natured camaraderie around her, balloon-speak the common language of tourists from near and far.

If she were on vacation, and not hunting an old friend who might be a serial killer, she might be able to join in the fun, laugh with strangers, step into a balloon basket and float above it all. Gleeful as a child, free as a bird. Or not.

The plethora of color, and all the people who looked to be having fun, reminded her of the circus Uncle Charlie would drag her to as a child. Even then she hated it, especially the clowns. They scared her. She didn't believe their slapstick, forced-gay merrymaking. She pretended to like it because Uncle Charlie so enjoyed himself.

But today wasn't about fun or working out her childhood issues, she was there to find Jerry. Before Kate did.

Confident that Jerry was still nervously skinny helped her scan through the crowds and eliminate the majority of overstuffed Americans. The Europeans in the mix hadn't yet caught up to their corpulent hosts, but they were gaining on them. Their costumes and accents shifted them away from Alex's keen, discerning eyes, especially their shoes. Those were always un-American.

Every lanky, fortyish American male caught her attention. There weren't many of them without a child attached, and she easily shuffled through the groups collected around each balloon. She was making good progress. Two text check-ins came and went. No sighting of their target.

She froze mid-stride at the sound of his Brooklyn tongue behind her. "H'v'you seen her? You seen her?"

She knelt as if to pick up something or tie her shoe. Stayed close to the ground till she could be sure it was him. He was asking people if they'd seen her. She peeked over her shoulder, he was showing them a photo of someone on his phone. *Who is he looking for? I can't let him see me yet, but damn, I want to see that picture. Is he looking for Kate? Here? That doesn't make sense.*

Jerry moved to the next group, scanned the crowds, searching for someone, a mirror image of the four of them. Except that he looked like shit, like he hadn't changed clothes in a week, patches of unshaved hair on his face—*he never could grow a beard*—white sneakers that looked like he'd been running through red clay—*definitely American shoes*—and sunken cheeks. *Looks like he smells pretty ripe, the way people are moving away from him, hardly looking at the photo.*

"I've found him," Alex whispered into her phone.

"Is he contained?" Guy asked.

"No, I'm about to move in."

"Where are you?"

"Shit, I don't know. Near an orange and purple half-filled balloon."

"What section?"

"Oh, right, let's see." She looked around for markers. "I think it's row D, I can see the RV parking lot nearby, off to the south."

"I'm heading over there now. I'll call Kate and Skip."

"No!" *Damn, he hung up.*

She kept Jerry in sight. *No need to move in too quickly, he's not going anywhere and Guy's on his way.* Together they could usher him away from the throngs with little disturbance, nobody the wiser. *No sense causing a scene.*

Text from Guy: *almost there, I can see u.*

Alex looked up from her phone and Jerry was staring straight at her. She smiled and waved. Started slowly walking toward him. He wasn't stupid. He turned and bolted. She took off after him knowing Guy was right behind her.

Jerry sprinted into the RV parking lot, ducking, bobbing, weaving around the houses on wheels. She spotted him crossing Alameda, darting into the larger RV park, a tangle of alleyways and narrow lanes. With bulky behemoth metal boxes blocking sight, sound and movement. *Damn, this is worse than city streets.*

She kept spotting him, then losing him. He was running in circles or more like rectangles. She could smell him, she knelt down, saw his feet two RVs away. Saw other feet walking here and there. People lived there. They were coming and going oblivious to the two, maybe by now five, intruders, some with guns. If Jerry had killed Sam as Kate suspected he too might have a gun. His and Kate's weapons were the most dangerous at the moment. *Let this not get ugly*, Alex prayed to the gods of crime and punishment.

He wasn't moving. Then he was. He crawled underneath an RV and lay down. *Maybe you're not stupid, Jerry, but you're not too bright either. Never were.*

She saw Guy approaching. Pantomimed Jerry's location. They made their way over, one on each side.

"Jerry, it's over, you can come out now. Let's talk. Why'd you run, Jerry? What're you running from?" Alex asked.

A bullet shot out on Guy's side.

"Fuck. Guy? You okay?"

"Yeah, it hit metal siding. S'okay."

"Damn, Jerry, you want to kill someone else? What the hell? One of those damn bullets could ricochet back on you for God's sake. Give it up Jerry. Let's talk about this."

"I didn't do nothin'," Jerry whined.

"Fine, I believe you, but hiding under there makes me think different. You know what they say about actions speak louder than words, don't you Jerry?" Alex said.

"Come out from under there and we'll talk about it. I'll be very cranky if I gotta crawl on the ground and drag you out. Won't be pretty for either of us."

"Fuck that." Kate came from out of nowhere. She laid her body on the ground, cocked her gun and pointed it straight at Jerry's eyes.

"Don't do anything you'll regret here, Kate." Alex sprawled down next to her.

Guy snatched Jerry's gun from the other side as he stared at Kate. She reached in, grabbed him by his shoulder and pulled him halfway out headfirst. Pushed her gun into his third eye.

"You killed Sam, you motherfucker. Didn't you? Say it. Why couldn't you leave me alone?"

Jerry lay there with a dumb, defiant grin across his face.

"Kate, this won't help. You know that," Alex said. "You're not like him. Sam wouldn't want this. If he killed Sam, we've got him now. That bullet he shot in the side of that RV will prove it. He'll get what he deserves. Think about Sam. What would he do?"

Kate reluctantly backed off.

Skip and Guy dragged Jerry up. Alex half-heartedly held her gun on him. She could see that he was whipped, no longer a threat. Kate kicked him in the gut. Drew her leg back to do it again.

"Kate!"

"Fucker deserves worse."

"Look what you did." Jerry raised his shirt up as he struggled to stand, his pale white skin rapidly turning bright red. "I'll show them what you did. Fucking police brutality."

"Yeah, and they find out you killed Sam, that's gonna be the least of it, you bastard. You couldn't just leave me alone? Why wreck his life, someone you didn't even know?"

"You both deserved it, thought you could just throw me out like trash. Well, I showed you, didn't I?"

"Oh my god, it was you. Fucking ..." She drew her arm back to throw a fist in his face. Alex got between them.

"Kate. We got him. He all but confessed just now. You guys hear it?" Nods all around.

Kate crumbled into Alex's arms.

"Shit, how the fuck did I ever hook up with that piece of garbage?"

"He wasn't always like that."

"I shoulda known. I shoulda warned Sam."

"Kate, none of this is your fault."

Guy was on the phone getting help, reading Jerry his rights. Jerry twisted and turned, there was a bit of fight left in him yet.

As Skip patted him down, all he found was a phone.

"Hey Skip, lemme see that." Alex walked over with an outstretched hand. "He was flashing a photo of someone around, I want to see who it is."

She tapped the phone to light up the screen. Cissie's face smiled up at her. *Fuck.*

She tried to hide it from Skip but she wasn't fast enough.

"You scumbag." Skip grabbed Jerry's shirt at the neck and lifted him up to his face. "What the fuck? How do you know my wife? Why do you have her picture? You kill her, too?"

"What you mean kill? She ain't dead." Jerry stared right back at Skip, spittle from both of them flying back and forth. "She's here someplace. She was s'posed to meet me. I been looking for her."

"How the hell do you know her?" Skip was angry still, but confused. "Kate, isn't this dirtbag your ex?"

"'Fraid so, and before you ask, I haven't a clue how the hell he would know Cissie."

The sirens were close. Four officers of the law plus one possible criminal. The way things were going, they'd be lucky at the end of the day if only one of them ended up behind bars.

Alex was tending to Kate, but knew if she didn't speak to Jerry now, once the guys in blue had him she'd lose her chance. She had a few questions of her own.

She caught Guy's eye, asked with a look and a shrug if he'd take Kate so she could take Jerry. He didn't skip a beat.

"Kate, help me out here. I got your precinct on the phone—least I think I do, but I can't get through to your captain. Can you talk to them?" Guy held out his phone.

Kate took it and walked off. She wanted to prepare them for Sam's killer, wanted to know what they'd dug up, if there had been any more related homicides. Did they already know about Jerry?

Alex jerked Jerry away from Skip. "Sorry, Skip, I gotta talk to this guy before those guys get here."

Skip raised his arms in surrender. He was beside himself, messed up in his mind, he could taste blood. He needed a minute away from this guy and knew it.

Guy walked off to meet the cops, shooing away gawkers as he went. "Nothing to see here, folks. Move along now."

Alex had a firm grip on Jerry's skinny arm. "Look, Jerry, I don't know what the hell you did, who you turned into, none of it, but you gotta answer a few questions. Maybe I can help you out later. You understand?"

Just as all the balloons floating above them now would be later in the day, he was deflated, had lost all his hot air, and looked even thinner than he was a half hour before.

"How do you know Cissie?"

"We're cousins."

"Cousins?"

"Yeah, cousins. I swear." Jerry kept a nervous eye on Skip. "Not blood cousins, but we shared some relations." He laughed at his own wit.

"Nothing funny here, Jerry. Were you here to see her?"

"Where, here?"

"New Mexico, here."

"Yeah."

"Not to torment Kate?"

"Well, that too, since I was here. That was like a gift in the cereal box."

"Did you kill Sam? We all heard you, you've been read your rights now, so think carefully."

"Maybe."

"Shit." Alex took a breath.

"Did you kill Cissie?"

"Why's everyone talking about that? She ain't dead, I just got a text from her this morning to meet me here. She loves those fucking things." He looked skyward.

The uniforms were three RVs away.

"You know anything about Cissie and the monks up at the monastery outside Abiquiu?"

"She used to go there. One of 'em was nice to her. One of 'em was the devil—what she said."

"What'd she mean by that? You know names?"

"I don't know, and no. Why don't you ask her? Where is she, anyway?"

"She's dead, Jerry."

"No, no, no. That's not possible. No!"

The guys in blue had him now. There was meanness behind their eyes, thinking they had Sam's killer in custody. It was gonna be a long ride to the station. She almost felt sorry for him.

18

Thwack! Thwack! Thwack! Renku Roshi struck Shoju's left shoulder with his shippei, a short, bamboo switch he used on wayward monks to assert his authority. *Thwack! Thwack! Thwack!* Three times on the right shoulder.

"You left last night without permission," Roshi said. "A flagrant abuse of your vows."

"I didn't think I needed your permission. You weren't around, I had no idea where you were. And I had a lead on the gong. Thought you'd be delighted."

"So, where is it?"

"It didn't pan out. Don't worry, we'll find it." Shoju's shoulders burned from the beating. The sting fueled his determination to get the hell outta there. He was tired of being lackey to a mad master.

***

Alex felt a wash of relief as she gazed up at the gliding orbs and heard the far-off squeals of delight. As if the scene in the parking lot had never happened. How many such scenarios were playing out nearby or far away at this moment? She didn't want to know. She wanted to lose herself in the surrounding gaiety, her fella by her side.

Maybe that's why there are circuses and storytelling and entertainment? To take our minds off the burdens we carry, to ease the pressure in our hearts, to let in a spark of joy?

She felt her body relax and let herself be captured by the sheer beauty and lightness. Her mind floated along with the balloons, free for the moment from earthly gravity.

She was never able to enjoy the circus because she couldn't unclench her heart from the pain of losing Daddy. It wasn't the circus or the clowns that were so terrible. It was her fear of letting go, her fear that if she had fun she'd forget Daddy, she'd be punished somehow. So she held on even when she knew he wouldn't approve. That was the grip of anger. *Oh, what I've missed!*

They took their time getting back to the car, clear on the other side of the Balloon Park. Strolling along the green, most of the balloons airborne, they gazed upward at the kaleidoscopic sky. The onlookers left on earth were mesmerized by the quilt of color overhead.

"My father would have loved all this," Alex said softly to Guy.

"Yeah? Makes him a cool dude in my book. What about Uncle Charlie?"

"Oh my god! He'd go bananas. He loves circuses, parades, roller coasters, shit like that."

"Mmmm, me too." Guy kissed her hair. "Weird, right? All your men liking kid stuff? You hating it all."

"I wouldn't say all. I'm kinda liking this right now."

"Maybe there's hope for you yet." He dropped his hand from her waist to her right butt and gave it an affectionate squeeze. She reciprocated in kind.

***

At dinner, Skip was all business as he talked with Alex and Guy about what they knew and didn't, his grief about Cissie's murder tucked away for the moment on a shelf in his mind. There'd be plenty of time to investigate that, once the SOB was behind bars. The racket in the busy restaurant kept their words private, as if they were in a soundproof box.

Alex scanned the menu for something besides rice and beans, having reached her daily limit of that Southwest staple at lunch. She settled on salmon and salad. During the meal she kept sneaking forkfuls of Guy's yellow and black side dish. He ordered a second helping. Alex couldn't believe how full she was at the end of the meal. Guy didn't enlighten her. Denial being what it was, sometimes it was thicker than the wall of sound enclosing them.

"How do you explain the text Jerry got from her?" Alex asked.

"He must have her missing phone, texted it himself. That phone you found, I never saw before. That wasn't any phone I ever saw her use. We search his place we find her real phone," Skip said.

"I don't know. I just don't think he's that smart. Foresight's never been one of his assets. Besides, we have no clue where his place is and if the cops know they're already there."

"Check his phone, what time did the text come in? You still got it?" Guy asked.

"Yeah, here, I can't bear to look." Skip offered it to Alex.

"You know the police ought to have this." Alex's cop mind felt a twinge of guilt for not following protocol.

"Yeah, well, no one asked, and I wasn't in a generous mood."

Alex scrolled around. "8:05 this morning. She couldn't have sent it, she was ... gone by then."

"Can't know that," Guy said. "That coulda been when he turned his phone on. No telling when it was sent. Unless we find her phone, or some forensic electronic geek to help us out, we can't know for sure."

"So, you're saying she could've sent it. Maybe last night? Before ..." Alex couldn't finish the thought out loud with Skip right there.

"I'm not buying it," Skip said. "It was him. He killed her, took her phone, sent the text after the fact. If she'd sent it, the phone would've been there this morning and I didn't see it."

"Wasn't in her purse when I searched the place either, when she went missing," Alex said.

"Maybe he took it with him," Guy said. "Maybe he couldn't find the other phone, if in fact it was what they used to be in touch. Maybe he thought later to send the text, maybe he didn't mean to kill her. Didn't strike me as a calculating killer.

"Not to mention the fact that he's slight of build. How the hell could he have had the strength to subdue her, get her up on the counter, with no signs of struggle? That's what you said, right Skip?"

Skip nodded.

"He might be a creep," Guy continued, "but I don't see him doing this to Cissie. Sorry, Skip. Now Sam, that's a different story. A surprise attack with a bullet? That's just how someone like him would operate."

"I gotta agree with Guy here. And maybe Jerry's crazy now, but I knew him once upon a time. He clearly has feelings for Cissie," Alex said.

"Yeah, feelings is what gets people killed," Skip said. "He's just the kind of guy Cissie would feel sorry for, be nice to, especially if they had shared history."

"Nice enough to ... have sexual relations?" She was going to say fuck, but she was staring at the bereaved husband, someone she knew, someone she liked, just had dinner with. This business of tact was complicated—people took things way too personally—she just wanted to speak her mind without consequences. No such luck. Even Zen told her that the law of cause and effect was always in play.

"There was something more than cousin in their kissing is what I think, for what it's worth," Alex said.

"Don't mean to offend, Skip. I liked Cissie, but there was definitely something going on that maybe you didn't know about."

Skip let that comment hang over the table as he let out a deep sigh and plopped his forehead onto his clenched fist.

The background din lulled while Skip collected himself.

"It took Ciss a while to get along with the idea of monogamy. She didn't think it such a big deal to give her body away—especially if you were nice to her. She had a rough beginning. But she was changing and we'd been talking more about what it meant to be faithful."

"This may be a non-sequitur," Alex said. "But those unnamed clients you told me about—they got anything to do with the monastery up by Abiquiu?"

"Why're you asking that? What the hell's that got to do with this?"

"Okay, I'll ask it another way ... how friendly was Cissie with the Roshi up there?"

"Don't know why the hell this matters, but, if you must know, she met him once at the house, by accident. She was s'posed to be out all day ... came home early. He was pissed at first, someone else walking into our meeting."

Alex recalled how Skip had ushered her out the back door. *I'll bet the client at the front that day was Renku Roshi.*

Skip continued. "But she flirted with him to cut through the tension and he fell for it. She had that sorta effect on men with a pulse. That's it. Beginning, middle and end."

Alex sat back. *I don't want to be cruel, this guy just lost his bride, but ...*

"You are the epitome of the truth in the love-is-blind cliché. Jeez, Skip, what do you know about your wife and her friends?"

"Don't be so fucking fresh. Tell me what you know, goddammit."

"I know what I saw. Cissie in a photo with Roshi, hanging in his tearoom. First time I was there when I wasn't supposed to be there, so no one knows I saw it. Second visit it was gone."

"It wasn't her, couldn't have been."

"I know what I saw." Alex had a flash of doubt. *Is my mind playing tricks?* "Why couldn't it have been her?"

"After that brush with Roshi I warned her to stay away from him. He was my client and something was off with him. I wouldn't've trusted him with my cat, never mind my wife."

"He's a Zen priest for god sakes, isn't he? Aren't they s'posed to be holier than the rest of us mortals?" Guy asked.

"Ha!" Alex said. "In a perfect world, maybe. You forget already what happened back in New York with my monks?"

"What happened?" Skip asked.

"Murder's what happened. Zen students and monks behaving like common criminals," Alex said.

"So, what'd this Roshi do to spook you?" Guy asked Skip.

"Wasn't so much what he did, was how he comported himself," Skip said.

"Comported, eh?" Alex said.

"Yeah, comported. ... Words between us were normal, assignment was pretty normal, it all appeared on the up and up—like any other client and business arrangement."

"But ..."

"But ... there was something dangerous behind his eyes, like he was itching to draw swords or karate chop my head off, or someone else's."

"You watch a lot of Kung Fu movies, do you?" Alex asked.

"Very funny ... this had nothing to do with his being Japanese. I got nothing against Asian people, fact is I spent time over there years ago and never met anyone like him. Fact is, never met anyone, anywhere quite like him. And I met lotsa psychos in my time. I don't know if this guy's psycho, but he's definitely menacing. Something off about him. Just can't put my finger on it yet.

"Sorta like a ripe apple, looks perfect on the outside, crack it open it's filled with worms. Never was able to see what he had going inside, but worms'd be the least of it," Skip said.

"I know exactly what you mean," Alex said. "All charm on the outside and creepy under the veneer. There is something going on with him and his monks, if they are monks at all. Something Buddha never intended.

"I gotta go to the bathroom." Alex got up and stood behind Guy, leaned over to whisper in his ear, but spoke loud enough for Skip to hear. "While I'm gone, tell him what I saw going on up there yesterday, would you?" She kissed him on the cheek.

"Gladly."

"Whoa, wait a minute now. I don't wanna get off track here from finding whoever did this to Cissie," Skip said.

"Listen to what I saw up there first before you decide. I'll bet there's a connection. By the way, what were you hired by Roshi to do?"

"Find an ancient bell that had been stolen right from under their squeaky clean little noses."

"I know about that gong. Muin said it was recovered."

"Who's Muin?"

"A monk friend from New York—doesn't matter. You found the bell and returned it, right?"

"Wrong. We think we know who's got it, but there's no proof, yet."

"That's weird." Alex turned to walk away. "When I get back I want to know about client number two."

"Don't see how that's gonna help ... we're just wasting time here," Skip said.

"Tell him." Alex locked eyes with Guy and cocked her head toward Skip. "Maybe he'll change his tune by the time I get back."

***

Alex dialed Muin and Uncle Charlie on her way back to the table. Voicemail, both. Time difference threw everything out of whack.

"You're shitting me," Skip was saying as Alex slipped back into her seat.

"What'd I miss?"

"I just told him about the nun you saw with Roshi—she was coming back from a trip or something and they had words, right?" Guy said.

"I'll say. That was the cherry for me. Got my ass outta there pronto."

"Is this her?" Skip held out his phone, picture of a frowning bald-headed woman on the screen.

"Jeez, yeah, that's her. You know her?"

Skip covered his face with his hands and rubbed his closed eyes with his fingertips, sighing all the while. He took a breath, dropped his hands to his lap and leaned back in his chair.

"This is getting weirder and weirder." He sat and stared down at the table. Alex and Guy didn't hurry him.

As if in a trance he said, "You asked about my second client, then I show you a picture and there's a connection ... everything is connecting here but who killed Cissie." He stared down at the table, not moving, hardly breathing. With little emotion in his voice, he continued, "Okay, client number two as you call him is the monk Shoju ... he hired me to locate a nun, she calls herself a monk not a nun, I guess they all do now... so's you can't tell anyone apart but maybe that's the point... went by the name of Enjou, was part of the group up there at the monastery, she and Shoju were like oil and water and for some reason he wanted to make sure she was far away and not coming back ..."

Skip closed his eyes and covered his face again. Alex fidgeted in her seat, about to say something, when Guy placed a gentle hand on her arm and whispered, "Let's give him a minute," which, despite her wanting to get to the end of the story straightaway, calmed her down and ushered into her body a modicum of patience.

A moment later, Skip sat up and leaned into the table. "I don't know what this has to do with anything, but I found her deep in the mountains of Japan in a secluded monastery ... looked like she was there for life and now you say she's back, so I imagine that Shoju is pissed. Nice guy, Shoju. She on the other hand is a piece of work. ... Now please explain to me how this information will help us find my wife's killer." He looked up and stared with his pale blue eyes straight into Alex's hazel green ones.

Alex's phone rang. She let go of his stare and looked at her phone.

"It's Kate." She answered before the second ring.

"Hey, Kate, what's up?"

Alex listened, Skip and Guy all eyes and ears.

"Calm down, Kate." Alex bit her lip. *That is exactly the wrong thing to say to anyone in the throes of hysteria. It always escalates the pitch, always.* "I don't understand. Who sprung him?"

"Where is he now?"

"We'll be right over."

Alex ended the call.

"We gotta get over to Kate's right away, she's frantic. They released Jerry. The bullets don't match."

19

E n route to Kate's, Alex finally reached Muin.

"I just hung up with Shoju and he's worried about you." Muin said. "Wondered why you left so suddenly, no goodbye, no explanation."

"Worried about me? Ha! That's kinda funny given what I witnessed up there. We should be worried about him," Alex said.

"Please enlighten me."

She told him about the warrior monks, the eerie chanting, the battering clubs, about Roshi's evil-laced scolding of the nun.

"Is that all?"

"That's not enough weirdness for you?"

"Yeah, I guess it's a little odd, but nothing to worry about."

"Okay, then, as you would say ... please enlighten me."

"Most Zen Masters aren't as gentle as Setsu Roshi, *our* Roshi. You've been spoiled. Lots of them are rather fierce—unnecessarily so, especially if they're American they think they gotta be dogmatic and severe. They end up just being cruel.

"They misinterpret some of the old stories about monks getting hit by masters and turn into harsh monsters wielding their power in unorthodox ways."

"This Roshi here isn't American."

"Why I'm not worried. He is supposedly the real thing, authentic and all, imported from the East. So while his stern scolding may seem harsh to you, it's not deep and it's not personal. Blows over in a second and is replaced with tender-heartedness."

"I don't buy it. I saw what I saw." *Am I being overly sensitive, exaggerating in my broken brain what actually transpired?* She recalled Roshi's smile after the berating when he hugged the nun. *Damn. Am I losing my instinct along with my memory?* She squeezed her eyes shut to drown out the internal chatter. "And what about the warrior shit, the clubs, the tattoos?"

"I only know what Shoju told me and I trust him. It seems Renku Roshi imported some ancient warrior discipline from Japan—sohei I think he said."

Muin kept talking. Alex wasn't listening.

"Hold on, Muin, sorry. I was just distracted by something. Have you told me about this sohei cult thing before?"

"I don't think so. And it's not a cult, exactly."

"Then what is it?"

"It's an ancient warrior art, used to discipline the mind and strengthen the body in order to become fierce meditators. So one can reach enlightenment faster, or some such bizarre notion. It's all harmless."

"Didn't look and feel that way to me ... hold on a sec, Muin. We just got to Kate's, I'm gonna go out to the backyard ...

"... Okay, where were we?"

"I think that maybe you need a real vacation, Alex—go to a spa or something. You still haven't recovered completely from that head trauma thing."

"Maybe you're right. 'Cept, dead bodies keep popping up over here and I can't just leave, pretend not to notice."

"Yes, that is a shame. So then, why not make a plan to go off with your new boyfriend as soon as things settle down a bit?"

There was absolutely no hint of jealousy in Muin's tone, which gave Alex pause, given their once-upon-a-time romantic interlude. She was convinced he was of the same stripe as Kido, her very first, now dead, favorite monk. The two of them were born that way: Full of love, forgiveness and compassion. *A shaved head does not a monk make. Those qualities do.*

"You can't save your friends from suffering, you know," Muin said.

"Yeah, but I can lend a hand to get them through the worst of it."

"Fine, long as you don't hurt yourself too much in the process, leaving you completely bereft of compassion."

"I'll work on that and check in with you every now and then to see how I'm doing. That be okay with you?"

"I wouldn't want it any other way."

***

When Alex walked into the house, Skip was alone in the living room. Sounds emanated from the kitchen but she couldn't tell if they were from two busy hands or four. Her stomach clenched in jealous dread. She ignored it and forced an upbeat tone from her throat.

"Okay, Skip, you win. Let's get off the monastery angle for a minute, see what else we might have to get the bastard that did Cissie.

"D'you know if the cops have any leads?"

Kate walked in from the kitchen carrying a tray with cups, creamer and sugar bowl. Guy trailed behind gripping a pot of coffee in his fist.

All nonchalance, Alex turned and said, "Kate, tell us what happened with Jerry, why he's out. Maybe we do need to look closer at him after all."

.   ***

Enjou held her breath and sat as still as Mount Fuji behind the shoji screen in the locked room of the monastery, listening as Renku Roshi disciplined Shoju. Her focus strayed for a moment, but she remained rock solid without even a breath sound.

She waited for Shoju to exit the room and Renku Roshi to close the door and secure the locks before she stepped out from her hiding place in the corner.

"Why are you wasting your time with him? He's useless. Doesn't know anything—"

"Enjou!" Roshi barked.

"Sorry, Roshi." Enjou bowed her head and put her palms together in supplication. "But you promised if I came back we'd be partners, we'd do what has to be done ... together ... as a team."

"And you will be my queen, once we gather a few more—" He stopped abruptly and closed his eyes.

"Roshi, it's time to tell the others ... you need me, you—"

"Enough!" His eyes flashed open wide and glared at Enjou.

"I say when it's time, not you! Not anyone else! They are not ready. I will decide when."

"I just thought we had an agreement."

"We do. But I get to say when and how!" Stern master gripped his voice. He clenched his jaw and teeth against his rage.

"Yes, Roshi." Enjou softened her voice. "And as the true master always says: In good time. All in good time."

Renku Roshi's jaw and shoulders relaxed. A soft smile lit up his face.

"You are a good student. And you will be rewarded. Come." He spread his arms wide.

Enjou walked into his embrace. Her body gave in. She turned her head to the side and rested her cheek against his chest, the scowl on her face hidden from her master's eyes.

***

Shoju paused outside the door, heard the locks click into place, and listened deeper. He couldn't hear a thing but knew she was in there, had been the whole time, behind the screen. His old post, watching some innocent monk get beaten, berated into submission for some higher cause. Shoju now knew that this cause was just Roshi's ego. Nothing grander.

Best place for him to be right now was out in the open. Best thing for him to be doing right now was sitting in meditation. Best person for him to avoid right now was Roshi.

He texted Muin on his way to the zendo. Only person he could trust. *Call me after your sit 2nite or ring me in the morning 1st thing. I'll be up. Something 2 tell u might need your help.*

Whatever the hell had happened to turn this place into a prison in the past twenty-four hours he didn't want to think about. Maybe it was the return of She Dragon. Maybe Roshi had slipped over into madness—he was always on the brink, Shoju could admit that now. Maybe the veil had finally lifted from his own eyes and he was able to see clearly that the whole enterprise called "Renku Roshi, Zen Master of Abiquiu Desert Monastery" was a sham, a front, and not for the eventual reign of true spiritual power, but for an evil, megalomaniacal thug to exercise his delusion. Shoju knew he too was complicit in some way, but that was about to change.

Zazen would help him dig down, find the answers to what his next move should be. He trusted that the evil hadn't poisoned every living soul there yet and meditation would still be sacrosanct, not to be disturbed. This left him free of worry that he'd be conked on the head and dragged off. He was being watched, guarded by two of Roshi's enforcers, hiding in the shadows just outside the zendo. How long could they stand attentive to his every breath? How did he end up here playing this deadly game?

He felt a cramp in his leg, and with it came the aha! moment. Roshi had discovered his affair with Cissie. That was it! Nothing else would have turned him. He prayed that Roshi's wrath was only raining down on his head and not Cissie's.

Hunger, thirst and the need to pee assailed him. He sat through it. Monkey mind was rampant, then a sharp unrelenting pain in his right anklebone focused his attention. It felt like it had been pierced with an arrow. Still he didn't move. The sun set. Darkness descended. There was no movement around him. He felt rather than heard his two guards breathing in the shadows. It was time for the evening sit. He remained alone, none of the other monks joining him. Time ticked by. He stole a glance at his phone: 7:12. Roshi must have cancelled the evening meditation.

The two goons would be replaced by two more when they got tired. He couldn't outlast them all. He uncrossed his legs, took a moment to stretch before standing. His bare feet took him slowly down the buffed wooden floor to his room. He had no way to lock himself in or them out. They would come for him in the middle of the night, of that he was sure. He wouldn't be there. He'd find a way out. He had to. For Cissie's sake, if she were still alive.

He changed into his yellow warrior pants and a faded black T-shirt. He scanned his room for what to take. He needed none of it. The only thing he wanted was the photo of Gempo Roshi, his old teacher in Japan. He slipped it out of its frame and into the waistband of his pants. All the rest of it was just stuff that could be replaced. He couldn't afford sentiment.

He eased into the hall and silently glided his way to the office. He was the only thing moving, his guards lurking somewhere in the shadows behind him. The rest of the men were by now in the arena for night training. He'd helped design the sohei tactics, so he knew. She Dragon was still within the walls.

Shoju figured he had about ten minutes to grab the car keys from the office, get his club, walk toward the arena as if he were going to join the others, dart into the garage and get the hell out of there.

The car keys were gone. Plan B clicked into place. Take the truck. Those keys were always left in the ignition. It was slow and loud. He'd have to lose his two shadow monks. He'd use his advantage, they didn't know that he knew they were following him. This is not why he became a monk. And in his mind, Roshi didn't even deserve that honorific. Sociopath, or maybe psychopath, came to his mind. Along with the resolve to think of him only as Renku, no more Roshi.

Once inside the garage, Shoju waited for his two minders to arrive and deftly put them into a twelve-hour sleep.

A minute later, he was startled by a disembodied voice.

"Going somewhere, Shoju?" Enjou asked. Bitter hatred laced her tongue.

"It's none of your business." Shoju turned his back and opened the truck door.

"Oh, but it is, indeed it is my business." She walked closer in, raised her left arm and pointed a gun at him. "Step away from the truck."

She gestured to her ladies in waiting. They moved in and held him.

He didn't resist. Even he knew he was no match for a bullet.

20

Alex and the rest of the foursome were up early the next morning without a plan. Too many bad guys running loose, no clues, too many ideas between them, no clear path. Kate cared only about Sam's killer, Skip only about Cissie's. Alex wanted to assist in their efforts, but before she could she had to calm down the mess that was her brain, unscramble the synapses gone haywire or she'd be of no help to anyone. There was something they all knew that would square the puzzle but it was out of reach, and Alex sensed they were moving away from it, not toward it.

If this were her case, she'd work it alone. It wasn't, and solitude was gonna be hard to come by.

Guy, well, Guy, he was along for the ride wherever Alex wanted to take him, tossing in his two cents when it mattered.

It was a delicate balance.

They sat around drinking coffee saying nothing, hoping someone would come up with a plan.

"Kate, you say someone paid Jerry's bail, picked him up?" Guy asked.

"Yeah."

"Any idea who?"

"None. It all happened so fast I can't figure how he maneuvered it. He's not that smart."

"Maybe that's a place to start."

"I suppose, though I can guarantee whoever put up that money's gonna lose it. Jerry's in the wind by now."

"Maybe not," Skip said. "Maybe Guy's got something. Why don't we head to the station, see if we can track down Jerry's benefactor—he's gotta know something—or maybe it was a she?"

Good idea, then me and Guy could ... do what?

Alex's phone chimed.

"Morning. How'd you know I was up this early?" She walked into the kitchen.

"I didn't, but I was hoping," Muin said.

"Has something happened? You okay?"

"I don't know. I'm worried. It's Shoju. He's not answering his phone."

"And that surprises you ... why?"

"He sent me a text last night, asked me to call him, said he needed my help."

"Help with what?"

"He didn't say. Doesn't matter. Wasn't his text got me worried. ... When he didn't answer I called the monastery phone, asked for him, they couldn't find him. Said he wasn't at morning service. Student who answered the phone didn't know where he was. I finally got Roshi on the phone—he told me Shoju was off on a solitary three-day retreat, that I shouldn't worry."

"Okay, so, isn't that what monks do? Go on retreat?" Alex had never heard Muin so upset, so close to hysteria. Or maybe what he was telling her struck her own internal hysteria bells and she only thought she heard it in his voice.

"Shoju hated solo retreats. Did one once. Vowed to never do it again. He wasn't the cloistered monk type—always too much of the world. Yes, I know, he lives in a monastery, but he really belongs in a soup kitchen helping the homeless, not where he is sitting for his own enlightenment."

"Then why the hell is he there?"

"Out of loyalty to Renku Roshi—or more like Gempo Roshi, his old teacher in Japan."

"Maybe he changed. Maybe what he wanted to tell you was he was going into retreat like he swore he'd never do."

"No, he would've just told me that. Listen, my gut says something's wrong. I just know it. You have to do something."

Hysteria might have been in Alex's brain, but it was also most definitely in Muin's vocal chords.

"When I called the monastery and they couldn't find Shoju, and Roshi wasn't available, I kept calling Shoju's phone. Eventually, Roshi picked up on that phone. He saw that it was me calling so much and wanted to let me know about Shoju."

"Is it normal for a Roshi to hold onto a monk's phone when they go on retreat?"

"No monastery I know of does that. It's fucked up."

"Maybe it has something to do with that warrior shit you told me about?"

"Maybe ... I don't know. I got a bad feeling. And the fact that Enjou, dragon-lady-nun, is back, is bad news."

"How can I help?" Alex asked, just as Guy walked into the kitchen.

Alex mouthed "Muin." Guy nodded and leaned against the counter.

"I'll call you right back, Muin. Don't move.

"Muin wants us to go check on something up at the monastery."

"Us?"

"Well, me ... and you're invited. Kate and Skip don't need us. I think they should go to the station, check on the Jerry angle and we'll go for a drive. I'll explain it all on the way. It's probably nothing, but worth a look, Muin's in a frenzy. Maybe just a nice drive in the country, you and me. Are you game?"

"Course."

"Good. I'll tell Muin, you tell those guys, okay?"

"Yes, dear." Guy sprang off the counter and bounced toward Alex.

"Mmmmm ... I like that." She kissed him back and gently moved him toward the door.

***

Shoju kept losing consciousness, the pain knocking him out, his mind unable to absorb the shock of it, stay awake. His body on fire everywhere. As if it were being tattooed five layers deep. He tasted blood, felt it run from his skin, drying, clotting, opening up, pouring out. Stinging, oozing blood. Buckets of it. She and her goils—he chuckled at that—doing what they did best, inflicting pain to relieve their own suffering.

He almost felt sorry for them.

***

Alex was glad to be down to a twosome. Four on a case was three too many. One she could handle. Maybe. She'd do her best. She hated herself for wanting to be on the road alone.

By 10:00, she and Guy were at the monastery entrance. Everything looked normal, the way it ought to look. Monks tending the grounds, raking rocks, pushing wheelbarrows, stacking wood. White cloths were wrapped around their bald heads to catch sweat, and blue work outfits that would look sissy in a city reeked of masculine pheromones.

They hadn't called ahead. No one batted an eye. They were escorted to the tearoom to await Roshi. He was busy with something, would be with them soon. The whole place was a hive of quiet activity.

Indoors, windows were being washed and floors waxed, a vacuum cleaner hummed somewhere down the hall, blue-clad bodies scurried soundlessly here and there. Work practice. Alex recognized it and it calmed her mind. She felt at home.

"Did I ever tell you about the pleasure of cleaning toilets?" Alex whispered to Guy as she relaxed into the soothing sounds of Zen monks and students busily executing their cleaning assignments.

"Don't think you have. I figured all you did in a place like this was sit on your butt."

"*Au contraire.* ... Want to know the coolest thing about the Zen approach to cleaning?"

"I'm all ears."

"It's not about cleaning!"

"Ha! That sounds so Zen. And I have no clue what you're talking about."

"Well, okay, here it is in a nutshell: As Jon Stewart would say, 'your moment of Zen.' It's the doing of the chore that's important, not the end result."

"O ... kay ..."

"The outcome is that everything is clean and neat and in order at the end, and that matters, but it's more about mindfulness in action. It's about being in the moment, bringing your body into the chore, not thinking ahead to when it will be done. Just cleaning, even if it's already clean."

"Aha! So that's why your bathroom is always so sparkling."

"Yeah, I clean it every time I'm in it."

"No!"

"No, silly, course not. But I am a bit of a clean nut, maybe a tad OCD, especially when it comes to sinks and mirrors."

"Hmmm, good to know. I thought you were just being a good host, keeping your apartment so clean while I was there."

"Nope, that was all for me, not you, sorry to say."

"Okay then."

"I'm feeling better about this place." Alex was lulled by the familiar buzz of activity. "I think I'll be able to report back to Muin that all is well and normal here."

"Let's first see how the meeting with Roshi goes," Guy said.

"Right. I wonder where the hell he is?"

She looked over her shoulder. Then she saw it. The photo. It wasn't Cissie back up on the wall with Roshi, it was another woman. Same blonde hair, but definitely not Cissie. Nothing had been hanging there last time she was in that room, something had been the first time. A different picture. One with Cissie. She was sure of it. She looked again. The blonde looked like Cissie, but it wasn't. And Roshi's robes were black. She remembered his robes had been golden in the Cissie photo, close to the color of Cissie's hair. Cissie had been in pink. Different photo, different time, different woman. She was sure of it.

"Shit, see that?" Alex indicated the wall behind them. Before Guy could respond, Roshi arrived on a breeze and plopped himself down on a cushion at the head of the table. A puff of incense perfumed the air.

"You left us the other day, Miss Sullivan, without saying goodbye," Renku Roshi said. "I hope our foreign ways didn't chase you away."

"No, not at all. I felt a migraine coming on and wanted to get back to town quickly before it settled in. Sorry for the rudeness but I didn't want to put you to any bother."

"Don't even think about it. One must tend to your female nature of course."

That is definitely icky.

Enjou served them tea. They said nothing till all cups were filled. Enjou looked at no one, kept her head bowed like a good geisha, though she was clearly an American girl. When done serving, she knelt in the doorway and blended into the scenery, dutifully waiting till she was needed again. Her two ears tuned in to the players around the table.

They talked about Shoju's retreat, about the life of a monk. Roshi was gracious and charming. A belly laugh about something Guy had said. Alex wasn't listening. She was staring out the window, distracted by two monks embroiled in quarrel. Their body language shouted vehemence and it wasn't about which shovel to use. One kept looking straight at her—she was sure he couldn't see in but her spine twitched. All she could see of the other one was red and blue ink creeping onto his neck above the blue collar of his shirt.

"Alex, are you with us?" Guy interrupted her trance.

She snapped back into the room. "Uh, sure, sorry. I feel a bit ill is all."

"Another migraine coming?" Roshi asked. "Enjou can find you a place to lie down." His tone said: I am not happy that you're here, that you're sick, that we must look after you.

"No, no, thank you. It's nothing like the other day. I just need a little air."

"So, then we'll save the tour for next time," Roshi said.

"I'd still love to see what this place is all about," Guy said. "If you don't mind it's just me. You okay to wait by yourself for a bit, Alex?"

"Sure thing. I'll sit out in the garden. Just what the doc ordered."

"Of course, of course," Roshi said. "Enjou will keep you company."

He did not want Alex on her own, she got that, but sitting with Enjou even for a short time would be torturous, enough to give her a migraine.

"Thank you, I'll be fine alone."

"I insist—"

"Surely you understand the need for solitude, Roshi." It wasn't a question. She was pissed, felt as if her arm was being twisted out of its socket.

She caught herself, softened her tone. "I'd like to meditate out there alone while you're gone, find a little of that peace I came up here for the other day." She wanted to talk to the arguing monk, the worried looking one, and she didn't need a bodyguard. "If that's okay with you."

"Of course, of course." Renku Roshi was not a smiling Buddha.

They stood up. Enjou backed out the door, waited just outside in the hall.

"Who's that in the photo with you, Roshi? Is she someone special, or famous? Should we know her?"

"Well, she is special to us. One of our benefactors, very generous lady."

"Ah, yes. Was Cissie Hunter a benefactor also?"

Alex detected a slight tightening of Roshi's jaw.

"Who?"

He was used to being in charge in his own tearoom and definitely annoyed the way this was going.

"Cissie Hunter, wife of Skip Hunter. I think you know him."

"No ... no." He pretended to think about it, rubbed the top of his razored skull as if it were Aladdin's lamp. "I don't think I know him."

"Funny, last time I was at his house in Santa Fe I could've sworn I saw that car parked in the driveway."

They all looked out at the sparkling black Hummer now hovering in front.

"Ah, well, Shoju sometimes uses that car. Perhaps they are friends of his."

"Can I ask him?"

"As I said, he's in solitary retreat." His jaw twitched.

"Yes, I understand, but it's very important."

"Ah, you Americans. Always in a rush. Everything is so important."

"There's been a death, Roshi, and I think Shoju would want to know."

The tension in his jaw relaxed.

"Ah, dead. ... What, after all, is dead?"

"S'cuse me?"

"No matter. I have this habit of quoting koans when it's not called for. Enjou gets on me all the time about it."

"So then, may I please interrupt Shoju's retreat? Or can you get a message to him?"

"I am sorry, Miss Sullivan, but I do not know where he is. His retreat is sacred and no one knows where he is."

"If that's the car Shoju uses, how then did he get to wherever he is that no one knows?"

"We have people like Mrs. Johnson there to thank for that." Renku Roshi stood in front of the picture, paused and smiled. "We have more than one vehicle here for our use."

"But someone is dead, a friend of his, surely he will want to know. You mean to say that no one here knows where he is?" Alex asked.

"Yes. And she will still be dead in three days. There will be plenty of time for him to mourn her. Patience, my dear Miss Sullivan. ... As I would say to one of my monks, this is a wonderful opportunity to practice patience."

"You said she, Roshi. I don't think I said who was killed." They engaged in a staring contest.

"Killed, you say?" Roshi's tone and look softened. "How unfortunate. What we do to each other ..." He shook his head with an aura of compassion.

"It is the husband then, that is dead, not the wife?"

"I don't think I said anything about any husband or wife. Did I, Guy?"

Guy shook his head.

"You mentioned the Hunters, our vehicle at their house," Roshi said. "I drew a conclusion. I apologize." He put his palms together and bowed.

"Unfortunately, you are right. It is the wife that's dead. Cissie Hunter." Saying her name elicited nothing. "And I'm sure Shoju would want to know."

"My, you are persistent. You would make a good Zen nun. Have you ever considered that? Ah, no matter ... why don't you go have a nice sit in garden, see if you can find some patience. And I'll give your boyfriend here a tour of our magical desert sanctuary."

Before she could say another word, he was out the door with Guy in tow.

After a few steps Roshi swiveled around and with a tinge of menace said, "Be careful out there. The sun is hotter than it seems."

Alex's habitual reaction to threat sent her hand to clutch her gun. A second flash of instinct gave her pause. She wasn't under attack. Not yet. Not in this moment. But was it safe to send Guy off with Roshi?

Guy read her body language, looked over his shoulder and winked. As if nothing was amiss. He could handle himself.

What she had to do was find the arguing monk. The hell with patience.

21

Roshi and Guy walked toward the zendo, Enjou toward the exit. Alex followed her to the door. Before exiting, Enjou turned and stared into Alex's eyes. There was no warmth there, just two black hungry orbs, no spark of light to be seen. If she meant to intimidate, it was working. Enjou turned and walked out. Alex paused, stood just inside the darkened doorway and gazed out onto the sun-blazed driveway after Enjou.

Enjou stepped into the Hummer's driver's seat and whispered something to the monk holding open the door. To Alex he looked like the monk she'd seen out the window, but didn't notice any inky colors on his neck. From a distance and the back they all looked alike. What Alex did see was Enjou's face turning pink with rage as she listened to the monk. And then she slammed the car door and sped down the driveway.

Alex walked out to catch up to the now wandering monk. She wanted to know what bad news had been delivered to Enjou to cause such a reaction. Once she caught up to the monk, she strolled alongside for a moment before looking over, casual-like. Her eyes landed on a nun, not a monk. *Damn, they all do look alike from the rear.*

The nun ignored her, stared straight ahead.

"Hi," Alex said.

The nun said nothing.

"Can you help me?"

Still nothing.

Alex touched her arm to get her attention. The nun stiffened, looked over and pointed to a sign hanging around her neck: *Practicing Silence.* She turned and resumed walking.

But I just saw you speaking to Enjou!

"Sorry." Alex stopped her again. "You don't have to say anything, just nod."

The nun continued walking toward the garden. No expression. No interest in breaking her vow of silence.

Just leave her be. Alex's inner Zen voice ruled the moment and she let her go on alone. *Do as Roshi suggests, practice patience, respect this nun's desire to be quiet. Just go sit, be still. The right action will make itself known.*

Aha! Call Muin.

No service, not even one bar. She walked around. Nothing, anywhere, close to the buildings or nearer the butte. *Muin had said that Roshi had answered Shoju's phone. If he'd been here, then the signal had been here, and there was one the last time I was here. Someone must be controlling it. Damn. Is that even possible? I could go inside and use the monastery phone, but then I'd have no privacy. Muin will have to wait.*

***

Ten minutes sitting in the garden and her patience was exhausted, which was some kind of new record. No sight of Guy, no sight of silent nuns or arguing monks, no movement anywhere nearby except for the desert breeze and the monkey in her mind. Cleaning practice was done.

I could search Shoju's room, if only I knew which it was. A stranger strolling the halls back at her home monastery would be welcome, hardly noticed. Here she feared any one of the tattooed warriors, or worse, silent nuns, would stop and frisk her if she were caught snooping around without a hall pass. Maybe she'd get lucky. *I have to try something. I can't sit here all day waiting for Guy to return.*

It occurred to her that her life from ten on had been spent waiting for the right guy to walk in the room. *To what, save me? Goddamn. Can that really be it? My version of waiting for Godot? Waiting for Daddy to return from the dead?* He never would, she knew that. And yet no man ever quite fit the bill. Except Uncle Charlie, of course, but even he wasn't Daddy. *How does anyone get over a loss so huge? Easy answer is they don't. So, how to stop the longing?* Her heart went out to Kate and Skip, what they must now be suffering, mercilessly and brutally robbed of their ideal love.

She walked in through the unguarded front entrance as any anonymous guest would and headed toward the office. Her excuse for being there was at the ready: She needed to make a phone call. Maybe that wouldn't arouse suspicion. A student who still had his hair was manning the phones and working on a computer. *He must be Andy.*

"Hi there, are you Andy?"

He looked up from the screen and beamed a broad, toothy smile at her.

"I am ... how can I help you?"

"I'm Alex, we spoke on the phone last week."

"Oh hi, yeah, I remember. I was in the doghouse for a week saying you could come when Shoju didn't want anyone here."

"Right. What was that about anyway?"

"Sorry, haven't a clue. I'm new here so am just getting used to how things work." Andy looked around Alex to peer down the hall, a worried look replacing his smile. "Does anyone know you're here today?"

"Yes, don't worry, it's fine. I'm here visiting with Roshi, he's giving my partner a tour of the place. I wasn't feeling so well so I stayed behind.

"Okay if I use your phone for a quick call to Albuquerque? No signal here." She held her phone out, evidence that she'd tried.

"Yeah, sure. It's temperamental, the service here. One of the monks was trying to fix it about an hour ago, but no luck yet."

More like tampering than fixing.

"You can sit here while I run to the loo." He got up and offered her his chair. "Just don't answer the phone, let it go to voicemail."

"Sure thing. Don't mean to be rude, but I'm guessing with all that hair you're not a monk?"

"And you'd be right. I'm just a student." He offered his hand as he came around the desk. "Nice to meet you."

"Pleasure." Alex gripped his hand.

"How long have you been here?"

"Just arrived last week, couple days before you called."

"Big job you got not being a monk."

"Nah, it's just busy work, keeps me in one place, no one else wants to do it."

"Okay, Andy, I'll be your place-holder."

"Thanks, I'll be back in a jiff."

Before dialing, she took a quick look around, and noticed a camera mounted high on the wall over the window, focused directly on where she was sitting. She waved. *Damn.* She picked up the phone, pretended to dial, pretended to leave a message. She did not want a live call to Kate being recorded, no matter how innocent. *Why the hell are they spying on their own students, if that's what that camera is all about?*

She needed to find a list of room assignments, get into Shoju's space, have a look around. Her back to the camera, she stood up to hide the computer screen from view. A quick search got her what she wanted. 2GR. She quickly returned the screen back to Andy's document, sat back down and then swiveled around and stared out the window. *Nice view. Serene. Perfect place for contemplation. But what the hell is going on here under the pretty face?*

She spotted Guy and Roshi in the distance slowly strolling back toward her, flanked by Andy down the hall on his way back.

"You're in luck, no one called, thanks for the phone call." She was out and down the hall before he could wave so long.

She found Shoju's room no problem. Encountered no one en route, no aural or visual evidence of the prior work hubbub. Just as in her home monastery there was no lock on the door. She slipped in, unseen as far as she could tell.

Nothing was amiss at first glance, no sign of struggle. *What was I expecting? A dead body?* Everything appeared to be in place, as if Shoju had just slipped out for a sit or a meal. A faint scent of recently burned incense. *Normal.* Overnight bag on closet shelf. *Maybe he owns two, so maybe normal.* Bed neatly made. *Could be normal.* Empty, disassembled picture frame thrown hastily on top of his altar. *Not so normal.*

She executed her turning-in-place ritual. It was just after returning from her first weekend retreat at the monastery that she had initiated this practice, that soon became a habit, that turned into a ritual, that over time became de rigueur at every crime scene. She'd place herself in the middle of the site, turn in place, softly focus her eyes on the space in front of her, just as she did in zazen. Then she'd open up all her senses to the scene, without actually using any one of them, and slowly turn three hundred and sixty degrees. By the end of a complete circle she'd usually know something that she hadn't known previously and wouldn't have been able to "figure" out. She trusted and relied on this sixth sense.

Today she felt rushed. Guy and Roshi were probably looking for her and if she got caught in Shoju's room she had no good explanation. She heard movement in the hall. Hoped Shoju would walk in, catch her in the act. *We'd have a laugh about it. Anyone else, not so funny.*

At the end of her three-sixty she knew something was wrong, and had a clear sense that Shoju was some place nearby and in trouble. She took another look in his closet. *Robe, check. Rakusu, check. Wouldn't he want those for his retreat, if he was on retreat? Could have more than one of each. Possible. Two sets of work clothes. Hard to imagine he owned more than that. So what was he wearing?* She quickly rifled through his two drawers—underwear, socks, T-shirts, the usual. Something was missing, but she knew not what. Her brain wasn't clicking fast enough. She had to leave, get to the garden quickly. She took a photo of the altar and his closet to send to Muin. He'd know what wasn't there.

She headed toward the garden. Someone walked behind her but she resisted the urge to glance around. She tried to act nonchalant, as if she belonged and nothing was wrong. When she got outside, Guy and Roshi were sitting on a bench, their backs to her, like old pals. Her stomach turned over. *Not sure what that message is. Maybe just hunger.*

She slipped quietly onto the bench next to Guy. "Did you guys have a good tour? I was inside calling Kate—she's not answering—and using the bathroom."

"Well," Roshi slapped his thighs and rose with a grunt. "Time to say sayonara. I will tell Shoju to call you when he returns. He has your number, I presume?"

"Actually, no, but he can call Muin in New York," Alex said. "He's the most concerned and he'll get to me."

"Ah, yes, Muin. He's a good monk. I wish I could get him out here to visit us more often."

"Yeah, he's a real monk. Born to it I think." She placed her palms together and bowed to Renku Roshi, her stomach churning at the motion. *Is that disgust or am I really getting ill?*

"Thank you, Roshi. We'll be out of your hair."

He rubbed his bald head and smiled. They all laughed.

"Allrighty ... guess we'll be going now."

"Yes, thank you for the tour." Guy stood up and extended his hand. "Lovely place you have here. We'll be back again before we leave for New York, take you up on that offer of dinner." They shook hands.

Alex did not want to touch him. Roshi or not, Zen Master or not, he was just too smarmy for her taste. She liked her guys and her monks a bit more wholesome. *Okay, with a dangerous edge and a touch of bad boy, if I'm being honest. But this robed being in front of me has not an ounce of wholesomeness and his dangerous edge is more razorblade than sexy.*

"Oh, I almost forgot to ask," Alex said. "Time for one more question?"

Roshi barely nodded.

"I notice, just like back home at my monastery, there are no locks on any doors. Except for that one room with the barred windows. What's in that room? It's so mysterious. For a monastery."

"Ah, yes. Not mysterious at all. Just some ancient relics that we like to safeguard."

"Is that where the reclaimed gong now resides?"

Roshi's jaw twitched. She was getting to him.

"That and many other priceless objects." He clearly did not want to engage her.

"May we take a peek before we leave? Setsu Roshi would be so disappointed if I told him I was this close and didn't pay a visit to your museum."

"Why don't we save that for next time?"

"Only if you promise to show us then."

"Yes, of course, of course."

Guy linked arms with Alex and coaxed her toward the parking lot. "Till next week then." He waved and walked.

Renku Roshi stood still, eyes boring into their skulls, hands clasped behind his back till they were in the car, moving toward the long drive back to town.

***

Shoju wanted to scream away the pain. He marshaled all of his inner resources, everything he'd learned about pain over the years as a monk, to hold back, to not cry out. No one outside the room would hear him anyway. And he didn't want to give Enjou and Renku the satisfaction. He refused to think of him anymore as a Roshi—he is not venerable and is master of nothing. Ronin was more like it, a rogue samurai with no master. Even applying the term samurai to him denigrated the term.

He flitted in and out of consciousness. He had no idea what day it was, what time of day. It didn't matter. He heard the click of the locks behind his head. He couldn't turn to see who it was. He hoped it was Renku and not the witch. He might still be available to reason.

22

"What the fuck? You let him go?" Kate and Skip were back in Albuquerque standing in the door of her captain's office.

"Come in, sit down, close the door."

They moved inside but stayed upright.

"What the fuck, Captain? He killed Sam."

"There's no clear evidence of that. The bullets don't match, his prints aren't on anything from the church. We couldn't hold him."

"But he had a fucking gun. He shot at a cop! And he told me he killed Sam."

"Kate, sit!" She moved to a chair, poured herself into it. "Who're *you*?" The captain pointed his chin at Skip.

"Skip Hunter. Helping Kate out, she's helping me. My wife was killed a few days ago we think by the guy you cut loose."

"Look, let's get something straight here. We're all ripped up about Sam, but the guy we arrested yesterday is not our guy. Or maybe he is, but the gun he had doesn't match. We get cause to search for another one we'll do that, till then we got nothing." He looked at Skip. "Condolences 'bout your wife."

Skip grunted.

"Discharging a loaded gun at a cop? You couldn't keep him a bit longer just for that?" Kate's fury was palpable. Her wide, blue eyes were shot through with red, her blonde hair hung limply around her head and looked as if it hadn't seen a drop of water in weeks, and her green shirt and tan slacks were loose and wrinkled. The gun and badge hanging from her belt were the only things that had her looking like a cop and not a suspect or witness that had been through the wringer.

"He's got a charge pending, claiming self defense, says he didn't know your friends were cops. Had a Florida gun license in his pocket, had a right to be carrying. Discharging, that's another matter and he'll have to face that charge, but he got an attorney, made bail in a matter of minutes. Guess he knows someone here able to pull strings."

"Fuck, who the hell does he know? Bastard's never been here before in his life." Kate sank deeper into the coffee-stained seat.

"We'll go talk to his lawyer, you got a name?" Skip asked.

"You know anything about lawyers and their precious clients? He ain't gonna tell you nothing, 'specially not this guy. Good luck with that." Captain slid a card across the desk. Skip picked it up, showed Kate.

"Shit, he's right, he won't say shit."

"Anybody know where he's staying? Or who drove him back there, if that's where he went?" Skip asked.

"Some limo service picked him up, like he was fucking royalty or something. Must've been his prince charming, or princess, paid for that, too," the captain said. "Go ask Howie out front, he'll know the car drove him away.

"And let's not do anything stupid here. We don't want to blow the one charge we got against him."

"Yeah, yeah, yeah. We know the drill. Let's go, Kate."

"Go home, Kate, get some rest," the captain said with kindness. "We've got this. 'Sides, we can't let you get near this one, you know that. We won't stop till we get the guy who done this to Sam, you know that, too."

Kate didn't move. She was splayed out in the chair, all the wind sucked out of her.

***

Behind the one locked door in the monastery, Renku swabbed Shoju's face with a white cloth and leaned close to hear the faint murmur of words. "Why is she back?"

"She's loyal. I can trust her. Not your concern now. Just let go," Renku said.

"She's a monster."

"Ah, perception ... I see her quite differently, more like she's blossoming into her bestowed name. Enjou means Dragon Queen. Did you know that? Quite wonderful, don't you think?"

"Nothing wonderf ..." Shoju began to lose consciousness.

Roshi slapped his face. "Not yet!"

Shoju came to, focused on the morning light seeping around the edges of the shoji shades. Another day.

"Why, Ro—" He took a breath to disguise his falling into the name habit. Summoned up the five vows. Even if the whole sohei warrior bullshit was a sham, the vows were not. He would not name him Roshi. He would not name him anything. Stripping him of power in his own mind helped make it so, even if the relative truth was otherwise.

"... let her do this to me?"

"You? You? Ha! You betrayed me!" Hot anger stung Renku's tongue. He threw the rag onto the floor, and picked up his shippei. "Do you need reminder?"

"Been nothing but loyal—"

Thwack! The force of the strike reopened the cuts on Shoju's thigh.

"What you think I did?"

"I."

Thwack!

"Think."

Thwack!

"Nothing!"

Thwack!

"I know!"

Thwack!

His legs burned, stung, bled. He passed out, then came to, his face was wet, his old teacher dabbing it dry.

"There, there. You know the rules. Treading on my territory is not sanctioned."

"... lie did she tell you?"

"By she, do you mean Cissie?"

"Where is she?"

"If you mean Cissie, well, she is no longer your affair. Ha! I just made joke, a pun. Did you like that, Shoju?" He gently lifted Shoju's head, raised a cup to his lips and let him drink.

A loud click, like a gunshot, pierced the room, drew them both to attention.

"You gave her a key?"

Renku dropped Shoju's head, walked to the altar and began to chant.

***

About an hour before first light, the girls were in Kate's kitchen, the guys still asleep. The dark early morning wrapped around them and cocooned them in still timelessness. Soft light from a gold-shaded lamp on the counter cast a warm glow.

"Can't sleep?" Kate asked.

"Are you kidding? With this head thing I got going on? And all the other shit?" Alex whispered as she eased herself into a kitchen chair opposite Kate. "Can I get some of that ice cream before it melts?"

Kate pushed the pint of Ben & Jerry's over the white Formica. "I'll get you another spoon."

"S'okay. You don't have any contagious disease, do you?"

"Not last I checked."

"I'll use yours then, you don't mind. Sit. Mmmm. Cherry Garcia, my all-time favorite."

"It was Sam's, too. You would have really loved him, Alex. I just can't believe he's gone. It's like there's a hole inside me that aches for something I know can never be filled. Whenever I remember that he's really dead, the hole just gets deeper and blacker and angrier. I feel like I'm suspended in some sort of life that really isn't life. I know I'm breathing and eating and shitting, but I'm not in my body, I'm not me. I don't know where I went. I don't know where he is. I keep expecting him to walk in the door."

"I felt that for years after my dad died. I still experience the deep ache you're talking about. Not sure it ever goes away. It's like there's an organ missing that I need in order to feel complete, to love, to allow myself to be loved. Ah, I don't know..."

She ate a few spoonsful of ice cream. Kate watched her. The clock over the doorway ticked the seconds away. 5:37. They moved into the future with the sound. 5:38.

"Coffee?" Kate pushed herself to stand.

"Love some. And pleeeeze, take this away from me." Alex held up the sweaty pint of creamy sweetness.

Tick tock. 5:52.

"I like Guy, he seems good for you." Kate sat back down to wait for the coffee to brew.

Alex peered into the living room, and lowered her voice. "Yeah, he's pretty great. Might be a bit too *nice* for me if you know what I mean. Not enough of a bad boy streak for my taste. Maybe. I don't know, you know me, can't settle on anyone."

"You might be surprised at how *nice*, nice can be. I know I was. All I can say is, stay away from the fucking bad boys. That's what I liked about Jerry—his bad boy-ness—and look where we are now with that. He probably killed the only nice guy I was ever gonna get. My fucking ex-husband-bad-boy stole his life right from under me. I'm sick. We have to find him, Alex. *I* have to find him."

"We will, Kate, we will."

They sipped coffee and said little as the early morning light crept slowly into the room.

Tick tock. 6:21.

As soon as Guy and Skip crawled out of bed, shot some caffeine and ate something, they all headed to Santa Fe. Kate and Skip were in one car, going to quiz Jerry's chauffeur, to try to find out "who the fuck bankrolled that asshole," in Kate's words. Alex and Guy took Sam's Jeep to visit the monk who purportedly stole the gong from Desert Monastery. Alex had no idea in her brain why this might lead to Jerry, but they all agreed to trust her gut on that one. Meanwhile, the cops were working Cissie's case, so nothing to be done there, Skip prayed that all the dots would connect. The foursome made plans to convene at Skip's sometime after noon.

***

Shoju was sitting propped up on the massage table so that he could see the altar. "That doesn't belong to you." He could barely speak.

Renku struck the large gong a third time.

Shoju couldn't feel his legs. They were draped with a white sheet. The lack of feeling worried him more than the pain. At least with that he could assess his condition. Now he hadn't a clue if he could walk, even if the bonds strapping him to the table were cut. He couldn't be sure his ankle straps were still in place.

"Want me to gag him?" Enjou's voice assaulted him from behind, spittle landing atop his baldness.

"Leave it be, his words matter not." Renku's eyes alighted on Enjou with love and compassion. When they slid down to impale Shoju they transformed into cold, livid slits, his hungry, black brain burning through. It was clear that Shoju's old master was lost somewhere inside, beyond reason now.

If only his legs worked, he might have a chance against the two monsters intent on destroying him. Shoju saw the sheet move slightly before he felt his toes wiggle. Renku's wrath rendered him blind to the movement. Shoju could only hope that Enjou was just as unseeing. Hope sprang to his lungs and parried with Renku's depraved stare. He felt like an avatar in a video game, the stakes for real.

"You were always a slow learner. Don't know why I wasted time on you. Don't know why I'm still talking to you—"

"Let me finish the prick now." Enjou slammed the side of her fist down hard on Shoju's skull where his infant soft spot once resided.

"You will touch him when I order it!" Renku's venomous glare embraced Enjou, and his spit found Shoju's chin.

Shoju felt like a Shakespearean stage player, it was all so dramatic. This scene was a twisted version of the recurring nightmare he had had in college where he'd land on stage naked during a monologue. Today he had to improvise, no one had given him a script, and he didn't know his lines.

He tucked his fear deep into his belly. He needed all of his wits, and fear would most definitely be a liability.

He sensed Enjou recoil from Renku with hatred. *Atta girl,* thought Shoju, *keep that thought—just where I need you.* Maybe he could use their blind rage against them to help him escape. If his legs were working.

"Those don't belong to you either." Shoju pointed his chin at the altar. He needed to keep them engaged as he slowly worked on loosening the bonds on his wrists.

"Ah, allow me to educate you, you stupid monk!"

Renku was seized with a psychotic version of Tourette's, snapping in and out of Good Master, Evil Master with no apparent command of his brain, his words, his thoughts. He had written the script, but kept forgetting his lines.

Enjou let loose a frustrated, impatient exhalation onto Shoju's skull. Another loose cannon. He had to find a way to point them at each other.

"This is all mine now. It is written!" Renku swept the long sleeves of his robe out in front of him as if to wrap his arms around the icon-laden altar.

"Daigen Roshi is now impotent, all Roshis everywhere are in my power now. I alone know. I alone have tapped vein of true spiritual power. It is done!"

He pivoted back around to face his subjects, arms still extended, the sleeves of his robe draping down to his knees.

"Bravo! Imagine me clapping. If I weren't tied down I'd give you a standing ovation." Shoju began to chuckle quietly, as if he were alone and tickled by some funny thought. Slowly the chuckle turned to laughter, then a belly roar. The kind of laughter that quickly becomes contagious—you don't even have to know the joke. He kept at it until Renku's tentative smile turned into a snarl.

"Enough!" Renku nodded to Enjou. She reached around and smacked Shoju's stomach with a club. The blow set loose his fear. So be it.

"Not so hard! We don't want to deal with his corpse here," Renku said.

"You can't see it, can you?" Shoju asked.

"Don't be so cryptic—"

"You will never be master of anything. Your delusion ..."

Renku glared through slits in his face, his arms behind him now, hands resting on the altar, shoulders hunched, ready to pounce.

"That altar behind you? Filled with all the religious objects you stole that do not belong to you? Icons that are only of sentimental value to their rightful owners? ... It has no power. You have no power!"

"Enough!" Renku sprang off the altar toward Shoju while Enjou grabbed his chin and brought the club to his neck.

"Let me finish." Shoju choked out his words. "At least a last word. Gempo Roshi would expect nothing less from you."

Renku relaxed his shoulders and motioned for Enjou to stand down. As she released her grip she whispered "Wimp" loud enough for Shoju but not Renku to hear.

"If you have the power you claim, my words will have none. Words, words, just words!" Shoju's lines were now clear in his mind.

Shoju worked at his wrist ties as he spoke. They were looser now. He needed at least five more minutes—a very long monologue in his condition. A performance for his life.

23

"You got a warrant?" Dick Pride, owner of DP's Limo Service, was practically crying. "Can't give you a customer's privates without that, c'mon you guys, you know this."

"We don't give a shit what else you got going on here, Dick, and I bet you don't want us back here with a warrant." Kate smelled something shady, something not quite kosher with Dick's operation. "Alls we want is a name—phone and address if you got it—and the driver. That you can give us. Else we'll come back and make your life miserable. You know we can do it."

Dick mopped the sweat off his face with a red bandanna that looked as if it hadn't been washed since the 70s.

"Tell you what," Kate continued, "you give us the driver assigned to this job we're talking about, we'll ask him about your precious paying customer, leave you off the hook."

Dick had a little shock and awe in his eyes that Kate was being so nice. Relief swept over him like a freight train.

He wrote down an address and number, slid it across the counter. "Here. Maurice might know from the guy he drove around who was footing the bill, alls I got is a credit card and general location anyways, guy's up near Abiquiu someplace, s'all I can tell you. This way you get what you need, and if my customer asks, I gave you nothing. I gotta protect my business. Word gets out I'm giving names, I'm done for."

Kate waved the slip of paper in his face, nice cop gone. "And if Maurice doesn't give us what we need, we won't be so nice next time we gotta come back here. So maybe you better get Maurice on the phone, explain it to him."

It took Kate and Skip an hour to get to Frank, who'd filled in for Maurice to pick up Jerry, something about another gig, they didn't need details, just Jerry's driver.

"What the fuck?" Skip said when Frank finally came to the door. "You deaf or something? We been banging and ringing here for ten minutes, at least."

"Yeah, well, I sleep deep. Who the hell are you? And why'd the fuck you wake me?"

Kate flashed her badge, the bulge under her jacket obvious to anyone paying attention. "Okay if we come in? We got questions about a passenger you picked up couple days ago down in Albuquerque."

Frank held open the door and with a sweep of his arm invited them in.

The room they stepped into had a look and smell about it that was at odds with the gruff, disheveled Frank. Neat and pristine with whimsical flourishes about, leopard throw pillows on the couch and porcelain cat objects on most flat surfaces, it smelled softly of roses and lavender, not an unpleasant atmosphere.

"Your wife here?" Kate asked.

Frank's shoulders clenched up till he realized they weren't here for her. "She's in the shower, getting ready for work. Can we make this quick?"

"Sure thing. Mind if we sit down?"

"Hey, do you mind?" Frank winced as he looked at their shoes treading across the white carpet. "Wanda will have a fit. Did you not see the sign?" He pointed at a framed sign hanging in the entryway. PLEASE BE AN ANGEL AND REMOVE YOUR SHOES, with elegant cursive writing, and pictures of winged creatures. "Shit." Frank followed them in and sat across from them. "Will this be quick? I really don't want Wanda to see those." He pointed at their feet.

They ignored him, crossed their arms and relaxed into the sofa.

"Okay okay … what passenger you want to know about?"

They told him.

"I dropped that guy off in Fiesta Park, said his car was there. Weird someone even hired us, could have easily taken a cab, woulda been cheaper. Alls I know is that dude I picked up wasn't paying the tab."

"Any idea who was?" Kate asked. "Your boss says someone up near Abiquiu arranged and paid for the ride."

"Haven't a clue. I just go where I'm told, don't get involved in the money side though sometimes I can get a little extra, some of the more generous patrons. Just did a favor for Maurice that day's all. B'sides, guy I picked up prob'ly didn't have enough dough for gas, so wasn't 'bout to tip a dime. And he wouldn't shut up."

"What'd he say?"

"Thought I had the wrong guy first off. Didn't know why he was being chauffeured around. Didn't want to go to no address I had for him, wanted to pick up his car and check it out on his own. Kept asking who the hell was paying, was I sure I got it right, what was at the address I gave him. Said he didn't know anyone with enough money to rent a limo, didn't know too many people in the state. Asked how easy it was to get a gun 'round here."

"What'd you tell him?"

"Nada. Said I couldn't help. He was so nervous I thought he was cranked up on some drug. Was happy to drop him off, get him outta my backseat."

"You have any idea who his benefactor was?"

"His what?"

"Guy who paid the tab?"

"Nope. Like I said—"

"Your passenger say anything else of interest?"

"Like what?"

"Like who he knew here, where he was staying, why he needed a gun."

"He babbled an awful lot. I wasn't really listening, 'cept couldn't help but hear some of it, him leaning forward through the glass and all. Something about an ex-wife, a girlfriend ... guy just sounded crazy."

"You remember anything he said about the girlfriend?" Skip asked.

"Something about her maybe being dead, which he didn't believe. Went on and on about her gallery in Santa Fe, how they knew each other forever, how she had to be alive. I tuned out after a while. Sounded to me like he got jilted, had his heart broke. I know the signs, see it all the time, my line of work."

"You remember that address you gave him?" Kate asked.

"Someplace near Central Avenue I think, not sure exactly. Ask Dick at the office, he'll have it. Came in with the rez I bet, pickup and drop-off locations."

They were getting nowhere fast. And if Frank recollected accurately, Jerry wasn't Cissie's killer.

"You get many customers up near Abiquiu?"

"Couple, not too many."

"Anyone make an impression?"

"Like what?"

"You know, like something not quite kosher, like someone who might've paid the tab on this guy we're talking 'bout?"

"Not so's I remember. But I'll think on it, let you know."

Kate handed him her card. "Call me right away you think of anything, even if it seems far-fetched. Anything that nags at you more than once, you give a call."

"Sure thing."

***

Alex was driving up Hyde Park Road wishing she were alone, hating herself for that thought. Guy was in the passenger seat. It felt like he was atop all of her nerve endings. *What is wrong with me?* Since his arrival less than a week ago he'd been telling her—ad nauseam telling her—how lovely she looked, reaching out and touching her, taking her hand, or stroking her cheek or simply touching her arm. It felt like constantly. To the point where the Greta Garbo syndrome clicked in and she wanted to scream. She wanted to be alone. She needed more space. Muin would tell her to face into this feeling, this fear, not run away from it. She glanced over at Guy, who was peacefully staring at the scenery and paying no attention to her. She heard Muin's and Kido's voices in her head: *Just be in the moment and enjoy.*

The mountain they were climbing reminded her of home even though it looked nothing like the Catskills where perched her home monastery. A pang of homesickness caught in her throat only long enough for her to take notice. Zen Mountain Monastery, the one they were on their way to visit, would probably look nothing like the one back home, the one she knew so well. But the terrain, the stillness, the whispering tall trees, the ever-thinning oxygen, and the dense beauty wrapped itself around her lungs and sent a comforting breath to her belly.

Mountain terrain felt like a more suitable container for training monks and sitting zazen than a desert. She knew she wasn't the first to awaken to this idea as most monasteries in Japan and elsewhere were planted high up among tall trees. The clear, cool air was an aid to breathing deeply and sweeping clear the mind, as she herself had sometimes experienced back home. If the mountain Roshi they found at the end of this road was less weird than the desert Roshi, maybe when all this gong, murder and mystery business was over, she, and maybe Guy, could come up here for a retreat. But she would have to convince Guy it wasn't a cult and he didn't have to believe in any religious mumbo-jumbo to reap benefits.

I can't afford to get sidetracked now. They first had to interview the monks they were heading toward to see if the purported thief of the Desert Monastery's ancient gong resided amongst them. They hadn't called ahead.

Sloping rooftops, brown wood and stone encased the inner space of the structure that greeted them as they drove up the dirt and rocky driveway. Though she hadn't been to Japan yet, it was on her bucket list—*damn, I hate that term.* This place, two hours from Santa Fe, could have been on a Japanese mountaintop. *I wonder how many similar structures are scattered across the planet. Wouldn't it be great to visit them all?*

Two resident monks with warmth and graciousness greeted them at the door. A stunning and stark contrast to the reception she received at Desert Monastery. Here, there was no interrogation about what they were doing there and why they wanted to see the

Roshi, they were simply asked to wait till they could check on his whereabouts and schedule.

Ten minutes later, Daigen Roshi, the slight and frail Japanese abbot, received them in his tearoom with his head monk and translator, Tendo, by his side. Roshi's eyes twinkled with an inner joyfulness that Alex had only ever witnessed in Kido, her first monk. Like him, Daigen seemed a real monk. But then her cop brain warned her not to be taken in so quickly. She collected herself while the tea was being prepared and doled out in silence. Her Zen manners battled with her cop's modus of getting straight to the point.

"My English not so good. Please allow Tendo translate Japanese. I understand you." Daigen Roshi sat back and smiled at them to say what they had come to say.

Alex did the talking. "We've heard that an ancient gong is missing from Renku Roshi's Desert Monastery and that you might know something about it."

Daigen Roshi smiled and nodded.

"Do you have it?"

"No, but we will have it soon," Tendo said.

"Sorry? Does the gong in question not belong to Renku Roshi?"

Daigen Roshi closed his eyes, a broad smile lit up his face and he laughed deeply, as if Alex had just said something hilarious.

"Please let us in on the joke." *What the hell is so goddamn funny?*

While Daigen Roshi was speaking Japanese, Alex's brain was twitching. Two people dead and here she was sitting on top of a mountain talking to a Japanese monk about a gong. Her mind had lost all sense of why the hell they were there. It was as if she had a sentence to finish and had forgotten the beginning of it.

Tendo translated the story of the gong.

"This gong you are asking about was once Buddha's—or at least that is the lore attached to it. Because it was once in Buddha's hands, or so the story goes—there are accounts of other relics out there in the world with similar legendary tales attached to them—it is said to hold special spiritual power and whoever has it in their possession is gifted with this power.

"For centuries now there has been friendly squabbling between various lineages about the rightful ownership of this gong. It has moved from one monastery to another, from one country to another for many, many years. In the past fifty years or so, a game of sorts has begun whereby monks from one monastery steal or borrow it from another and so on. Whoever is in possession of it is said to be spiritually superior.

"No one takes it too seriously. It is just a friendly game. Something to keep the monks occupied."

"A game? Spiritual power?" Alex asked.

"Yes, rather silly, don't you think? Grown men and all? And monks no less ..." Tendo was now speaking for himself.

"I never underestimate the silliness of men," Alex said. "Has the competition for it ever turned deadly?"

"Oh, my, no. Ha ha ha!" Roshi said. "Simple entertainment."

"And you don't have it now?"

"No, we don't, but we're close to knowing its whereabouts," Tendo said.

"How many monasteries compete in this so-called game?"

"Hundreds I would say. Too many to count. We are especially happy now that it is rumored to be in the area. It feels like it's our time to take possession and the monks here are quite excited about it," Tendo said.

"Do you ever hire private investigators to track down this gong?"

"We never do, no. But there are some who resort to such tactics. We think of it as cheating and it is not condoned by true masters."

Alex's gut told her that she was sitting in the presence of a true master in Daigen Roshi. She'd never felt that with Renku down in the desert. She wanted to ask Daigen Roshi what he thought of Renku, but knew his Zen manners would have him say nothing ill of a fellow Roshi. But she could beat around that bush to see what flew out.

"Did you know Renku Roshi in Japan?" Alex asked Daigen Roshi.

"Was small group of monks in temples when we were young. We had not same teacher so paths rarely crossed, but we meet few times," Roshi said.

"How did you both happen to end up in New Mexico?"

"I quote one of your musical poets, Bob Dylan. I think was 'simple twist of fate' that we both like here."

"And do you see each other much now that you're both in America?"

"No, just few times. Each very busy, no time to visit." Daigen Roshi paused and stroked his chin. "You not Renku Roshi's student?"

"No, no. Actually, my teacher is back east at Nekoji Monastery, in New York. Setsu Roshi. He, too, is from your country."

"Ah so desu ka? Wonderful! He my true dharma brother."

Alex looked over at Guy and smiled. "Now I know why I liked this guy so much."

They spent the next half hour chatting, Daigen Roshi telling some funny stories about when he and Setsu were mere monks in

Japan. All talk of Renku Roshi, Buddha's gong and monks' weird games over and done.

When they were all bowing to each other and saying goodbye, Daigen Roshi gave Alex a big bear hug.

"Please give my brother Setsu a big hug from Daigen when you return home," Roshi said. "And come back to visit us anytime. Maybe next time we will have the famous gong. Ha ha ha." He winked at Alex, threw back his head and laughed. Then he walked down the hall with Tendo in his wake.

24

"You mind driving?" Alex dangled the keys out in front of Guy as they walked to the car.

"Love to." Guy wrapped his hand around the keys, his arm around Alex and kissed the side of her head. "Thought you'd never ask."

"I'm whooped. And much as it was pleasant enough meeting Daigen Roshi, this whole visit"—she glanced over her shoulder at the monastery—"feels like a wild gong chase."

Alex and Guy headed down the mountain no wiser. Until Alex finally got cell service and Muin on the line.

"I know about that silly gong game," Muin said. "Always seemed so infantile. Setsu Roshi never cared much for the whole idea, said some monks were trying to take shortcuts to enlightenment."

"Have you ever talked to Shoju about it?" Alex asked.

"No, not directly, but now that you bring it up, the whole business about the missing gong was strange. I had a feeling he wasn't being straight with me."

"What about those photos of his room I sent you? Anything strike you as out of place or missing?"

"Like you said, the empty frame was odd. Only thing I could think of that wasn't in your photos was his warrior garb, those yellow pants you told me about."

"Shit, you're right! How'd I miss that?"

"Well, it's not something you'd find in most monks' rooms."

"Guess my brain's not back to normal, damn it."

"You gotta relax, Alex. Take a vacation why don't you?"

"Ha! If only ..."

"What'd you think of Daigen Roshi?"

"Seems like the real thing, though I'm not inclined to trust my gut lately."

"He's the real thing all right. Much like Setsu Roshi, *our* Roshi," Muin said.

"Good to know. Daigen Roshi's affinity for our Roshi was clear, but he didn't seem to have much regard for Renku. Wouldn't say so directly though."

"I've done a little research since we last spoke and there's something that just doesn't add up about him," Muin said.

"About who? Renku Roshi?"

"Yeah. Thing is, I'm not sure he's even a Roshi."

"Damn." Alex closed her eyes, slammed her head into the seatback and exhaled loudly.

"You said it ... I can't find any evidence of his teacher, of dharma transmission, of any ceremony whatsoever that ever took place giving him the title of Roshi. He just sort of appeared on the scene about twenty years ago as if out of vapor."

"That could explain his obsession with this gong thing." Alex sat up and stretched her back. "Isn't possession of this damn gong supposed to impart spiritual superiority or some such nonsense?"

"Yeah, according to legend, but everybody knows that's apocryphal."

"Maybe not to an illegitimate Roshi. He could be grasping at anything to give him some credibility. Or maybe he's simply delusional or just plain eccentric."

"There is definitely something off about him."

"I just hope whatever it is he hasn't crossed over into criminal territory. If so, he could be the one responsible for Shoju's disappearance and Cissie's death—she did know him."

"Now let's not get carried away, Alex. He might not be a real master of Zen, but why would a cold-blooded killer pretend to be a monk for twenty years and then start killing people? I think he's just got a big ego."

"Maybe you're right. He is weird for sure and I didn't get the killer vibe from him ... but there is a mean streak and maybe something else that he hides under those robes, and it ain't just his manhood. I can't suss out what it is yet and I have no desire to spend more time with him to do that. I'm not sure I even care to know anymore."

"Maybe the two real Roshis, Daigen and Setsu, never called him on his masquerade because he's not harming anyone, really, and all those lineage rules are so ancient and antiquated," Muin said. "Maybe they thought it time to let go a little, let someone like Renku have some students if he could get them, teach the dharma, shave his head and wear robes. What's the harm really?"

"Yeah, and he probably gets lots of respect and special treatment at airports." Alex's voice relaxed.

"That is one advantage of being a monk." Muin laughed.

Alex and Muin chatted a little more and by the time she and Guy reached the bottom of the mountain she was feeling much better and more open to having Guy by her side.

***

"What the hell have you got in there that needs such safeguarding?" Kate was behind Skip at his front door as he turned lock after lock. "Looks like a pretty safe hood to me."

"Yeah, well ..." Skip shrugged. "Last one."

Kate was spent down to her toes. She hated the heat of the sun on her back, the stillness around her, the paranoia all those locks signaled. A longing for the streets of New York crept up her spine and lodged in her throat.

Once inside, Kate stopped short and her hand flew to the gun strapped to her belt. "What the fuck is that doing here?" She nodded at the Oni demon painting hanging above the couch and glared at Skip.

"Jeez, relax. It's just an ugly demon, belongs to Cissie, was a gift from one of her customers. Take it easy."

"Take your shirt off." Kate pointed her gun at Skip.

"What the fuck!" Skip said.

"I mean it. I need to see your back."

"Wha—"

"Do it!"

"All right, all right, hold your horses." He raised his arms in surrender.

Skip pulled up his shirt and bared his back to Kate.

"Okay, now sit and tell me about that painting."

"Like I said, it belongs to Cissie, someone gave it to her."

"Who?"

"I have no idea. Why'd you want to see my back? What's going on with you?"

Kate relaxed, holstered her gun and told him about Tattoo Jack and the John Doe stiff with his newly tattooed back that looked almost exactly like the painting, and his possible link to the spate of church robberies she'd been working on.

"There's a connection here, I just know it ... Cissie, Sam, John Doe, that ugly thing." Kate shot her eyes over to Oni.

Skip's front doorbell pierced the quiet. "Fuck!" Kate jumped to her feet and drew her gun.

"Kate, relax. It's just the door. Probably Alex and Guy." Skip got up and walked to the door. "You really ought to take your captain's advice and get some rest."

"Fat chance of that till this is over."

"Yeah, well ... for me too ..."

Skip opened the door to Alex and Guy. Soon as they were settled, they all got to work sorting out what they knew, what they didn't and what came next.

Oni, majestically ugly with horns, fangs, red body and fierce growl, was the only piece of art left on Skip's living room wall by the time they were done hours later. He had become the centerpiece of what Alex dubbed the "Oni Case." Taped up all around him were photos, diagrams, notes and clues that the four of them had put together after a tiring day of interviewing and gathering information. The floor was littered with pizza boxes, soda bottles, coffee cups. Trained cops and investigators, they felt at home in the mess of their makeshift investigation space, surrounded by chaos and all the facts as they knew them on the wall. Alex's brain felt a tad more organized.

"First, we got this Oni demon," Alex said, "tattooed on monks, partially tattooed on Kate's John Doe. If the dead guy, our victim number one, was one of Renku Roshi's monks—tattoo makes that plausible—it's not likely Roshi killed him, can't see the motive in

killing one of his own monks. Maybe what the dead victim had in his
backpack was the gong? Maybe the gong game has turned deadly.
Maybe we gotta look at Daigen Roshi, the one up the mountain, a
little closer. I wonder how many other monasteries in the area are
hunting that gong? Maybe Kate's sacred object thefts are just a
distraction from the mother lode, the gong?"

"*If* the gong is for real," Guy said. "We don't even know if it
actually exists. Google and Wikipedia couldn't say for sure what
Buddha's gong looks like. Whole thing seems like a fairy tale."

"Right ... then we got victim number two ..."—Alex paused,
didn't want to say Sam's name out loud, didn't have to—"... working
the scene of a church robbery. Anyone think there's a connection to
John Doe?"

"Captain said the guard at a church over near Old Town, ID'ed
the tattooed stiff, so alls we know is they were both in a church,"
Kate said. "Too flimsy for me to take my bet off Jerry."

"And Jerry's the only connection to Cissie far as I can see ... if
she even knew him," Skip said. "Fuck, I don't know what to think.
Maybe she knew Jerry, she met Roshi once ... fuck." He couldn't
wrap his mind around Alex's report of the Cissie-with-Roshi
photograph.

"Okay, moving on to our suspects," Alex said.

"Jerry first." Kate was obsessed with finding him, this fact
written on none of the pages tacked to the wall, but etched in
everyone's mind and all over Kate's face.

"Couple things just don't add up for me," Alex said. "If all three
vics are connected, how the hell did Jerry know John Doe? Doesn't
make sense. And he had some sort of association with someone near
Abiquiu. So, Jerry might be involved somehow, but if he is he's not
acting alone. I say it's gotta be a monk from the desert monastery,

maybe even the Roshi himself. Or Shoju. Maybe we find one we find the other."

"Limo guy, Jerry's driver, didn't know who paid the tab on his ride, and didn't think Jerry knew either," Skip said.

"I don't buy it, that guy was hiding something," Kate said. "I think we need to pay him another visit."

"Okay then ... we got Jerry as suspect number one." Alex wrote his name on a blank page on the wall with a Sharpie. "What about the monks? Or Enjou, the nun? Seems like a badass to me and capable of murder." Alex raised her hands to ward off any comments. "I know, I know, you guys don't think a woman did any of it, but hear me out.

"One: Shoju hired Skip to find Enjou, to make sure she was far away in Japan and not returning any time soon. Why? The fact that he took trouble to hire an investigator tells me it's something more nefarious than a personality clash.

"Two: She's back. Why?

"Three: Her eyes were black, hard and mean. No nun I ever saw looked like that. But an awful lot of perps do.

"So ... I for one want to have a little tête-à-tête with her." She wrote Enjou's name under Jerry's.

"Good idea," Guy said. "Who's next on the suspect list? Shoju?"

"Yup." Alex added his name to the list. "His manners leave something to be desired, and I don't see him as a killer ... but ... for now I say he stays up there. If he's been on retreat and returns tomorrow as expected, I think we can probably eliminate him.

"But if he doesn't show up at the monastery, he's either out playing warrior in search of the elusive gong, or out being a soldier using real guns and bullets in a war we don't have a name for yet. Whichever, it'll be easy enough to determine what sort of monk he is tomorrow."

"And if he doesn't show up in the flesh tomorrow, he could end up being victim number four instead of suspect number three." Guy said. "Let's not forget that Roshi has his phone, which Muin said was not monk protocol."

Alex turned her back to jot a note on the wall about Shoju's phone. They'd forgotten that detail, *damn it.*

She spun back around. "Last but not least, we got the two Roshis."

"Give us your Zen take on them," Guy said. All three stared at Alex and waited.

"Okay, Mountain Roshi first: I didn't detect any weirdness there except for the gong game. Could be boys being boys, a mere diversion from a monk's life. Plus, Muin vouches for him, and if I trust anyone other than the three of you right now, it's Muin.

"Only thing that doesn't add up is that Skip's search for the gong led him directly to Daigen and his monks, but he denied having it. So there's that. But I don't see how this links to any of the homicides. Yet.

"Then there's Desert Roshi: This is where it all gets weird for me. Let me count the ways." Alex ticked them off with her fingers. "One: I know Skip doesn't believe it, and I doubt my own recollecting skills these days, but I'm ninety-nine percent sure I saw a photo of Cissie with Renku Roshi.

"Two: The scolding he gave to Enjou was much more than a teacher chiding his student—there was something sinister in his tone.

"Three: The room locked down like a vault … this just ain't something a legit monastery would have, especially one way out in the middle of nowhere. A city temple with precious art, maybe, but not one so inaccessible. It doesn't make sense.

"Four: Hiring Skip to find the gong. Even if Roshi were only participating in the game, hiring a private investigator goes against the rules and for that alone we know he isn't completely honest.

"Five: The tattoos. And the warrior shit. I don't know, does that make six? Doesn't matter, it's now too many to chalk up to coincidence ...

"Not to mention having Shoju's phone, his lack of hospitality, wanting me and Guy to get the hell out of there and never come back, and the first time I met him there was something creepy about him. I got the sense that his relationships with women have always been twisted, if not kinky. And Muin couldn't find any evidence that he's an authentic master, as he claims. And much as I hate to see another, quote, spiritual place, not being so spiritual, everything seems to be leading to Renku Roshi and his desert monastery."

"I agree," Guy said. "Kate? Skip?"

A shrug and a nod had them maybe not on the same page, but not disagreeing. Kate was still convinced Jerry had killed Sam. And Skip had no theories at all about Cissie. Grief had carved a few more lines in his forehead this week.

"Shoju should be coming out of his retreat tomorrow," Alex said. "I say Kate and I pay one more visit to the desert, see if he or Roshi can explain some of this before we call in the big guns. Even though she's not officially on the case, Kate can make him think that she is, and she can question Renku Roshi about John Doe while I talk to Shoju.

"Guy, Skip, want to come with? Want to track down Jerry? What you want to do?"

While they were thinking about that, Alex stretched out on the floor. "God, I'm tired," she moaned.

"I'm not ready to be fired by Roshi if he's on the up and up," Skip said. "Chasing after mythical gongs and putting up with a little

Zen weirdness is worth it for what he's paying me. I'll see what I can
dig up on Jerry, find out where he's hiding."

"I'll keep Skip company, s'all the same to you," Guy said. "I'd
also like to chat with a couple of tattoo joints, see where that leads.
Maybe Tattoo Jack has a few secrets that he didn't share in his first
interview." He knelt down next to Alex and began to massage her
shoulders and head.

"That okay with you?" he whispered into her ear.

"Mmmmm." She melted into his touch.

Skip dragged a metal box out from under the couch, unlocked it
and flipped it open. "You guys need any more heat to carry, help
yourself to one or more of my little friends here. All licensed and
ready to go."

"Oooohhh ... I love you." Alex sat up and ogled the cache of
weapons. "I'll take this little baby for my ankle carry. Just like my
Hellcat at home."

"I'm good," Kate said.

"This nine-mill'll do me just fine," Guy said. "And just for the
hell of it, I'll strap this snub nose to my leg. Weird to think we're
dealing with monks and loading up like we're about to bust a gang of
dope smugglers or worse. Let's hope there's no one gonna shoot at
us so's we gotta use these."

Skip went to get their sleeping arrangements sorted. There
were a few hours left before sunrise for a little shut-eye.

25

Shoju was wasting his breath and he knew it. Trying to talk sense to Renku Roshi and his demonic acolyte was like telling a two-pack-a-day smoker that inhaling carcinogens would kill. If only he could get Roshi alone ... the truth trailing right behind that was that it would never happen. It was his own delusion telling him that he could get through to his teacher and tap into the bond they once had, reopen the communication they had built up over the years.

"Any chance I could have a private meeting with you? For old times' sake?" He looked only at Renku Roshi. "One last session to finish our student-teacher bond or whatever the fuck I was crazy enough to think we had?" His wrist bonds were loose now. There was hope in that. He wasn't sure about his legs.

Renku Roshi took a breath as if considering it.

"Don't even think about it," Enjou hissed. "You do, I'm gone for good this time."

No one moved. It was now or never. Roshi wouldn't let her go. Shoju had to act. They weren't expecting it. He threw a fist at Enjou, made contact with her left eye. Startled, she dropped the club. He rolled over on his side, reached down for it. She swiftly kicked his arm with her heel, but not fast enough, the club now in his grasp. He swung it wildly over his head behind him connecting with air, she now out of reach. His legs were limp and still tethered. He sat up, his warrior trained upper body still strong.

He twisted his body awkwardly so he could train an eye on both of them. Enjou stood on a chair to take down an ancient samurai sword from the wall.

"Don't touch that!"

"But Roshi, he has the kanabo. We need to defend ourselves."

"Leave it! A sohei warrior with a kanabo no longer invincible. With all this"—he smiled and gestured to the altar— "no one surpass my power. He is nothing. He cannot even stand up. Why you afraid of him?"

Enjou's eye puffed up and began to turn purple. Furious, she stepped off the chair, empty-handed, and stood rigid at the door.

While Shoju had the advantage he worked to untie his legs, still not sure if they would work. They were caked with blood.

"Roshi, do something," Enjou growled.

"Shoju, shame on you. I thought you were a smart one. Can you not see? Can you not just give up? You cannot compete with my power. It is over. Why make difficult for us? Hand me club. NOW!" He reached out his hand, palm up, toward Shoju, who was now free and shaking out his legs. He swung them over the edge of the table. Some of the wounds opened up and started to bleed.

"I am going to walk out of here and neither of you will stop me."

Roshi moved closer. "Give me that thing. You go nowhere."

Shoju swung, made contact with Roshi's hand. Roshi screamed out in pain, fell back against the altar. Enjou rushed to him. "Oh my god, you're hurt." Turning her head to Shoju she spat: "You bastard!"

Shoju gingerly slipped off the table onto the floor. His legs crumbled under him. He sat up and scooted himself toward the door, the pain like fireworks in his legs, up his spine into his brain. The club could help him walk but then he'd have no defense. He pulled himself up off the floor to unlock the door. The two lovebirds were distracted for the moment, cooing over the broken hand.

The sharp unlocking sound snapped Enjou to attention. She pounced at Shoju like an uncaged animal, toppled him back to the floor, grabbed the club and swiped it right at his sweet spot with all of her hundred and twenty wiry pounds. It found its target and rendered him immobile. The duo then turned back to licking their wounds.

***

"Awfully quiet out here," Kate said as she and Alex walked from the car to the monastery entrance.

"Why they chose this spot, I s'pose. Conducive to meditating," Alex said.

"Yeah, but not one living soul around? I don't like it. Where the hell are they all?"

"Was like this the first time I was here. Maybe they're all playing warrior over there." She cocked her head toward the butte.

"Alls we need is Roshi, best to get him alone anyways."

No one met them at the entrance. There were no signs of life anywhere. Not many shoes were left in the foyer, evidence that Alex was right about everyone out playing games.

"No way I'm taking off my shoes," Kate said. "And you shouldn't either."

"Not sure I could walk inside with them on, I'm so used to being barefoot inside temples and monasteries."

"Yeah, well, do what you want, but I'm keeping mine on. I'm a cop not a Zen student and right now so are you."

"S'pose you're right, but it sure feels wrong," Alex said.

They kept their shoes on.

First person they saw was Enjou outside the closed door of the tearoom.

"What're you doing here?"

"Hello to you too, Enjou," Alex said. "We need to see Roshi."

"He can't see you now." Enjou, arms folded, rooted herself in place. "And take your shoes off, have some respect."

She's like a pit bull in greyhound clothing.

"That's quite a shiner you got there. Did you run into someone's fist?" Kate asked.

Enjou stood mute and stolid, as if she'd had lessons from the sentries guarding Buckingham Palace.

Kate flashed her badge. "Look, we've got official police business. We'll wait while you tell him."

"I said he can't be disturbed right now. It'll have to wait."

"Think so, huh?" Kate reached around behind Enjou to open the door. Enjou body-blocked her.

"You don't step outta the way, this could get ugly," Kate said.

"Maybe I can help. How about we try that first? I can't help, I'll get Roshi."

Kate stepped back, relaxed her gun hand. "Only cuz I'm feeling generous today. You know this guy? He one of Roshi's monks?" Kate showed her the photo of John Doe.

Enjou barely looked. "Nope. What's wrong with him?"

"He's dead, that's what. Take another look."

"Well ... that's no business of ours. You can ask Roshi later."

"He's dead, it's not your business? Where's all the compassion you Buddhists are famous for?"

"I'm sorry someone's dead." Enjou put her palms together as if she cared.

"Okay, I'll tell you what, since I'm still feeling generous, you go tell your precious boss we're here to see him. Detective Sullivan and I will take a little stroll around—I've never been to a genuine Buddhist monastery before, love to see what all the fuss is about—and we'll meet back here in say fifteen minutes. Seeing as how you're so broke up about this dead guy, who is you'll no doubt discover, one of Roshi's monks, we'll have a little wake for him right here with Roshi and you and anyone else you wanna invite. Burn a little incense, say some mumbo jumbo, whatever you do for the recently deceased. And then I get to ask the questions and you and Roshi get to answer them."

"I'll inform Roshi."

"Good girl," Kate said.

Enjou squinted out a few hate darts and stared through their backs as they walked down the hall. Alex felt the hot glare on the back of her neck, turned and asked: "What about Shoju? He back yet?"

"Not yet."

Alex turned back around and fell into step with Kate and held onto her arm. The sudden pivot had her head spinning. "There's something seriously wrong with that girl," she whispered.

"If she is a girl. Now I get what you mean about her. Creepy and definitely capable of cold-blooded murder. The way she shrugged off the corpse? Being a nun and all? Something's not right about that."

"Yeah. Let's go check with Andy in the office, maybe he'll know something."

"Let's not go too far afield, I don't want those two getting any bright ideas about eloping or hightailing it outta here."

"Ah, Kate, I've really missed you." Alex squeezed Kate's arm and laid her head on her shoulder, just like two teenage girls walking down a school corridor.

***

Alex gave Kate a quick tour of the monastery: The dining hall, dharma hall and zendo. She insisted they remove their shoes at the zendo entrance. Walking through the halls was one thing, but the Zen in Alex just couldn't abide hard heels in the zendo. Kate complied though she wasn't too happy about it. They ended up at the front office where Andy was holding down the fort.

"Hey, Andy, how you doing?" Alex said.

"I'm okay, you?"

"Not too bad. Andy, meet Kate. Kate, Andy." They shook hands.

"We're here to meet with Roshi but he's not quite ready to see us yet. You got a minute?"

"Sure, time's all I got here," Andy said.

"You recognize this guy?" Alex held out John Doe's photo.

"I've never seen him before. Is he a monk?"

"We're not sure, we were hoping you could tell us."

"I ain't been here long, so you oughta be asking someone else. Doesn't look too healthy that guy."

"Yeah, he's seen better days. He's all out of breath," Kate said.

"He's dead?"

"'Fraid so. Any monk you know been missing for a couple of weeks?" Alex asked.

"Like I said, I only just got here."

"Right. So maybe you never seen him up close, maybe you know a room that's got stuff in it that no one's sleeping in."

"Come to think of it, Marco's room's still got personal stuff, but I've never seen him. And there's no space in the zendo with his name on it."

"That normal practice here?"

"Don't know about that. Never got a clear answer when I asked. Told it wasn't my concern. I trusted they had reasons."

"Which room is Marco's?"

"Right next to mine, why I even know about it. It's in Dogen Hall, Two-B. That building there." He pointed out the window to the second building out.

"Was Marco a monk?"

"Don't think so, Dogen Hall is mostly just students like me. Monks live over there in Rinzai Manor."

"Any chance you got a picture of Marco in that computer there? If this place is anything like my zendo back home, there's gotta be snapshots galore—all the sesshins, celebrations, birthdays, stuff like that."

"Dunno. I s'pose."

"Think you could find a couple of group shots and send them to my phone?" Alex handed him a card.

Andy took it and shrugged.

"That'd be great. And if Enjou comes looking for us—we got an appointment to see Roshi—you text me on that number, okay? And don't let Enjou know where we're at."

"Awww man ..."

"Didn't tell you last time we met, wasn't important then, but we're cops ... just need to have a look around Marco's room for a couple of minutes."

"Sheesh, don't you need a warrant or something to do that?"

"Don't you worry, we got what we need. We'll clear it all with Roshi."

"Jeez, I don't want to get in trouble with Enjou, ya know? She effing hits people. Does it with a stick that feels good when you're sitting, but outside the meditation hall she uses it as punishment. It's scary. She's like a mean girl squared."

"I'll stay here with you," Kate said. "That way we can face Enjou together. She gets outta hand I'll handle it." She patted her gun. "We'll say Alex is in the bathroom and no one will be the wiser. Okay?"

"This is all too weird," Andy said. "Don't think I like it here anymore."

"Can't say as I blame you," Kate said. "Tell me something ..."

Alex left them and slipped soundlessly out the back door to Dogen Hall.

***

Executing her turning ritual inside Marco's room made her dizzy. Which pissed her off, but that felt better than worry. Made her think she was on her way back to normal. And in her gut she knew this room belonged to the dead man in Kate's photo.

First glance, all appeared normal, except the one table in the room held only an incense burner, an empty vase and a water bowl. Dust pattern indicated there'd been two small icons there once upon a time, probably a Buddha, maybe a Quan Yin, or some other Buddhist saint. *Maybe Marco had left for good and only taken his valuables?*

Ten minutes later Alex stepped out into the darkened hall of the residence with two pieces of paper—the only things Marco, or someone else, had left behind that might have some value as clues. A wadded, discarded piece of paper with a phone number. And a beautifully written scroll that had been tucked between futon and wall. It had a colorful, detailed drawing of the Oni Demon with five vows in calligraphy.

Vows of the sohei warrior

1. Be Prepared

2. Be Obedient

3. Be Vigilant

4. Be AWAKE—Always

5. Trust no one outside the circle

If Marco had left the monastery and taken his personal treasures, this would surely not have been left behind. Her gut told her that someone else had pilfered the statues. Maybe the same person who had stolen his life. Looked like Marco hadn't been practicing his vows hard enough. Or, more likely, there was a killer within the trusted circle.

***

"We can't let them leave. You have to do something. You have to initiate the sohei plan." Enjou was caressing half her face with an ice pack.

"You not tell me what to do!" Renku ordered. "I decide when, where and how! We will visit with them, we will let them leave, we will begin plan once they are away from here."

"They have a picture of Marco. They will find out he was your student. They will return."

"We will be ready for them. Then ... not now ... not yet ... when I say it will be so!"

26

A half-hour later, Alex and Kate were sipping tea with Roshi, Enjou kneeling outside the door. As if this were a social call, a monk wasn't dead, and the two monks in the room didn't look like they'd just done battle.

"You" —Kate stared at Renku Roshi— "or one of your monks have to come to Albuquerque to identify Marco's body." She was sitting uncomfortably on two cushions on the floor feeling vulnerable without her boots, her ankle holster peeking out below her jeans.

Enjou had insisted that they both remove their shoes before stepping inside Roshi's room. "Least you can do is respect our custom here, bad enough you're even here announcing a murder," Enjou said.

"Murder? Who said anything about murder?"

Enjou hadn't bothered to respond to Kate's question.

"Just have the decency to take off your shoes."

Kate had enough of twisting herself into a pretzel. She stood up. "You don't mind if I move over to that couch do you? I'm not used to sitting on the floor. Don't want to be rude, but ..." She didn't wait for an answer. "You could ride back to town with us. We'll see that you're brought back here as soon as possible."

"That won't be necessary," Renku said. "I say it's him from picture. No need for anyone here to go all that way."

"That's not how it works. Someone will have to come. Paperwork involved et cetera. You do want his body?"

Roshi nodded and sipped his tea, his bandaged hand limp in his lap, eyes glazed over from painkillers. *Vicodin*, Alex guessed. *What the hell happened here?*

"Any idea when Shoju will be back?" Alex asked.

"Maybe today, maybe tomorrow."

"Or maybe never," Alex said.

"Or maybe never," Renku said softly.

Enjou coughed loudly, Roshi came to attention.

"Never? Really? You mean like Marco?"

"Ha ha." Roshi's laugh and smile seemed innocent and authentic, but neither cop was taken in. "No, of course, not what I meant. Sorry. Not so myself from injury and medication. Shoju be back soon. He good monk."

"And Marco ... was he a bad monk?"

"Marco not monk. He student only. Such a pity ... violence today ..." Renku shook his head. "Misguided young people ..."

"Enjou didn't recognize Marco. Can you explain that?"

"She gone for long time, he new student, she never meet him. Simple explanation."

"Tell us about the Oni tattoo," Kate said.

"How you know about that?"

"Detective Sullivan saw it on some of your monks last time she was here, and it's on Marco's back."

Roshi's tight jaw made it clear that he didn't like either reason. "Ah, so. Youthful enthusiasm is all. Reverence for tradition. Some monks like to reenact warrior practice, as you Americans do with your Civil War soldiers. Innocent diversion for rigorous life of monk."

"Any idea who might have killed Marco?" Alex asked.

"He troubled boy. Sure he not kill self?"

"We're sure. And what about the gong game that you and Daigen Roshi and others play? Is that another innocent diversion?"

"Ha ha. Yes, just that."

"When do you have time to be monks?"

"Ah, plenty of time. As Zen Master Dogen say: *Time is always being, all that is is time.*"

"Was Marco searching for the gong? Any chance a competitor could have killed him for it?" Kate asked.

Roshi closed his eyes as if in pain. Or thinking deeply. They waited.

"You smart detective, I think. That be possible. Sad, but maybe yes, that happen."

"You will have to come to Albuquerque, Roshi. We need to confirm that the body we have is Marco."

"Yes, I see now, yes. Tomorrow, we will come tomorrow. If that okay?"

Kate and Alex exchanged a glance. They agreed. "Fine," Kate said, "but no later than tomorrow."

"Good. I need rest now. As you see I hurt myself. Enjou will show you out."

Alex and Kate stood up, started to leave. "We can find our way, you take care of him," Alex said to Enjou.

Before Enjou had a chance to close the door, Alex held it open and popped her head back in: "Did Shoju have anything to do with your injury? Or with your black eye?"

They stared at her for a long *all-that-is-is-time* moment.

"Why you say that? No, we have accident is all." Renku's eyes were awake and harder now. "We not see Shoju since he go on retreat. We see you tomorrow."

Enjou shut the door before they could ask more.

On their way out they stopped off at the office to ask Andy one more question.

"I sent a couple of pictures to your phone," Andy said. "I found someone who looks like the picture you showed me. Must be Marco."

"Much obliged," Alex said.

"But our system is down again so you won't get them till you're back in range of a signal."

"S'okay. Roshi confirmed it's Marco," Alex said. "You know anything about the tattoo some of the students here have on their back?"

"Monks."

"Huh?"

"Monks, only monks have the tattoo."

"Hmmm. What would happen if a non-monk got one?"

"Dunno. Don't think Roshi would be too happy about it. But I really don't know. Like I said—"

"Right, you haven't been here long."

"Yeah, that."

***

"Okay if I drive?" Kate asked.

"Course." Alex tossed the Jeep's keys to Kate. "If you're sure."

"Not sure of anything right now, but I miss him so much my whole body aches. Maybe it'll help if I sit in his seat."

"I'll take over whenever you say the word."

They rode in silence till the monastery was lost in their rear view.

"Goddamn," Alex said. "I can't stand not having cell connection. 'Member the old days when we had to find a landline or pay phone to make contact with anyone? Shit. How'd we ever get anything done?" She stared at her phone, willing it to work.

"Yeah, easy adjustment that one ... shit, what the fuck is that coming up behind us?"

Alex turned to look. "Appears to be Roshi's black Hummer. Maybe he decided not to wait till tomorrow after all? Or maybe he has more to say to us, doesn't want us to leave just yet."

"Doubt that. I'm gonna move off the road here, let him pass. We'll follow him. Hold on ..."

They bounced over the rocky terrain, Alex holding onto her seat unable to fasten her seat belt. The front wheel hit a ditch, Alex flew out of her seat and hit her head on the side window before the Jeep came to an abrupt stop on its own.

"Shit. It stalled. This is why I always hated this hunk of metal." Kate hit the steering wheel with the heel of her hand. "Sam treated it like it was a person, called it temperamental ... goddamn. Maybe we should get a lift into town with the monks?"

"I don't think so. Let's find out what's up. Jeep'll start up again soon... happened to me last week. Just gotta be patient."

Alex braced herself for a rush of vertigo as she stepped out onto the dusty earth. Nothing. She let go of the car and moved forward ... still nothing. Maybe slamming her head against glass pushed her brain back to normal. Fact was, she felt clear-headed for the first time in weeks. The aha! moment followed: *Renku killed Marco as sure as I'm standing in a desert canyon miles from nowhere. Killed him for disobeying his rule that only monks are allowed the Oni tattoo. Maybe something else, too, but that was the kicker. Now we just have to prove it.*

They couldn't very well hide, so they stood away from the side of the road. They saw a frantic Andy at the wheel of the Hummer and waved him down.

"What's going on, Andy?" Alex asked. "Why have you got Roshi's car? Where're you going in such a hurry?"

"They're all nuts. I had to get outta there, only thing I could think of was to take this car, had no other way out. I gotta go, please, you should, too."

"Whoa, slow down. What the hell? We only just left a half-hour ago."

"Soon as you left Roshi called all the monks back from the arena, had everyone come to the zendo still dressed in their warrior outfits—that never happens, I was told it wasn't even allowed! Roshi said the sohei plan was in effect immediately and everyone reacted like a fire alarm had sounded and then scattered themselves like buckshot around the grounds. I didn't wait to see what it all meant, what was gonna happen. Took what I could from my room and got the hell outta there. Not sure how I got away with no one stopping me. They were all too focused on whatever the fuck they were doing to care about me."

"What's the sohei plan?" Kate asked.

"No fucking idea. Roshi looked possessed. Enjou by his side, mean as ever, like she was a queen or something ..."

"Was Shoju back?" Alex asked.

"Dunno, didn't see him. Look, I gotta go. You see anyone, you tell 'em the car'll be at the bus stop, okay?"

"Sure thing. Listen, do me a favor ..." Alex wrote Guy's number on the back of her card. "Soon as you get a signal, call this number, tell him what happened."

"You're not leaving?"

"Not yet. Think we'll go back, have a look around, see what's going on. You don't get an answer on that number I gave you, call the state police, tell them what you saw. ... Have them call that number ... Kate, lemme have one of your cards ... and give them this card, too. They'll know what to do."

***

Guy's FBI pals helped him and Skip find Jerry through the car he'd leased. He was getting ready to jump bail and hightail it out of town when they drove up. They cuffed him, threw him in the back seat and attached him to the door. It was good they stopped him from leaving town, but bad they had to put up with his whining and blabbering all morning. They weren't going to let him out of their sight till they knew the truth.

By noon they'd turned Jerry over to the cops, had a chat with Tattoo Jack, and another one with Frank the limo driver—who had a come-to-Jesus moment, by which he told them about his evening with Renku Roshi outside Cissie's gallery. A very productive morning. At the end of it they were tearing up Route 84 to get to Abiquiu Desert Monastery as fast as four wheels and flashing lights could get them there. No one was answering the phone, Alex and Kate were out of range, and the state police decided to do nothing till Guy and Skip arrived. Then Andy showed up and changed their mind.

By 2:00 they were all headed into Chama Canyon toward a cluster of monks playing at warrior games. They had no clue how real it all was.

27

It was just after noon by the time Alex and Kate approached the perimeter of the monastery grounds. The Jeep wouldn't start so they walked the three miles. Hotter than normal for that time of year, they arrived thirsty and hungry. And except for the weapons they were carrying and their years of experience chasing bad guys they were unprepared for the colony of warriors awaiting them.

About thirty soldier monks, barefoot and garbed in yellow pants, their backs naked but for the lurid Oni tattoo, had taken up position in a semicircular stance on the outskirts of the property, facing the only road in from the outside world. Behind them at every entrance to every building stood one or two warriors. The rest of the army walked back and forth and around the grounds. They each carried a metal-studded club. Some of them had guns strapped to their bodies. There was no sight of Renku, Enjou or Shoju.

Outnumbered and outmuscled, Kate and Alex decided to sit behind some sagebrush and wait for reinforcements.

"This is fucking unbelievable," Kate whispered. "Maybe they did kill Sam. All this time I was sure it was Jerry, but now I don't know."

"I should've known something was off the first time I saw these guys swinging their clubs," Alex said. "Even after what happened back east, I still can't get used to the idea of monks being monsters. Not to mention my head was messed up so I wasn't thinking straight.

"The first precept of a Buddhist is to be reverential with life, to not be violent or kill any living being. I expect anyone in a robe to follow that one, at the very least. I guess that's my Pollyanna attitude. Come to think of it, these guys commanded by Roshi have probably violated all ten precepts. There's one about not stealing, one about not deceiving, one about not giving in to anger. What the hell."

"We should go back to the Jeep, wait for backup there," Kate said. "Nothing we can do here and if our guys drive up like everything's hunky dory, like they're just dealing with a few crazy monks, someone's gonna get hurt ... or worse."

"You go. I'll stay here."

"Not a good idea."

"I'll be fine. If this gets outta hand I'll retreat back to the car. I promise. I just want to keep an eye on things, see what they're up to, so we can be prepared, know exactly what we're up against."

"Okay, fine, but don't do anything crazy. Really, I mean it. I already lost Sam, I can't lose you, too."

"Don't worry, now go."

***

A half hour later there was still no sign of Guy or any other friendly gun. Alex was hot one minute, cold the next. She had to pee, she was dying of thirst and her stomach was growling so loud she was afraid someone would hear it. It would be better if she walked in and asked for help with the Jeep. She could pretend that their military behavior was normal monk activity, part of the gong game nonsense. Better than being caught hiding in the bushes. Kate and Guy would be arriving soon anyway. She couldn't just sit there and do nothing.

Kido had often used that phrase years ago when he first taught her how to meditate. Just sit, do nothing. And his very favorite teaching was: Expect nothing. On that score she was aligned, after what she'd witnessed and what she'd learned about monks playing find-the-gong game, she had no expectations about what would come next. But she had to do something now.

Other than being hungry and thirsty Alex felt renewed, like her old self, her brain back to normal. Maybe an example of two negatives making a positive—one conk, messed up grey matter; two conks, back to normal brain function. And her intuitive gut was churning faster than ever and told her that Renku Roshi wasn't a real, ordained Roshi. That term was reserved for those who merit the title. She knew it would be confirmed at the end of all this, and that right now thinking of him as a Roshi would only interfere with lucidity and detachment. From now on she'd drop the Roshi honorific and refer to him only as Renku.

What her belly knew about him: He'd killed Marco, a student who'd defied him, and Cissie, for a reason not yet clear. Still a cloud around Sam's killer, she hoped it wasn't Jerry, but she couldn't come up with a reason the monks would have done it. And what about Shoju? If he wasn't dead yet he soon would be at the hand of Renku or Enjou, his malevolent mistress. She had to get to him, but to do so she had to get around her. There was no telling how long before her backup would be there and by then it would take forever to penetrate the wall of monks. *Damn it, they are not monks! I don't know what they are, but they aren't monks! I have to start thinking of them as gang members or worse. From the looks of them they'd kill me as soon as look at me if they thought I'd harm their precious leader. No spiritual monks here.*

She spotted Enjou in the courtyard talking to one of the men. There were no other women in sight—perhaps they were inside protecting Renku. Maybe Enjou was now in charge, maybe her cohorts weren't protecting Renku at all, maybe they were holding him prisoner. *Maybe that's what all the bruises were about.* Body language told her the monk wasn't down with whatever Enjou was saying. She had to get closer.

All the men were now at alert, paying attention to the Enjou/soldier exchange, whose voices were loud enough to reach Alex. But all she heard was the angry heat of it, none of the words. The distraction gave her the opportunity to skirt around the edges and make her way toward the main building. The men were consulting with each other in small groups, focused inward, moving slowly toward the center, toward the one talking to Enjou. They wanted to hear what was going on, they weren't watching out for intruders. They appeared menacing but confused about what they were supposed to do.

Desert brush offered cover for most of the way, but the last stretch to the side zendo door was a flat rock garden that would be noisy and leave her exposed. Kneeling behind a bush at the edge of this area, she had a closer view of Enjou and the monk. They were finishing up.

The monk's face was tense, angry, defiant, the white scar across his cheek in sharp contrast to his ruddy complexion. He was of an age to be grey if his skull hadn't been razored smooth. Enjou was a foot shorter and younger by half. That and her gender were probably enough to enrage him. The fact that she was doling out orders raised his shackles even more.

The men who'd been guarding the door she was eying had walked to the corner of the building to watch the hubbub in the courtyard, their backs now to her. Adrenaline pumped through her body. She crouched and scuttled across the wide-open rocky terrain praying to whatever deity was listening that no one would notice.

She reached the building, flattened herself against it and got control of her breath. The monks' backs hadn't moved. She palmed her Glock, slinked over to the door and cautiously pushed her way in.

***

Renku was now outside addressing his flock. "What do you think we've been doing here? This is it! We have it now, just as the old scriptures promised."

"Roshi, may I speak?" The monk who'd been quarreling with Enjou stepped forward. Two gun-strapped men hovered behind him. "Speak without consequence?" he asked as he peered over his shoulder at the bodyguards.

Roshi signaled to the two guns to stand down. They relaxed their grip on their rifles and stepped back a foot.

"Denshin, you know there is always consequence to our actions," Renku said.

"Yes, and I'm willing to accept the cosmic consequences of my words and actions, but there is no way to call back a bullet. Once it's released, it kills. We never agreed to guns," Denshin said.

Murmurs of assent rustled through the body of monks.

"They are temporary, impermanent, just as all things are. Until the world acknowledges my spiritual dominance we must demonstrate power. Bullets are a language they understand."

"The old texts never mentioned using such force to convince. We ought only be concerned with our own personal spiritual power."

"Ah so." Renku was still in good humor, but the cracks were beginning to appear. "There are some writings I saved for just this moment. Tonight we will meet and read together."

"What writings? There are no other writings."

"Enough!" Renku's two goons readied their weapons. "You are all trained to be warriors. Now is the time. If you cannot see that—"

"But we were not trained to kill!"

"Your kanabo is a killing weapon, you know that."

"Yes, but its purpose is to put us in touch with our killing instinct, our shadow self, our murderous impulses. As monks we learn to embrace the dark side and control it. Not give in to those impulses. It is wrong to kill."

"There is no right and wrong. There is no difference between dead and not dead. Have you learned nothing?" Renku's patience was wearing thin.

"You're crazy," Denshin said under his breath.

"What did you say?" Renku started to strut over to Denshin.

Denshin didn't back down. "Shoju said something was up with you, that you'd lost it. I didn't believe him. You're nuts ... and where the fuck is Shoju?

"Did you make him dead or not dead or whatever your delusion says not breathing is? Huh? Where's Shoju?"

"He's taken care of. As you will be." Renku stood three feet in front of Denshin now, Enjou just behind him on his left flank. The two gunmen hadn't budged. The other monks had formed a wide circle around the five of them.

Renku nodded to the guns. One of them drew a pistol from his waist, walked up behind Denshin and shot him in the head. He fell without ceremony. Everyone froze as the shock waved its way through the group.

Feet began to move, voices to rise up. Someone struck the bonsho bell. Its toll resounded through their hearts and quieted them once more as Roshi raised his kanabo high in the air.

"Be prepared!" He waited for the echoed response from his warriors. No one opened his mouth.

"Be obedient!" A few murmurs could be heard.

"Be vigilant!" Renku called out the third vow and punctuated it with his kanabo. More voices now in the choir, warrior training taking over their better sense.

"Be awake!" Renku added. "Now more than ever!"

"Trust no one ..."

Most of the men with him joined in the call-and-response ritual. "Trust no one."

"Outside ..."

"Outside ..."

"This circle!"

"This circle!"

Renku lowered his club. All was still and silent now. A coyote howled far off in the canyon. The sun beat down. The chill in the air wafted over their bare backs and into a few of their souls.

Renku walked back to the entrance, turned and spoke softly to his men.

"If any of you want to revoke your vows and leave us, please step forward. Now or never."

No one moved, they hardly breathed. There were a few more than ready but knew without a doubt that he'd never let them leave breathing. The hell with his proclamation that dead and not dead were the same—they knew otherwise and breathing was something they were still attached to.

"Good," Renku said. "Now, let's protect what we all worked so hard to get. What we deserve."

He punched the sky with his club. All the others followed suit.

"We will have service for Denshin tonight." He turned and walked inside.

Enjou waited till he was behind the closed door. She pointed to Denshin. "Prepare his body. Then resume your positions."

She swiveled around and disappeared through the heavy oak door.

28

Scrambling softly through the lifeless halls, Alex felt a twinge of guilt treading on monastery floors with shoes on. Meeting room, zendo, dharma hall—all rooms behind unlocked doors—void of monks and nuns. Even the kitchen was vacant, except for the steaming food atop the stove. The monks hadn't eaten their lunch yet. She was tempted to help herself to some sustenance but knew she couldn't risk it.

As she neared the courtyard side of the building she heard Renku and one of his monks exchanging angry words. The windows were too near the crowd to peek out so she just listened. An angry monk asked about Shoju, the ensuing gunshot jangled her nerves for a second, and the bonsho bell brought her cop's brain into sharper focus. The chorus of voices shouting out the vows softened behind her as she made her way to the tearoom to wait for Renku.

As soon as he returned and sat down she stepped out from behind the door and pointed her gun at his heart.

"If Enjou shows up you tell her you need time alone, make her go away or you'll both be dead by the time your thugs get here. Understood?"

A blink of his eyes told her he did. Any surprise at her presence was held stoically in check some place deep inside his brain. She couldn't help but admire his cool, and immediately realized it was his megalomania or psychopathy and not his Zen mastery that was operating.

A minute later Enjou darkened the doorway. "What now, Roshi?"

"I must prepare for tonight. Leave me now. Come back later."

"But—"

"Now! And close the door."

Enjou left in a huff, the noisy slamming of the door expressing her anger at being dismissed. All monastery etiquette was forsaken, replaced by some other rubric.

Alex kept her gun trained on Renku and sat down on the couch facing him.

"Now that it's just a matter of time, why don't you tell me about Marco and Cissie, what you hoped to gain with all this warrior shit?"

"Ah so, time ..."

"Don't give me any of that fake Zen Master bullshit. I happen to know a few masters and you're not even close to being in their ranks."

"You know nothing!" She'd touched a nerve.

"Then enlighten me, please. We have a little time before the good guys get here to lock your ass up, and shut down whatever crazy cult you got going on here."

"You Americans ... so righteous about your world view. You have no idea what goes on beyond your borders. What true religion is ...what spiritual mastery is ...what truth is."

"Hmmm, and that attitude isn't all righteous and superior? Only we Americans are guilty of that?"

"I don't have time for this. I have work to do."

"Ah so, time ..."

Renku smiled at her. "Perhaps I underestimate you ... I would like to have dharma battle with you, but right now I must tend to other matters." He reached behind him for a bell on the altar.

"I think you want to put gun away. I ring this bell, my warriors come running. They see gun they will shoot. If you value your life you will put away."

"Don't even think about ringing that bell. One chime and you're dead," Alex said.

"Ah so." Renku nodded. "I think I know you better than you know you. That is where I have advantage. Your bullets cannot touch what I know ... you will not shoot me. I am only simple monk holding a small bell. If you were to shoot me and survive how would you explain to your superiors killing an unarmed Zen priest, a Zen Master? Killing me? The rightful owner of that title now, above all others!"

Alex rose from the couch and slowly moved toward the false monk.

"There are so many other ways this can play out. I'm surprised that a powerful Zen Master such as yourself can only think in black and white... killing you, or not killing you. I could create so many other scenarios that my superiors would believe. I suspect I've had much more experience with psychopaths than you've had with police detectives."

They paused in stillness for a silent second.

"It's just you and me here, Renku, or whatever your name is."

"It's Roshi to you!"

"In your dreams, maybe. Nope, just the two of us here. ... Who would the world believe? A false prophet leading an army of crazed warriors pretending to be monks or a decorated police detective?"

"You can talk all you like, but there is present reality ... this bell or that bullet? Either will draw attention, bring one or more of my monks."

"And I could do a lot of damage to this side of your lungs expiring. I know exactly where to strike to keep you alive in a life no one would want, especially not a world famous Zen *Master*.

"And anyone comes through that door that's under your spell, any bullet they fire will have to go through you to get to me. And despite that hand injury that tells me one of your acolytes isn't too pleased with you right now, I expect who's left is still loyal and won't want you maimed any further. Am I right?"

Alex was now behind Renku, gun trained on his head.

"Now put that bell back down without a sound."

"Another place, another time, you would make fine opponent, Detective Sullivan."

"There's that fucking time again! You don't even believe what you preach. You ought to be a little more careful with your words. We are here right now opposing each other."

"You don't know a thing."

"And that's another example of how wrong you are. Maybe I don't have a clue about time being time or being being time or whatever the fuck you said. But what I do know is that right now in this moment of time, as I understand time, you are one fucked-up narcissistic, grandiose, arrogant bastard who thinks he's the second coming. Ah, sorry, that's a Christian reference. In your case it's more likely you think you're the first incarnation of the true Buddha.

"And I know that it's about to be over for you, this little fantasy you're play-acting. So it's up to you whether you want it to be bloodless or you want more people to suffer. Then again, it doesn't really matter to you, does it? Who gets hurt? Long as you get what you want ... well, here's a newsflash ... you are not going to finish whatever this is that you started ... it's over. Men with guns, the good guys, the ones with the law and sanity on their side, are on their way here now.

"That means, now, this moment. As we sit here with my gun pointed at your head."

"Enjou will be back to check on me soon so we'll just have to wait, see who gets here first, your men or mine. I'm betting mine."

"Okay, here's what we're going to do ... we're gonna get up nice and easy, we're both gonna walk outta here, and we're gonna go into that locked room of yours while we wait. I know my gun is no match on its own against the muscle of your disciples out back, so behind a locked door'll be the safest place for both of us." Alex nudged him with the barrel of her gun. "Get up and start moving. And remember, my finger is faster and deadlier than your tongue, so if we happen to run into anyone on our way, use your charm to convince them that all is well. You may not care about what happens to any of the others here—just so you know that's a common trait of creeps like you—but I know you're not ready to die, and despite what your deluded mind tells you, you cannot repel a bullet. So don't fuck up. Got it?"

Renku grimaced with pain as he awkwardly raised himself up, his right hand limp and unable to assist in the effort. "You are more than clear. No worry. I know what to do. None of it matters. I will prevail before day is over. And I will own you."

***

"We need more men with guns." Kate was talking to the two state police who'd pulled up as she was zipping up her jeans after taking a leak behind a cactus. Guy and Skip arrived three minutes later. She described the monastery scene to them. "There were at least forty men that I could see, some with rifles and handguns, not sure how many, all were carrying clubs that looked like fat, iron-studded baseball bats. Get too close to one of those it'll do serious damage. They might be monks, but they looked more like a mutant group of martial artists—from another century, past or future. Nothing I've ever encountered before."

"Any idea what they were doing exactly? Who they were protecting or defending? And from what? Why they needed so much artillery?" Derek, one of the state troopers, fired off questions.

"Not a clue. Alex and I had just visited with the boss monk not a half-hour before and all was peaceful. No sign of anyone else about."

"Think it has anything to do with that silly gong game that Daigen Roshi down in Santa Fe told us about?" Guy asked.

"Dunno, 'spose there could be a connection, but they all looked too fierce for game playing. I say we play it safe, expect the worst and be happy if it turns out to be a game. We need more backup before we make a move."

They all agreed. The uniforms radioed in, spoke to their boss. They could round up a half dozen men, tops, who could be on scene in about thirty-five minutes. Any more than that would have to come from Espanola, ninety minutes away moving at cop speed.

"I'm going in, keep Alex company," Guy said. "Let her know what's going on. Can't leave her there on her own for too long, she's liable to get antsy and do something crazy."

"I'm going with you," Kate said.

"Count me in," Skip said.

"Okay, the three of us'll drive in a little closer, hike the rest of the way. You can hear a car coming a mile away in this canyon. Good for security, bad for us." Guy looked over at the uniforms. "You guys okay waiting here for backup?"

"Sure thing," Derek said. "We'll come along soon as the first wave of reinforcements gets here, couple of them can wait for the rest. Should have all we need 'bout eighty-five minutes max. Let's hope they don't get trigger-happy 'afore then."

"I'm still hoping they don't have bullets, that it's all a game," Guy said.

"From your lips to God's ears," Derek said looking skyward.

"Amen," Derek's partner, Bob, said.

"Bet you guys don't see action like this much out here in the desert, do you?" Guy asked.

"Nah," Derek said. "But don't you worry, we know how to shoot straight. Lotta time here for target practice, so's we're ready for whatever awaits over yonder."

"Good to know," Kate said.

"We'll see you fellas soon." Guy slid behind the wheel and turned the ignition.

"How long's it been since you left Alex?"

"Shit, more than an hour. She is definitely getting antsy. You guys got any food with you? I'll bet she's starving by now. That, combined with the monk madness'll have her fit to be tied."

29

A loud, slow drumbeat emanated from the courtyard as Alex and Renku made their way to the altar room. The rhythm coursed through Alex's body and pulsed in concert with her heart. Adrenaline kept fear at bay. The afternoon chill in the dark, old building made her shiver. She clenched her teeth to keep them from chattering and held one question in her mind, *where the hell are they?*

With no interference from Enjou or any other monk, Alex and her prisoner were safely behind the first locked door.

"Good boy. Now, gimme the keys and put your hands behind your back ... slowly."

The space between the two doors was tight, only enough for two bodies standing. Alex estimated it to be about four feet by five, too small for her liking. She needed to restrain him before rushing through the second door. No telling what awaited them there.

She untied the rope at Renku's waist with one hand, quickly holstered her gun and began to bind his wrists. He winced with pain, and rammed his foot into her shin. She buckled and fell back into the door behind her. The tiny space was to her advantage. Without a gun she knew she'd be no match for him mano a mano. His body was trained to kill, hers only when the law and a gun were in her hand and she had no other choice. Even at his age his body was a deadly weapon.

"You fucker." She drew the cord tighter. He remained silent but she knew that pain streamed through his body. She turned him around and slammed his back against the wall, delivering more pain to his brain. She then drew her gun and poked it into his now bare belly, his open robe exposing red warrior pants, a bare, hairless chest, and a sheathed knife dangling from his waist.

She turned him around, pushed his face to the wall and patted him down. The knife was all he was holding. She stuffed it into her jean's rear pocket.

"Don't move."

She unlocked the inside door and kicked it open, gun outstretched in front of her. No one was inside. A blood-stained white sheet draped over a pile of something on the floor was the only evidence of danger.

She pulled Renku into the room and shoved him against a wall. "Sit!" She closed and locked the door behind them.

Weapon in hand, she moved over to the sheet and snatched it off Shoju's body. Gun trained on Renku, she knelt and felt for a pulse. It was weak, but he was still alive.

"This how you treat your monks? First Marco, now Shoju? Someone gets in your way, you torture, then kill them? That your perverted idea of the first precept? How many others have there been? How many piles of bones we gonna find when we dig through this place?"

"Being a cunt, how can you understand the way of a master?"

"Shut the fuck up."

She could hear a faint drumming from outside, but had no eyes to what was going on in the courtyard.

"Who else has keys to this room?"

"Never mind that. Someone will be coming soon. You cannot win this."

"You're right about one thing. Someone will be coming soon." She hoped the first someone through that door would be on her side. Alex dug out her phone. There was a half bar of service. She speed-dialed Kate. The reception was too crackly for her to hear clearly, but Kate was on the other end. "I'm in the locked room with the so-called Roshi ... and Shoju. He's hurt bad." She hung up. It was useless, the half bar had disappeared.

Shoju moaned and moved ever so slightly. She gently stroked his bald head. He was slowly coming to. He needed to drink something. She looked around for a teapot. No luck. The altar was so cluttered with artifacts that she didn't see the water bowl, but she knew it had to be there, every Zen altar had one. She finally found it behind a statuette of some Christian saint, St. John she thought. Then it dawned on her. *Renku and his monks are responsible for the sacred object thefts around the state. Holy shit.* She didn't have time to dwell.

The bowl was only half full of water, but it would help. Her own thirst and hunger were now driven away by circumstances. She could wait, Shoju couldn't. She propped his head on her lap and fed him some water. He responded. A good sign. Maybe the water, after being surrounded by all the saintly items, would perform a healing miracle. If some mysterious energy were her only partner right now, she'd take it. Much as she liked solo police work most times, now was not one of them.

"Ain't that sweet," Renku said. "Maybe if he'd been fucking you instead of Cissie you'd both be on my side."

Alex ripped off two pieces of the sheet and formed the rest into a pillow for Shoju's head. She moved over to Renku and tied his ankles together.

"That is unnecessary. Even immobile I am superior to you, stronger than you. I will vanquish you in the end. You will see ... in good time." He looked up at his power altar and smiled. She used the second strip of sheet to gag him.

After leaving Renku's knife with Shoju, who was gradually becoming more alert, Alex slipped out into the hall, gun in hand. Uncle Charlie always reminded her that her impatience would one day put her in a position that she couldn't control or back out of. Today, he was in her head repeating himself. She thanked him for sharing and proceeded on guard through the halls.

***

"I think she's inside." Kate held her phone to her ear.

"Goddamn it." Guy slammed his hand against the steering wheel.

"I can't be sure. All I heard was 'room' and what I think was 'Shoju'... maybe she found him... maybe he's on her side."

"Or maybe he came back, caught her lurking, and took her captive."

"I don't think so, doubt she'd still have her phone and be able to call, that were the case."

"Let's hope you're right." He pulled the car off the road and turned off the ignition. "Okay, this looks good. Let's go."

By the time they got to the edge of the monastery grounds, a dozen warriors were sitting on the ground near the kitchen door eating from bowls held close to their mouths, chopsticks shoveling food down their gullets. The rest of the group was patrolling the same way as Kate had left them. Lunch break in shifts, it looked like.

"Who the hell are they expecting?" Guy asked.

"Fuck if I know. S'not like they know we're here. Even if they have Alex, we saw them like this after they thought we were long gone, so it started as something else."

"Maybe there's a rival group on its way, something to do with that crazy gong game you mentioned?" Skip chimed in. "Could be it's not as serious as it looks."

"I don't like it," Guy said. "I'm gonna try Alex again. Looks like there's some service here." He punched in her number, listened to the endless ringing and then the voicemail prompt.

***

Alex got to her phone before the third ring and turned it off. She couldn't risk answering. The sound ricocheted off the walls, shattering the silence. She froze and listened for movement around the next corner. Her own breathing was all she heard.

She took her next step and chaos rained down on her. A club attached to a monk's hand knocked the gun out of hers. Two warriors grabbed her from behind and restrained her. In seconds she was contained.

Enjou walked around the corner and slapped her hard across the face. "What the hell are you doing here? And where is Roshi?

"Pat her down, see what else she's holding, then take her over to Soto House with the rest of them. He'll like this one."

As soon as the altar room keys were found in Alex's back pocket, Enjou stormed off to rescue Roshi, ending the body frisk and leaving her ankle piece safe for the moment. *I hope Shoju is alert enough to defend himself.*

She was taken around back to an outlying building she hadn't noticed before. It was a small two-room cottage that blended so perfectly into the landscape that it was rendered virtually invisible. The path they took held no view of the courtyard or the entry road so she had no idea what was going on out there or if Kate and the others were closing in.

A door was unlocked and she was thrown into the front room. The door slammed shut and bolted behind her. Six women, in varying degrees of agitation and physical discomfort, greeted her. The practicing-silence nun was among them, her vow long forgotten.

"What's happening out there? Why are you here? Is anyone else coming to help us?"

Alex got up off the floor, twelve eyeballs staring at her brimming with hope that she came bearing good news.

"Never mind about me, why the hell are you all locked up here?"

"He's crazy you know, Enjou too. We had no idea till yesterday how insane he was. He plans to rape all of us."

"And then probably kill us," said a frightened ball of flesh on the couch.

Alex's mind raced, wanted to dismiss the hysteria, pictured Shoju, and knew there was truth in what she was hearing. "Tell me what happened."

"Come with me, I'll show you." The once-silent nun led Alex into the back room.

"I'm Choro. Sorry about being so rude the other day."

"I'm Alex ... s'okay."

The futon on the floor of the bedroom held a bald woman tending to a long-haired young woman lying so still Alex wasn't sure she was alive. Her arms and legs were marked with multiple bruises, some old, some fresh.

"Mandy was a student, came here about a month ago, disappeared shortly after. Everyone thought she'd gone home. Been in here since as Roshi's sex slave. We think there've been others. He intends the same fate for us."

"My god, this is so much worse than I imagined. Did you know a woman named Cissie? Used to come here to visit?"

"No, but most of us were away for six months, only returned recently after Enjou convinced us that things were changing and that Roshi had come around and would treat us the same as the monks," Choro said. "We like this place, we trusted her. Mandy there, and Sherry, who's in the other room, filled us in on what happened after we left. You could ask Sherry about Cissie. Yesterday we were all rounded up and locked in here, told they had plans for us."

Alex and Choro moved back into the front room closing the bedroom door behind them.

"Why didn't you guys escape through the windows? This is hardly a fortress," Alex said.

"Guess we were stunned into inertia and we didn't want to leave Mandy. Truth is we've been wearing blinders for so long, had become so used to obeying Roshi without question ... it took twenty-four hours for reality to set in. And now you're here."

"There are more on the way, though I'm not sure how many or where they're at right now. From the looks of things out there we might be in for a battle. You gals up for that?"

"More than up for it," Choro said. The energy in the room buzzed, even the ball of flesh on the couch uncurled herself and sat up attentive. "All of us except Sherry there are trained for it, good as the men."

"What about weapons? They're armed with clubs, some with guns. You got any of those?"

"Not here, of course, but we got knives and swords in our rooms. No guns though."

"S'okay, we should have plenty of those coming." Alex straightened her spine.

"Okay, here's the plan ... Choro, take two people with you, go to your rooms, get your weapons. I'll try to get over to the main road, see if I can get a fix on what my people are up to. We'll meet back here soon as we're done.

"Don't take any chances. If we're smart about this, and if my guys are ready, maybe we can end this without anybody getting hurt or killed."

"Someone's coming," said the nun standing watch at the window.

Alex leaned over to unhook her ankle holster.

30

As the door opened, it flashed through Alex's mind that whatever went on in the cabin had been going on for some time, the lock only accessible from the outside. How many women had been Renku's victims? What perverted sense of Zen mastery was he operating under? And for how long?

Guy slipped in and closed the door behind him. Alex's heart leapt and her stomach fluttered at the sight of him. She raced over and wrapped her arms around his neck.

"Damn, it's good to see you," she said into his neck. She pushed herself an arm's length away. "Where are the others? How'd you know we were here? Is it over? Have you found Shoju?"

"I saw them taking you here. Kate, Skip and two cops are at the front. More will be here within a half hour, then we'll move in. So, no, it's not over and we haven't seen Shoju. What's going on here?"

Alex gave him the quick version. He escorted Choro and two of the others to their residence, the closest building to the cabin. They returned quickly, armed with swords and knives, ready to face the men.

"I'll go back around to the front," Guy said. "The extra cops should be here by now. Why don't you guys take position this side of the courtyard, surprise the shit out of them once we make our move?"

A loud gong echoed off the canyon walls, and a booming drum roll followed. It got faster and louder, adding to the tension in the cabin. The sense of urgency escalated, as everyone was anxious to get moving so they wouldn't lose the element of surprise.

"Anyone here know what that could mean?" Guy asked.

"That's the ogane bell and the hokku drum. Usually means Roshi's about to give a talk. Maybe he plans to address the monks. We should get out there now, hear what he's got to say," Choro said.

"Right, let's go. Take your cue from us, once you see us enter the courtyard, make yourselves known," Guy said.

"You got an extra gun?" Alex asked. "Enjou took mine. Alls I got is my ankle piece."

"Take this one. The cops'll have extras." He handed her his 9mm.

"Thanks, let's hope we won't have to use them. Maybe once they see the uniforms some of the monks will realize how off the wall this whole thing is. Maybe their monk training, if any of them really are monks, will prevail."

"I think the only ones you gotta be extra wary of are the two goons who brought you here," Choro said. "Don't know where they came from, but they only just arrived while we were away those six months. I doubt they're even monks."

"They're the ones with rifles strapped to their chests," Alex said to Guy.

"Yeah, by the looks of them, they're ex-military with scrambled brains. ... Okay, ladies, after you." He opened the door and they left the cabin to take up their positions. Sherry stayed behind to tend to Mandy and keep out of harm's way.

***

Renku was just outside of the main entryway standing on a wooden platform looking down on his minions, who were gathered round listening to his every word. He was bare-chested, garbed only in red flowing pants cinched at the ankles and a cone-shaped headpiece with wings, gilded and sparkling in the late afternoon sun. He looked like a cartoon wizard.

Enjou was behind his left shoulder decked out in a shiny black skin suit that accentuated her lean muscular body. A hood was pulled down over her forehead, shading her eyes. She had a large sheathed knife and sword dangling from her waist.

The warriors had lost interest in guarding the perimeter in favor of attending to their leader. This gave the girls and cops an opportunity to spread out without fear of detection. Alex heard only bits and pieces of Renku's speech: "The time has come ... our vows ... rightful master ... sacred object ... long ago." She noticed a few small clusters of monks talking amongst themselves, not rapt in every orated word. It looked like they weren't exactly buying what he was saying.

One of these monks, abandoning all Zen decorum, interrupted Renku in mid-sentence and shouted, "Where's Shoju?"

So there's dissension in the troop ... that could be useful.

Alex whispered to Choro, "I'm gonna go inside, check on Shoju, see if he's still alive."

"Want some help?"

"Nah, I'm fine, you guys stay here. I'll be back in a jiff."

Alex got close enough to see the dark cloud settle into Renku's cheekbones. Enjou gripped the hilt of her sword, ready to strike anyone who got near her Buddha incarnate.

Murmurings wafted through the gathering like the buzzing of bees. The two rifle-bearing soldiers flanking Renku hardly blinked.

"Enough!" Renku shouted.

The crowd quieted down.

"You will all see Shoju this evening. But first we must—"

"Attention!" Guy's voice boomed from a bullhorn and bounced off the canyon walls. Alex heard it as she approached the altar room.

Cops in blue and nuns in black drifted into the outer ring of the courtyard and formed an arc enclosing the monks between them and the building behind Renku.

"Put your weapons down and no one will get hurt."

Renku shouted something in Japanese. It galvanized his men into a Pavlovian attack. A gaggle of monks rushed at the cops with their clubs. Arms and heads were struck, a few shots were fired, the nuns surged, whipping their swords at monks who had once been their dharma brothers. Many of the monks dropped their clubs and stood with hands on their heads, confused and disoriented. The nuns too were dispirited. They never planned on their martial training coming to this.

"Shoju is here!" Alex was back outside with the bullhorn to her lips, Shoju hanging off her left shoulder.

"Look at him. This is what your master has done to him." Two monks came forward, took Shoju off her arm and supported him in their strong arms so his brethren could see him.

"And where is your fearless master now? It looks like he's disappeared and left you to fight his fight, whatever that is." The monks looked around to find Renku, but he was gone, had disappeared during the melee.

"He's run like the coward he is. Look at Shoju, all of you, this is how he treats loyal monks."

The men lowered their clubs and listened to Alex. Some had already given up the fight. They were bewildered, had no idea how they'd come to be fighting with cops. This wasn't the plan. This wasn't one of their vows. This was most definitely not the Buddha way.

"Let the cops move inside to go find your boss, who is attempting to flee as we stand here fighting each other."

"Let's all go find him," one of the monks shouted.

A rallying cry rose up and most of the congregation surged toward the entrance.

"Stop! Now!" Officer Derek had taken over the horn. Conditioned to obey orders, the monks stopped in mid stride. "This is our job. Let us do it. Move aside, let our men through." The mass of monks parted into two streams, opening up an aisle for passage. Derek sent four men around back to cover the two back exits.

Alex, Guy, Kate, Skip and three cops rushed to the building, weapons drawn. They stopped outside of the door to quickly strategize.

"I think it's only three of them in there," Guy said, "the monk, the nun and a mercenary. Derek's got the other hired gun contained."

"Not sure how Renku plans to flee the area, but I do know he's not going anywhere without that precious gong and all the other artifacts he worked so hard to get," Alex said. "He thinks they give him some sort of magical, invincible power, so his first stop'll be the altar room."

"Okay," Guy said. "We'll split up. Alex, you go round that way with Skip and two officers, I'll take Kate and this guy."

They moved in without another word. Like the monks, they were all well trained, but with different skills for a different purpose.

Alex's group got to the locked room first, meeting no one on the way. The first door was ajar, the interior one closed and locked. They had no key, they couldn't be heard, they had no way in. Shooting a bullet into metal in that small a space might've worked, or it might've ricocheted and killed the shooter. They couldn't chance it.

"I have some experience with these locks," Skip said. Alex's mind flashed to all the locks on his front door. He pulled out a small leather case from his jacket pocket, flipped it open to reveal tools for picking locks. Within a short minute the door was kicked open and Alex and Skip were through it, guns first.

Enjou and the bodyguard were shoveling the contents of the altar into two huge bags. There was no sign of Renku or the gong.

Hired gun was quick on the draw, and got off one bullet into a cop's leg. Guy darkened the doorway and shot him in the heart. Enjou swiftly surrendered.

"Renku's not here. He must've gone out the back. Gong's missing too, so he can't be moving too fast," Alex said.

"I'll tell Derek, you guys go," Kate said.

Alex and Guy raced down the hall to the rear exits. They scanned the horizon for an escape route, and all they saw was a mile of desert brush leading up to canyon walls. A few meandering footpaths were visible through the maze.

"Andy took his Hummer, so maybe he's got a helicopter or some other escape vehicle hidden out there," Alex said. "And he's not waiting around for those two inside. He's got a Plan B that only includes him."

"Listen, you hear that?" Guy said. "Hard to tell where it's coming from, but I hear an engine out there somewhere."

"The only road out of here is the one we came in on and he doesn't have too big a head start. Let's borrow one of Derek's cruisers—we'll catch up to him before he reaches town."

They checked in with Derek, raced out to where the cars were parked, jumped into a black and white Ford SUV and sped down the dusty road after the fleeing monk.

31

The dust kicked up by Renku's wheels was getting thicker as they gained on the Lexus that was the same color as his pantaloons.

"Looks like he's had this planned for some time. I never laid eyes on that vehicle the few times I've been here. Must've had it hidden for weeks, maybe months, for his escape," Alex said.

"Guess he wasn't too confident he'd be able to pull off whatever this fantasy of his is," Guy said.

"And I'll bet no one else knew about his hidden wheels, typical narcissistic psychopath that he is. Looks like a custom paint job, never saw such a color. Whatever his plan, it didn't include blending in."

They fell into silence with only one thing on their mind. Catch the bastard.

"Think we can talk this guy into giving up?"

"Not a chance," Alex said.

"Okay then, fasten your seat belt and hold on." Guy clipped his into place. "Let's see how much he cares about his chariot."

He sped up behind Renku, rammed into his backside and pushed him to the left of the road, then pulled around and came up along the passenger side. Renku slowed down to about thirty, still fast for the rough terrain but perfect for his pursuers. Guy nudged

Renku's side and pushed him further to the edge of the road and up against the prickly desert brush that lined the way.

Renku tried to push against the two-ton mass of metal at his side and Guy pushed back, each of them thinking that they had the advantage. Guy with his experience and lack of attachment to the vehicle he was abusing. Renku with the power-inducing gong in the back seat and his rightful mastery of all things human.

They rode in tandem, two hunks of metal driven by two purpose-driven men, in a motorized tug of war for what seemed like many miles and minutes to Alex but was only two and ten before they came to the point of who would be chicken. This was a parallel version of the game played by reckless teenagers, who needed to prove something or win the girl.

They approached a bend in the road that curved to the right. If Guy took the turn too soon Renku would have a chance to avoid crashing into the desert brush. If he waited too long, he too would end up immobilized.

Renku blinked first and began to slow down. Guy felt it but didn't ease to the right and stop till the last second. Alex and Guy jumped out of the car, guns drawn before the Lexus came to a complete stop. Renku couldn't exit the driver's side but also couldn't admit defeat, his delusion about his superior strength still operating.

"He's not going to give up," Alex said.

"I got that," Guy said.

"Doors are locked, looks like he's settling in. I'll bet the car's bulletproof, too."

"Shit."

"I got that," Alex said. They looked at each other and smiled.

"What the hell? He thinks we'll just go away, get tired of waiting?"

"Real monk or not, he does know how to sit still for long periods of time."

"Okay then, let's go to Plan B."

It took Guy three minutes to find a stick and a rag with which he fashioned a torch. He then soaked it in gasoline and lit it up with matches he found in the glove compartment. The flame got Renku's attention. Guy threw Alex the car keys. "Move that down the road a ways." He walked over to the Lexus.

Renku rolled down the rear window. "You think that scares me?"

"What I think matters not. What I know is you will burn to a crisp in no time once this reaches your gas tank."

"You know nothing." Renku started shooting.

Guy was caught off guard and had no cover. He knelt down and drew his gun. Too late. One of the bullets got him in the shoulder. He dropped the torch and rolled out of Renku's line of vision.

Alex walked straight toward the Lexus, gun outstretched in her hands. She knew her bullets wouldn't penetrate the glass but neither would his. Renku laughed out loud, started the car and slowly backed it out onto the road. The rear window was still down. It was a small porthole into the car, but it could be enough.

Alex sprinted into position, and got off a few bullets straight into the open window. The Lexus continued to move. She shot out two tires and it finally rolled to a stop. She wanted to check on Guy but couldn't take her eyes off the maniac in the crippled red car. She inched her way toward the vehicle, moving the still-burning torch off to the side of the road on her way. It didn't look like Renku was moving, but Guy was, *thank Buddha.*

She heard a moan from inside the car. Either one of her bullets had found its mark or he was baiting her. Approaching from the rear didn't give her a good line of sight to the driver's seat. She ducked under the open back window and peeked into the front passenger window. The car was still running so if Renku was alive he could roll down the window and shoot her. She didn't have that advantage.

She saw blood. He'd been hit. But she couldn't tell how serious it was. His chin was resting on his chest.

She reached up and unlocked the rear door, opened it and slid into the back seat. No reaction from up front. Renku's gun rested in his open palm on his lap. She put her gun to his head and reached around for his. He made a move to resist but had no muscle control left. He was done, vanquished. It was over.

Before stepping out of the car to tend to Guy she checked carefully to make sure there were no weapons hiding anywhere. She found a small pistol in the glove compartment but that was it. Renku was still alive and she hoped he'd make it. Not only because she hated taking away any life, but also because she wanted him to pay in this life for all he'd done. She knew he'd never show remorse for his actions, he was too sick a human being for that, but it might help those he'd hurt to know he was locked up and unable to cause any more harm.

***

Three days later Alex and Guy were having breakfast in bed in the best room in the swankiest hotel in Santa Fe high up on a mountain. The view was spectacular, the food was gourmet and the spa facilities were extravagant. They planned to stay put for a few days.

"I can't cook for you like you did for me when I was hurt, but at least you can let me feed you." Alex spooned a forkful of frittata into Guy's mouth.

"I still have one hand that works but I do love this, so okay." He chewed happily. The bullet hadn't done much damage to his left bicep but the soreness hadn't completely disappeared yet and the doctor had told him to avoid lifting weights for a few weeks. He was willing to baby it for a while if it meant such attentive care from the woman he hoped to marry. He also decided not to spoil it by whipping out the green gem quite yet. There was plenty of time for that.

Renku was in custody and would be going away for a very long time, the rest of his natural life if there was any justice left in the relative world. The stories of his treatment of women were becoming more bizarre as his victims began to surface and come forth with damning evidence. The authorities had no idea yet how many bodies, dead and alive, he'd left in his wake and they were not in any hurry to find out. This was going to take a while.

Shoju was in hospital but was going to be fine. The monastery's doors were closed for the time being until everything was sorted out and they could find a teacher willing to step in and bring it back to life. Shoju wasn't interested. He had plans to head west to a soup kitchen.

Sam was buried. The service was one of the most beautiful and touching sendoffs Alex had ever witnessed. Kate was still deeply sad and would grieve the loss for a long time, but the ceremony helped her to express her feelings and begin to move forward into the next day.

Skip had a private ceremony for Cissie and left the next day for a month in Europe. Cissie had always wanted to see Paris and Rome so he thought he'd take her there, bring some of her ashes to scatter around the world. She would like that.

Jerry was on trial for Sam's murder. Kate would keep her eye on that, make sure he got what he deserved. The evidence was mounting and it looked like a done deal but she wouldn't rest until he was behind bars without any hope of parole. Least she could do for Sam. Maybe she'd move back to New York now, or she'd stay and help out with the youth organizations that Sam had been involved with. She didn't have to decide anything today. There was time left for her.

Alex didn't want to rush time, as if she could, and was determined to savor and luxuriate in every moment of this well deserved vacation. But she sure wished she knew what her next move in life was going to be. She had no idea what she even wanted.

As she sat naked in the hot tub on the top of the mountain it began to snow. This, right now, was a perfect moment. She didn't have to figure anything out. She just had to be in beauty.

About the Author

Nancy O'Hara is a meditation coach in real life who kills people in her fiction. She is the author of six books on the subject of mindfulness and meditation, including the bestselling *Find a Quiet Corner*, and her first mystery novel *One Hand Killing*. Along with her writing, Nancy shares her experience through her Mindful Life Coaching practice, meditation classes, workshops, and retreats. This is the second book in the Alex Sullivan Zen Mystery series. She lives in New York City with her perfectly imperfect husband, trees outside her windows and noisy upstairs neighbors.

Connect with Nancy online at www.nancyohara.com

Other Titles by Nancy O'Hara

One Hand Killing – An Alex Sullivan Zen Mystery

Find a Quiet Corner – A Simple Guide to Self-Peace

Just Listen – A Guide to Finding Your Own True Voice

Work From the Inside Out – 7 Steps to Loving What You Do

3 Bowls – Vegetarian Recipes from an American Zen Buddhist
    Monastery

Serenity in Motion – Inner Peace: Anytime, Anywhere

Zen by the Brush – A Japanese Painting and Meditation Set

www.ingramcontent.com/pod-product-compliance
Lightning Source LLC
Chambersburg PA
CBHW020047180626
46812CB00006B/2226